Ready Or Not

(The Redfern Series Book 2)

By Ste Sharp

'Like pebbles on a beach...'

Ste Sharp

"Someday you will find me, caught beneath the landslide"

Friday 13th December 1996

Richard III – Supergrass

The nerves kicked in when the stage lights swung round and lit up the hundreds of people facing us. This was the biggest gig we'd ever played. We weren't in Brighton anymore.

'Evening,' I spoke into the mic and my voice boomed around the cavernous hall. 'We're Beachhead…' a few people cheered which was a good sign, '…and this is *Sunmaker*.'

James ripped into the bassline, Rob kicked into his funky beat and I let rip with a heavy barre chord. The sound was *amazing*! The set up was spot on and the acoustics of the hall amplified every nuance as Andy tore into the opening lead riff. Whenever he played, I found it hard to keep my eyes off his finger work. He had a mesmerising, lazy style and was way better than Mike had ever been. Subtle. Paced. Crisp.

Heads bobbed and the crowd rocked to the beat. So much was riding on this gig. Keep calm, I told myself as I stepped up to the mic, opened with the first verse and felt the buzz fill my chest. This was what it was all about.

Of course, most of the crowd were only here to see Skimrider who had two top twenty hits back in the summer and had just done a live set on the Evening Session. Beachhead were riding in their wake and making steady progress. John Peel had played *Avalanche* on his show, so we were getting known and we'd recorded the tracks for our album in the summer, which was still being mixed. First step, release the *Shift* E.P., which was why we were gigging.

Despite everything going to plan, I still felt nervous. I was wary that anything could go wrong and we'd have the rug pulled from under us, and my relationship with Jeff, the head of the record label, hadn't healed since the 'incident' during the summer, which I was still too embarrassed to apologise about. I'd been told to be careful with Jeff because he liked to watch his bands' gigs and often made snap decisions. That's why I hadn't smoked tonight. Apart from a pint of London Pride and what Andy had given me, I was playing clean.

'*And all of us were made by the sun…*'

I caught James' eye after the first chorus and we shared a smile. This was it. The stage was ours and we were buzzing! All our hard work had been worth it. We were running so fast we could take off and fly!

When we got to the second chorus, I nailed the new bit with the extra two bars, repeated the chorus and we finished with a neat stop, all cutting out on the same beat. Split-second perfection. Professional. It usually catches the crowd off-guard and, for that long second of silence afterwards I could feel the blood buzzing round my ears… then the roar erupted. Fucking brilliant! The mass of young, music-addicted, half-drunk, Britpop-mad revellers loved it!

Don't talk yet, I told myself and took a swig of beer which tasted weird with gum.

Straight into the next song.

I nodded at Andy and he tapped a few pedals with his blue Converse and started the hypnotic lead he'd created for our newest song, *My World Came Together*. Rob came in with an off-beat rhythm and we were sounding like the Jimi Hendrix Experience, then James brought in a Stone Roses style bass and I sang the opening lines.

'*Girl, I've never seen you before, then our eyes meet across the bar…*'

I was focussed, but all I could think about was Lisa. Her smile. Her eyes. Lisa in her cotton dress the first time I saw her in my bookshop. Lisa in her bikini in Australia. Laughs as we zipped around in a mini-moke. Waking up to her sleepy face every morning. Sunshine. Making plans. Decisions. Saying goodbye… her sad eyes. The tears. I could still taste the Aussie beer. Big decisions were always made over a few pints. No music playing though. Just insects chirruping.

Stop. Push the thoughts away. Concentrate on the music.

The next verse flowed from my mouth: the lyrics fastened to a gossamer string drifting across the heads of the bouncing throng of revellers. The memories flittered away as the song progressed, leaving me with an occasional impression of Lisa's face while I watched the audience reacting to the chorus. They loved it! I was getting a good feel for which songs went down the best and had an idea to extend the middle four to eight.

We were determined to play as many songs as possible but the crowd probably only knew us for *Avalanche*, so we'd pushed it up the playlist.

'You might know this one,' I said as I switched over to the semi-acoustic guitar. 'Avalanche.'

The roadies had already tuned the guitar, so I got stuck in. A strum of the opening chord and a few people cheered, raising the energy up a notch. I sang and played on my own, a single spotlight on me, and felt my skin tingle. Every note was spot on. Rob crept in with the drums, then James and Andy let rip when the chorus morphed into our rockiest track.

'And we were swept awaaay!'

My thoughts went back to earlier in the evening when us four were getting ready in our house. The label had suggested we share a place when we moved to London, to get to know Andy better. It wasn't like we were the Monkees or the Beatles living a crazy life in a party house, but it worked. After a few nights down the local boozer we got to know each other, ironed out our differences, and our sound tightened up. It was a bit weird living with people after having my own flat above Red Books, but it worked. We were all focussed on the music.

A couple of hours before the gig, we'd watched Supergrass on TFI Friday, who were playing a new tune, *Richard III,* from their second album. I was transfixed for the whole song as a rush of inspiration danced a twist with the pre-gig anxiety nerves in my stomach. That was where I wanted to be – on the big stage. Gaz was doing exactly what I wanted to do… these guys were what we were up against. Yeah, I knew our bands weren't really in competition with each other but it drove us to play better and write smarter. Jeff had said the music scene was like a rainforest, the more diverse the music scene's ecosystem was the stronger it was, but these guys were the pinnacle. This is what we had to aim for if we wanted to be at the top. The apex predator. The Leopard.

'A huge thanks to Skimrider for asking us to support them tonight,' I said when *Avalanche* ended.

Mentioning the main act received a roar. Good move. I was still learning how to create a good rapport with the crowd, but needed help. Andy used to chip in when he played with his old band, Lightback, so he was always happy to help out. I remember seeing them when the label first mentioned nabbing Andy from Lightback. Chris, the lead singer was pretty good at chatting and creating that relationship with the crowd. I'd heard Chris was going to sue us, but the truth was, his songs were crap and Andy knew he had a better chance of making it with Beachhead than with Lightback.

'You're such a lovely audience,' I said and switched back to my black *Les Paul* guitar.

'We'd like to take you home with us,' James sang and I joined in. 'We'd love to take you home.'

It got a few laughs and helped calm what was left of my nerves.

'This one's called *Loud and Clear*,' I said.

Andy started with his vocals and the song built up around his guitar riff.

It sounded different now we'd re-worked it. It had always been good but Andy's touch had raised it up a level. The set was sounding good. Every song had a different start, they all built well and each had a catchy chorus. Our album was going to be awesome, I could feel it. Not being big-headed, but we sounded better than a lot of bands I'd heard recently whose songs just sounded the same. Predictable. Three-chord wonders.

'Right, this is the last song.'

I heard a few boos and someone shouted for more. This was great. They were loving it and we'd done our job. They were properly warmed up for the main act. I squinted and could see to the back of the hall and it was packed. Some of the people at the front were properly getting into it, so I pulled a couple of spare Beachhead plectrums off the mic stand and flicked them out for them to catch.

Time to leave on a high.

'This one's called *Cobra.* You've been awesome… have a great night!'

The song went down a storm, setting up the beginnings of a mosh-pit in the centre, and we left the stage with the sound of cheers ringing in our ears.

'That was bloody amazing!' Rob said, beaming like he'd won big on a scratch card.

'Yeah,' we mumbled back, each floating in our personal cloud of chilled euphoria.

We shuffled down a dark corridor past the roadies who were heading out to change the drum kit, amps and guitars. Some avoided eye contact but most were friendly.

'Nice set,' one said to me, patting me on the shoulder.

'Yeah, good work man,' a long-haired guy said and it took me a second to recognise Dave, the lead singer of Skimrider.

'Cheers,' I replied. 'Have a good one.'

I shook my head. Last summer I would have been going crazy after brushing past Dave, let alone him talking to me, but my band had just bloody well supported Skimrider! I poked my head in their room and breathed in the heady scent of fresh weed. A half-empty bottle of Jack Daniels lay on a chair next to a surf mag and the discarded hoodies outnumbered the packs of Marlboro Lights, evenly scattered around a bare patch in the scuffed carpet, like petals on a dead flower.

'Come on Luke!' Rob shouted down the corridor, beckoning me to our room.

Smaller than Skimrider's, with more graffiti on the bare walls and more stains on the carpet, we'd had to share the support room with the first band, Krunch, who'd buggered off to watch the main event. I grabbed a fresh Budweiser from the tray and raised it.

'Cheers guys. That was fuckin' awesome!'

'We're getting better,' James said, full-grinned.

We clinked bottles and I waited for Andy to say something. He was quieter than usual and, as the front man, it felt like I should ask why.

'You okay, Andy?'

I didn't want him to feel like an outsider.

'Yeah, sure,' he said with a forced smile. 'Just tired.'

Rob swung an arm around Andy's shoulders. 'Come on man, you were amazing!'

Rob had dealt with Mike leaving the band better than I thought he would – but that was probably cos we'd moved to London, so were closer to where Mike lived now.

'Cheers,' Andy replied and took a swig of his beer. 'It was alright.' He nodded and started to loosen up a bit. 'I don't know… there were just a couple of things I wasn't happy with.'

'What like?' I asked, trying not to get defensive. This was killing the mood and getting my back up.

'Just… we missed the extra bit in *Sunmaker*.'

'No, I was ready for that,' Rob said. 'But Luke went back in after two so…'

James nodded and looked at me. Shit. It was supposed to be four.

'Oh,' I said. 'Sorry.' I nodded at the Guarana chewing gum on the table. 'I guess that stuff was stronger than we thought,' I said, trying to lighten the mood.

'And the lyrics in *My World*,' Andy continued, keeping his eyes on me. 'You repeated the verse.'

I winced. I couldn't remember but he was probably right. My cheeks were feeling warm. What if Jeff had been watching and picked up on all this too.

'But the crowd wouldn't know would they?' I said, taking another swig from my bottle.

'Maybe, but we need to be tighter,' Andy said with the slight accent I couldn't place it when I first met him. It turned out he and Chris were from the same town in Suffolk. 'And where's our manager?' He slumped into an armchair and picked up his mobile phone.

Andy was more like Mike than I'd first thought, with his flashy gadgets. I mean, how did he afford a mobile phone if he was getting the same pittance from the label as we were?

James gave me a look and said, 'He's right. Our manager should be here. In case we need stuff, right?'

'True,' Rob said, twiddling with his drum sticks.

I felt hassled, but I was also feeling guilty: our choice of manager had been my idea.

'He does a lot for us, okay?' I said.

'But he should do more,' Andy said and pushed himself up out of the chair. 'Look, I'm going out to listen to Skimrider. See you back here after?'

'Sure,' James replied, patting him on the back as he left.

We stayed in silence for a minute until Rob said, 'I think Skimrider have got their names down at some club tonight, so maybe we could join them later?'

'Cool,' I said and downed my beer, still feeling the cloud hanging over us. 'Maybe we should all get out there then, yeah? Have a listen.'

'Yeah,' James said and opened the door, letting the sounds of Cornish surf-rock invade our room.

We strolled back down the corridor and our summer surf trip came back to me: the tents; the waves; the cider. I felt the buzz coming back. We could get through this. Ride the bumps, get tighter. Get the E.P. out and then the album. There'd be less pressure on us when we were better-known, surely?

'Listen,' I said as we filed out into the dark corridor. 'We still need a name for the album, don't we?'

'Yeah,' James said. 'I've had an idea about that-'

An ear-splitting shriek blotted out what he was about to say.

The three of us clasped hands to our ears and winced as the sound of a thousand Valkyries battered down on us. Flashing red lights lit up the corridor, turning silhouettes of people into speeding zombies. A blast of white light made me flinch, followed by a gust of fresh air as a rush of sweaty bodies swept us outside.

'What the…' I mouthed and slowly released my hands from my ears.

We were in a freezing dark alley out the back of the venue, surrounded by roadies and bins full of stinking beer bottles. I stared at dog-ends floating in a steaming puddle and heard someone say, '…triggered the bloody fire alarm.'

Rob looked as bemused as me and James was shaking his head.

I sighed and looked up at the grey clouds. I thought it'd been going so well, but after what Andy had said and now this, I felt the weight return. The weight of expectation pressing down on my shoulders. Everything was riding on me, the songwriter… the front man. James, Rob, Andy, Jeff, the label, Mum and Dad, Stephen… Lisa. Sacrifices had been made and everyone was expecting great things from Beachhead. This was our only chance and I couldn't fuck it up.

The cold air had sobered me up and I needed a spliff to chill me out. I stared around, taking everything in. James lit a cigarette and Rob chatted to the roadies about drum kits. More doors were opened further down the alley, spilling disgruntled revellers into the December night in a haze of smoke. Most were just wearing t-shirts like us.

A shudder ran through me as I watched them, but it wasn't from the cold. Everything Andy had said came back to me as I spotted Jeff, but it wasn't our performance that worried me now. He'd brought his daughter with him.

Saturday 14th December 1996

The Riverboat Song – Ocean Colour Scene

The wind tore up the Thames, buffeting our boat as it headed east from Tower Bridge, carrying a hundred party-goers in the main event room, who revelled in a cloud of drunkenness, snug in the vessel's belly. Groups of five or six people huddled in chats, drinking and shouting over the live music, while some stood at windows, pointing out lit-up landmarks as we slipped past.

'Hair of the dog!' Rob shouted, raising a glass of beer.

James shook his head, lit a cigarette and said, 'I'm keeping a clear head.'

'But it's a party!' Rob's eyes were glinting. 'We're here, we've-'

I cut him off. 'Don't say we've made it.'

His face dropped and I felt like I'd kicked a puppy.

'Sorry.' I raised a hand. 'Look, I know what you mean… we're *here*, right?' I turned and looked at the executives from the label mingling with agents, journalists and members of the other bands signed to the label. Some famous. 'But our work's not done yet.'

James nodded but Rob still looked stern. He took a swig of his beer and looked around, gathering his thoughts. 'I don't have the… words you do, right? And I know we've got more to do… the pressure gets to all of us, okay? But we are here now and we might never get this far again. We need to embrace it. Enjoy it.'

James put an arm round Rob's shoulders and I sighed. He was right.

'You put it perfectly mate,' James said in his Mancunian accent. 'Come on, Luke, we're ready for this. Let's have another beer and meet some cool people.'

'I know, sorry,' I said. 'I just… you know.'

'You're missing Lisa.'

I laughed, trying to hide my unhappiness. 'Yeah, she'd love this.' They knew better than to ask about Lisa: they knew it had been hard. 'And I just don't want to mess this up for us lot, you know?'

'You won't,' Rob said.

I caught a glimpse of Jeff on the other side of the room and winced. We hadn't cleared the air since what happened in the summer and although I managed to avoid him last night at the club with Skimrider, it was going to be hard work to avoid him on a boat of only a hundred people.

'Listen,' James said to me. 'You're surrounded by important people in the music industry – this is your perfect audience! You can bore them with every detail of your songs… your chord shapes and fingering techniques!' He gave me a wink. 'We'll give it a go too… although as I'm the only black guy on the boat everyone'll assume I'm a bloody drummer.'

'Oi!' Rob said, giving him a punch in the arm. 'We're the foundations of Beachhead. We should stick together. Drum *and* bass.'

'Nah mate, we're definitely not drum and bass!'

'I'll get some beers in,' I said as we laughed. 'And try to find Andy, wherever he's gone.'

'Well he won't be at the bar, that's for sure,' Rob said as I walked away.

He was right. Andy fitted well in the band musically and as a friend… but he wasn't much of a drinker or smoker. Bit of a health-freak to be honest. Up early. Green tea. Morning jogs. Meditation. To give him credit, he always had energy. Or was that just his Guarana gum?

'Hey, Luke, isn't it?' A middle-aged man wearing glasses and white shirt held his hand out to shake.

'Yeah.' I shook it. 'Luke Redfern, from Beachhead.' I tried to use my professional voice like I'd heard Stephen and Detective Mellor use. The memory of Mellor threw me for a second and an image of Grandad came and went.

'That's right! Jeff was telling me all about you. I'm Nathan.'

'Ah, Nathan, good to meet you!' I said, having a vague recollection of Stephen mentioning his name once. I was treating everyone here as important, so I gave him my full attention.

'How's everything going with the E.P.?' Nathan asked with genuine enthusiasm. 'I heard *Shift* the other day – love it. Got a touch of The Doors about it, good beat too.'

'Yeah, top song,' I replied, unsure of how much I could say without boring Nathan with music-talk, but like James said – this was the perfect audience for all that. 'We built the song around the beat actually… Rob was trying out something new-'

'The drummer?'

'Yeah,' I replied. 'I had this old chord progression knocking around that fitted and James created the bass on the spot.'

Nathan was nodding.

'Then the lyrics formed themselves really… once we had the chorus.'

'Interesting, so do all your songs come about like that?'

'No,' I replied. 'Most are just me and the acoustic. Traditional song writing really. Lonely man singing the blues,' I said with a laugh. 'I bring the songs to the band and see what we can make of them.'

'Yeah, cool,' Nathan sounded enthused. 'Makes sense, although how you guys come up with something new every time I don't know!'

'That's the tricky bit but usually someone, Andy or Mike, our original lead guitarist, would add a riff that could change the whole song!'

Nathan raised his eyebrows and said, 'I bet he'll be kicking himself after leaving the band.'

'Who, Mike? Yeah, I guess.' I said and felt a hollow echo inside my chest. 'Andy's been great though. Turned that riff into what it is now…'

Nathan nodded again. 'Great song,' he said, but I felt the energy dissipate. 'Good luck with it!' he smiled and moved away, leaving me to carry on to the bar.

What was the issue? Was it Mike? My stomach tensed like I'd said something wrong but, no, it was the feeling of… guilt? Yeah, that was it. Here we were, mingling with the music elite, but where was Mike? He'd been a part of what had got us here hadn't he? Would he have any rights over the lead breaks he'd created? Andy hadn't changed everything…

'…not even a proper bloody manager.'

I recognised the voice and kept my head down, squeezing into the crush of people at the bar. I could still hear Andy, a few people away to my right.

'And I never got a say… I know I wasn't there at the start, but I'm a full-paid member now, you know?'

I angled myself to see Andy was talking to Jeff and clenched my fists. I caught a glimpse of his concerned face. Why didn't Andy say something to me about it? No, it was obvious why. Still, I was annoyed.

'...best man for the job...' was all I heard Jeff say before I made it to the bar and ordered three bottles of free beer.

I took a different route back to avoid Jeff and saw Dave from Skimrider surrounded by a trio of slim beauties hanging off his every word. The rest of Skimrider were lounging on sofas behind and I thought about joining them, but had to get back to Rob and James... and then I saw her. Charlotte. Jeff's daughter.

I diverted my route again, this time behind a gaggle of journalists huddled around a singer I vaguely recognised and made the long way back to the boys. Yes! I'd avoided her again.

'Here you go.' I handed the bottles over, keeping an eye on Charlotte.

'What's up?' James asked straight away.

'Charlotte's here,' I whispered, despite the noise of the chatting, music and boat's engine.

'Where?' James peered around.

'Don't look!' I hissed. 'The last thing I need is-'

'What is it?' Rob started looking around too.

'Nothing,' I said. 'Just Jeff's daughter and… after what happened in the summer, I…'

'You're still worried about that?' James said with a laugh. 'It was all natural.'

'Yeah, that was the problem!' I said and Rob laughed too.

'Don't worry about it, she'll be fine,' James said.

'It's not her I'm worried about, it's Jeff!' I replied.

'Don't sweat it,' Rob said. 'Anyway, did you see Andy?'

'No, I… well actually yeah I heard him,' I said. 'Listen, did Andy ever say anything to you guys about our manager?'

Rob and James shook their heads. 'No.'

'I know he's feeling guilty about leaving Chris's band and all that,' Rob said. 'Like we feel about Mike, I guess.'

I could see the pain in Rob's eyes. We'd talked about it openly and Rob knew he'd never be with him because Mike wasn't gay, but that didn't stop Rob worshipping the ground he walked on. It was like me not being with Lisa, I guessed, and felt some of his pain. At least I'd been in a relationship with Lisa.

'We gotta see it from his point of view,' James said. 'I mean, how would you feel if you went off to another band and left us stranded?'

I shrugged. 'Lightback could get another guitarist… like we did.'

'Yeah, but they knew each other from school,' Rob said. 'We need to look after Andy or he'll quit.'

'Yeah, I know,' I said, feeling an ache squeeze my temples. 'He's great.' I didn't need this extra pressure. Not now. 'Then Jeff would pull the plug and we'd be screwed.'

'Yes mate,' James said. 'No E.P. No Album. All that hard work for nothing.'

'I know,' I replied. 'I just don't want him undermining us when-'

A pair of long arms grabbed me, cutting me off, crushing me in a bear hug.

'Hey, bruv!'

I felt eyes turn to us and I tried not to wriggle like a schoolboy getting a wedgie. 'Stephen!' I said, trying to sound more surprised than annoyed by my big brother's attempt to embarrass me.

'Here he is - the most famous brother in British music,' Stephen said with his usual sarcasm. 'Good night lads? You didn't bring your girlfriend, James?'

'Nah, she's out with her mates...'

'Ah, shame. Alright, Rob?' Stephen said. 'You been to any of those clubs I told you about?'

'Yeah, a couple,' Rob replied with a glint in his eye.

'Cool, cool,' Stephen said and looked around. 'Anyone seen Andy? We should get the band together. Get a photo. Hey, listen,' he focussed on me. 'I saw Mum and Dad yesterday – had to pick something up – they asked how you were. Give them a call sometime, yeah?'

'Alright, alright,' I replied. 'You're not my boss.'

'Well, actually,' Stephen replied, 'I kind of am. Just call me Sir!'

After Andy's comments and now this, I was starting to regret suggesting having Stephen as Beachhead's manager. I looked away and saw Andy heading our way.

'Here he is,' I said and shuffled to give him some space.

'Brilliant, how's it going Andy?' Stephen said. 'Nice gig last night, didn't see you after?'

'No, I didn't fancy a big night,' Andy replied and took a swig of what looked like orange juice.

'Right, cool. So, are you all ready for tomorrow?' Stephen asked, looking at each of us in turn, like a school teacher.

I'd completely forgot and winced at the thought of it. Nerves or excitement I couldn't tell.

'Yeah sure, should be good,' James said.

'Yeah, exciting times,' Rob said.

'There's nothing to worry about,' Stephen added. 'Everything's sorted. The car will pick you lot up early doors and I'll meet you there, okay?'

'Sounds good,' Andy said, looking like he was cheering up.

Maybe Stephen would prove to be a good manager after all?

'And you've phoned everyone you know to get as many people as possible there, right?' he asked. 'I know loads of these guys will be there.' He nodded at the party around us.

'Yeah,' I said, trying to remember who said they could make it.

'I've messaged a few people,' Andy said, tapping the phone in his pocket.

Everyone else was nodding and Rob said, 'Mike's able to come along, I hope that's alright?'

'Of course,' Stephen said. 'The more the merrier. We need a big crowd. Nice one, right I'm off to schmooze a bit… you should too. Get out there guys – get your faces known!'

I looked at the boys and smiled. I'd dreamt about this for years, yet something was missing. The pressure I was feeling was taking the fun away and I couldn't stop thinking about Lisa. If she was here, she'd calm me down and get my head in the right place.

I remembered what my Mum used to say about thinking time and guessed I just needed some space.

'I'm off for a ciggy,' I said.

Stephen gave me a look saying 'just a ciggy, I hope?' which I ignored and made my way to the sheltered rear of the boat, careful to avoid Charlotte and Jeff along the way.

I squeezed through the heavy glass door, took a lungful of the fresh air and spotted a hooded figure leaning on the rail. 'Alright?' I said and pulled out my pack of Marlborough Lights.

'Alright,' he replied and I recognised his Cornish tones.

'Good night last night, Dave,' I said and lit one up. 'Cheers.'

'It's cool, good to have you there,' he replied and we smoked in silence for a bit.

'You're like me mate,' he eventually said. 'Prefer to smoke outside, yeah?'

'Yeah… and it's doing my head in there,' I replied, trying to act cool.

'I know what you mean,' he replied. 'Plus last night pissed me off… fucking fire alarm. Really killed the gig.'

'Yeah.'

He looked at me as though taking me in for the first time and I saw him as he really was: he was me in a couple of years' time. He'd lived through what we were going through now – the pressure, the uncertainty, the art, the first album, the rise, worrying about the fall - and he'd made it out the other side.

'You know what it's like, right?' Dave continued. 'On stage… you're *in it*. That bubble.' He looked away. 'Like being out on your board when a good set's rolling in and you can read the swell. If anything stops that it feels…'

'…broken,' I said, staring at the lights of the London river side, sliding by.

'Yeah, exactly. Like you've cut a film in half – it's a whole show, not two parts.'

'But we carry on,' I said, remembering the number of times I'd been thrown by Mike's antics or a broken string. 'That's being professional, right?'

'Yeah man. Doesn't feel the same after though. Missed that wave.'

We smoked in silence again, watching the city pass by. I thought of the trip we'd taken down to Cornwall where I'd given surfing a go. I'd been terrible but could see why people were drawn to it. The calm between the waves; the power of nature; being immersed in the real, natural world.

'It's all fake you know?' Dave said, catching me off guard.

'What?'

'All this.' He waved an arm back at the bobbing silhouettes through the window.

The bass rumbled through the floorboards, the drums mixed their vibrations with the boat's engine, and the singer's melody drifted in and out.

'It's fake,' Dave continued. 'All hype for the sake of hype… just to make money.'

'Like any business, I guess.'

'But for us, this is the big one. You and me, Luke, we have to ride it because *this is it.* We have to paddle hard and be the first up… for the band's sake as much as ours.'

'Yeah, I feel that,' I said, glad to have someone who understood.

'Soak it up,' he said. 'And keep writing man!' His face broke into a smile. 'I'm really getting into *Cobra* this week… love that chorus!'

'Cheers!' I said, stubbed out my cigarette and we went back inside.

The beery, smoke-infused air wrapped around us and drew us into its warmth.

I thought about Dave's surf analogies and remembered how hard paddling through the breaking waves had been, then trying to stand up on the board with an eight-foot vertical cliff of water beneath my board's nose… it had all been a struggle. But, in the end, I'd caught one and, as the fins bit in and the board did its job, I rushed down the bank of water, feeling a rush of pure exhilaration. I wiped out of course, rammed underwater, holding my breath for long seconds, desperately trying to find which way was up, but I was still buzzing when I returned to the beach. But when I was up, surfing, all I could think was how small that huge wave really was.

It was all about perspective.

'Ah, Dave and Luke!'

Jeff walked towards us ahead of a cloud of journalists.

'The future of British Indie music right here,' Jeff said to the group, patting Dave on the shoulder and gave me a wink. 'What I'd give to hear a song written by these two, hey?'

'Any chance of a collaboration?' one of the journos asked.

'Yeah, that'd be cool,' Dave replied. 'I was just saying to Luke how much I liked *Cobra*, so a track like that would work.'

'*Cobra*, is that on the Shift E.P.?' another asked me.

The gaze of countless eyes turned to me, like Medusa's snakes, and I tried not to freeze up.

'*Cobra's* on the new album,' I said. 'I think it'll be track eight so it'll kick off side B on vinyl.'

The music journos loved that, nodding and beaming, but all I could think of was Lisa and of our camping trip the summer before last when we argued over the best track number on classic albums.

'Have you got a release date for Beachhead's debut album?'

'Not yet,' I replied, feeling awkward that I was taking the limelight off Dave. 'We've got the *Shift* E.P. first and *Top Up* is still riding high in the charts, isn't it?' I looked to Dave, who took over for a few questions, answering with charm but rarely giving anything away.

'And the name of the Beachhead album?' A journo turned back to me but Jeff stepped in.

'We're keeping the album title under wraps for now,' he said. 'Let's give these boys a chance to get back to the party, hey? Thanks guys.'

The gaggle drifted away.

Dave looked at me, said, 'Hype for hype's sake,' and disappeared into the throng.

I felt sweaty and a bit dirty, but underneath I could feel a little thrill bubbling away. People wanted to know about my music… no, not people - music journalists wanted to know!

I drifted towards the stage at the other end of the room and took in the tunes by some band I'd never heard of, watching the finger-work and chord changes. Another group of lads, who'd just been given the key to the door. They sounded okay, but I found myself tearing their songs apart in my head. They were three steps behind us.

Lost in thought, it took me a second to register the warm hand on my shoulder, and double-took when I saw Jeff beside me.

'It may not feel like it now,' he said, keeping his eyes on the band. 'But these are your biggest rivals.'

I swallowed and my arms turned rigid.

'If you fuck up.' He turned to me and held my gaze. 'They will be in your place. They will get the house, the contract, the records, the marketing genius that accelerates your career from zero to a hundred in thirty seconds and *they* will get the gigs supporting our top bands.'

I blinked and felt my cheeks burn. What more could I do? I thought. Or was this about Charlotte?

'Krunch are hot on your heels too,' Jeff carried on. 'And you can be dropped for any misdemeanour I see fit.'

So this *was* about Charlotte.

Was this the time to be humble or show come backbone? I couldn't tell. I thought about everything I'd done to get here. Everything I had sacrificed. All of us in the band. An image of Isaac flashed before me – him rushing at me with his animal rage. I'd faced him and won. I could face anything.

I took a swig of beer, looked Jeff in the eye and said, 'The truth is, Jeff, with the material we've got, after our album comes out, we'll have Skimrider supporting us.'

Jeff didn't blink. An eyebrow twitched, followed by a crease by his mouth and he burst into a full grin.

'Ha! That's what I'm talking about Luke. Fighting talk, yes!'

He punched me in the arm.

'Look, you had an okay gig last night but you can do better. You've got the event tomorrow and the gig Tuesday night haven't you?'

'Yeah,' I replied, trying to remember the tiny venue Stephen had booked us into.

'Cool. I'm glad Stephen's keeping you boys busy. Which reminds me. We've got a little surprise for you in a minute – you'll love it.'

'Really?' I said, wondering whether I could trust this mood-swinging man. Half of Stephen's stories about him were starting to make sense.

'Yeah, totally,' Jeff said, his eyes wandering across the crowd now. 'And don't worry about all that shit with Chris, okay?'

I nodded back.

'Nathan in Legal's got it all sorted.'

'Brilliant,' I replied, realising that was why Nathan had acted so cagey when I mentioned Lightback.

'Oh, look, we're docking,' Jeff said, pointing at the lights out the window.

I could see a few silhouettes on a metal pier. More guests joining the party. Someone famous maybe?

'Let's go and greet them,' Jeff said, ushering me over.

'What? Okay,' I said as we pushed through the crowd.

Stephen was waiting by the exit and had his *'I know something you don't'* look on his face as a few deep clunks signalled the boat connecting with the mooring.

'We're all set,' Stephen said and opened the door. 'May I introduce the latest member of the Beachhead management team…'

A light mist had risen off the cold Thames, obscuring the people walking down the gangplank, but I recognised the one at the front straight away.

'Hello gorgeous,' she said, engulfing me in her arms and perfume as she kissed me on the mouth.

'Lisa?' I whispered.

'She's a keeper this one,' Jeff said with a wink.

Sunday 15th December 1996

Going for Gold – Shed Seven

'Get up, Luke!'

Lights flashed in front of my eyes like white fireworks and the real world came crashing into my consciousness. I'd been dreaming… maybe. My heart was racing. Lisa was standing over me and, for a second, I lost myself in her eyes.

'Come on, get up. The car will be here in half an hour.'

'Car?' I said and coughed.

'For the shoot, come on famous boy, you've had your beauty sleep, let's get a move on.'

I sat up, rubbed my head and grabbed the glass of water Lisa held out for me. It'd been a late night, but I'd only had a few beers on the boat so didn't have a proper hangover.

'Ah, that's better,' I said, finishing off the water.

'Get in the shower and don't worry about your hair – the make-up guys will sort that out,' Lisa said and ruffled my blonde spikes.

I glanced at the record player and stack of vinyl in the corner.

'Don't even think about it, Redfern!' she said. 'We haven't got time for setting the mood – crack on!'

I shook my head. 'I still can't believe you're actually here.'

'Believe it. Now get a move on!'

She ripped the duvet back, exposing me to the cold.

By the time I made it downstairs, the rest of the band were milling about, eating toast, drinking tea.

'Do you want a coffee, Luke?' Lisa called out from the kitchen.

'You've got her well trained,' Andy whispered.

'Oi, I heard that!' She shouted from the kitchen. 'Just remember I'm doing this as part of my new job.' She walked in, deposited a mug of Colombian heaven on the table in front of me, next to a bacon butty, and faced the boys. 'I'm part of the management crew, okay? I'm not a spy from the label or your boss.' She picked up a dirty plate and handed it to Rob. 'Or your Mum.'

'Got it,' Andy said, looking sheepish.

'I'm here to get your arses into gear so you can be bloody rock and roll stars, alright?' Lisa said.

I chomped on my butty, swigged the coffee and kept quiet.

'Gotcha,' James said, lying on the sofa. 'So this thing today… do we get clothes?'

'Yeah,' Lisa replied, softening. 'Stephen's got it all sorted – seriously, it's going to be amazing.' She caught my eye and I smiled. I didn't know if it was her natural energy or because she'd just come back from travelling, but Lisa was in her element. 'So, you've called everyone you know, yeah?' She held up the mobile phone the label had given her.

'Yep.' Andy tapped his phone in his pocket, while James and Rob both nodded.

'Good. So I'm guessing we'll get about seventy or eighty in total,' Lisa said.

'How does this fit in again?' I asked.

'Don't worry – the director will explain everything,' she replied.

'A director…' I whispered and shook my head. This was starting to get very real.

'Yeah,' James said. 'We're living the dream mate.'

A car horn beeped outside.

'Right, let's go lads!' Rob said, grabbing his sticks and a rucksack.

'What the fuck you got in there Rob?' James asked as they left.

'A few snacks and…'

Andy hot-footed it behind them and I crammed the rest of my butty into my mouth.

'Today's going to be great,' Lisa said, kissing me on the cheek. 'Everything you dreamed about. Soak it up, yeah?'

I nodded and finished my coffee. 'I'm buzzing,' I said. 'And so glad you're here – this is what we talked about all those nights in Australia, isn't it? It's finally happening!'

'It really is.' She beamed back. 'Come on – let's live it.'

I grabbed my bag and we rushed out to the waiting car. We'd been treated well in the summer when we recorded the album, staying in a hotel down the road from Jeff's huge mansion, spending days recording in the converted barn on his estate or chilling by his pool, but I wasn't expecting a car like this.

'It's a bloody limo mate!' James said when Lisa and I climbed in the back.

'Bloody hell!' I said and collapsed in the reclining seats opposite James, Andy and Rob.

'It's a Mercedes,' Rob said, stroking the leather seat and playing with a set of knobs and dials built into the walls. 'And here's the sound system – what shall we have?'

'Is it just radio?' Andy asked.

'Don't know,' Rob replied, poked a couple of dials as a mellow guitar riff reverberated from a dozen hidden speakers. 'Surely a limo from a record label would have some decent tracks plugged in…'

'The chilled Champagne is in the centre island, Ma'am,' the chauffeur said before closing the door for Lisa, enclosing us in our bubble of music and laughter.

'Turn it up!' James said as the drums started up, then the lyrics.

I never said never, ever…

'You took the words right out of my mouth!' We sang along with Rick Witter.

Lisa pulled out a huge bottle of champagne and handed out glasses. 'Cheers guys!'

'Rock and roll!' I said and gulped half a glass down, nearly choking on the bubbles.

Or are you going for gold…

'So where're we going again?' James asked.

Lisa pulled a folder out from a door compartment and read from a list. 'We've got three locations… starting off at a warehouse down by the docks.'

'So we're heading east then,' Andy said.

'Yeah, shouldn't take twenty minutes on a Sunday morning,' Lisa replied.

I sighed, trying to take it all in, staring out the window while the others chatted. I didn't need to know too much about today – that would make me feel nervous. I thought about having a smoke and eyed my bag, but knew what Lisa would say, plus this was a day for energy, not artistry. Lisa had everything covered and I was sure she and Stephen would let me know where I was needed.

'So that's why we need everyone there for ten o'clock, then a break while Luke films his bit and back again for the cars,' Lisa said.

'And they've got our guitars and amps?' Andy asked.

He was always asking questions, I thought. It got some people's backs up, like he was questioning *them*, but I'd learnt he just liked to know everything. Made him feel comfortable, I guessed.

'Yes, everything will be there – it's fine,' Lisa replied. 'Could have done with a bit of sun though,' she said, looking out the window.

'London in December, hey?' Rob said.

'You don't know you were born mate,' James replied. 'It'll be hailing in Manchester!'

By the time the car pulled into the barren and broken concrete desolation of the East London dockyards, we were half-drunk, which took the edge off the disappointing view.

'It's very… industrial,' Andy said as we clambered out.

'Gritty,' James said, nodding.

'Not the sunny beach video I was expecting,' I said with a laugh. 'Come on, let's pretend we're famous.'

I didn't see any cameras but Lisa told me they were rolling when we left the car and captured us strolling across the grey landscape to the derelict shell of a metal storehouse where a hundred people cheered our arrival.

'They've been told they'll open the burger van when you get here,' Lisa whispered in my ear with a giggle.

'Genius,' I replied, waving at the horde of eager twenty-somethings.

There was a two-foot high stage at one end of the space, where out instruments sat tuned and eager, framed by a set of lights. I nodded, taking it all in. The lads were beaming too.

'This is going to be great,' James said, smirking.

'Hey, there's Mike!' Rob shouted over the noise and waved at our ex-lead guitarist.

A pang of guilt hit me, but I forced it down: it'd been his choice to abandon us and he still got to be in the video, I thought. Plus a part of me liked the idea of him seething when he saw Andy playing an upgraded version of his old lead break. He needed humbling.

'We'll just go to the van to get you guys powdered,' Lisa said, directing us through a rear door to an open space that looked like a classic car rally.

'What the hell?' I said and slowed down.

'That's an original twenty-one window campervan!' Andy said, pointing at a sweet splitty with narrow windows running down either side of the roof. 'And is that a 1970 Karmann Ghia?'

I looked to see where he was pointing and spotted Grandad's old car.

'Yeah, that's my… that's Stephen's car,' I said, trying to stay cool. That's why he'd been to our parents recently, I thought. Brave of him to drive it all the way to London!

'Awesome,' Andy said, his eyes as big as saucers.

I turned to Lisa. 'You sorted all this out?'

'Some of it,' she replied with a cute tilt of the head. 'But Stephen's been organising this for weeks. He wanted the driving scene to be shot in Brighton, but the budget was tight.'

I nodded, realising how much work Stephen was doing behind the scenes, and felt butterflies in my stomach: Beachhead had a video budget! No wonder Jeff was putting pressure on us with the amount of effort and money being ploughed into our band.

I took a deep breath and we strolled over to a caravan in the far corner.

'Hello.' A man with curly hair welcomed us. 'Let's get you lubed-up for action.'

'And she said… Shift! You know we gotta… SHIFT!'

We were playing the song live on the stage for the second time while the sound engineers linked up the speakers to allow us to mime to the recorded track. None of us were keen but the director, Jason, explained how it had to sync up, so we went with it. I wasn't sure how many times I could sing the same song over and over though.

'Nice one,' Jason called through his megaphone. 'Now we're going to give it a live run through with the cameras, so this is it.' He'd hopped onto the stage to talk to the crowd, his long hair flowed, mimicking his flared jeans and opened shirt. 'Just go crazy for the chorus and mental during the lead break, okay?'

The throng of cold-but-excited revellers yelled back. Happy now they had food in their belly.

I'd been people-spotting while we played, recognising a few. I recognised Chris, from *Lightback* and gave Mike a thumbs-up, standing with James' ex, Rachel, and the other girls we knew in Brighton, including Sarah, the girl who'd dumped a pint of cold lager over my head when I left her for Lisa.

I breathed in deeply.

Lisa was on the right flank with a group of her mates… including Jim, her ex who I'd dobbed in to Detective Mellor for dealing drugs. Jeez, the audience was peppered with guilt-trips! I tried not to catch their eyes again, focussing on Stephen instead, who was at the back, making up the numbers with some other guys from the label.

'Right, here we go from the top!' Jason called out from the crowd and the speakers crackled into life.

An hour or so later, we'd played *Shift* about seventeen times and tried all sorts of random stage antics, getting wilder with each play, until we broke a speaker and Jason called it a day. The lads took a break and the crowd were given more food while I was whisked away for the most embarrassing scene. Sure, I'm the front man and this is what I'm supposed to do - I'm the face of Beachhead, I sing *my* lyrics. But it's hard not to be self-conscious mouthing words to a song coming from a tinny-sounding speaker taped to the bottom of a huge video camera shoved in your face.

We filmed it in the concrete wasteland we'd been dropped off in. I could see the photographic appeal. Black and white shots of broken histories and a giant's lost strength. Moody. But I felt ridiculous. It was just me and two cameramen – one filming and the other guiding him as he walked backwards – it felt amateurish.

'How was it?' Lisa asked when I strolled back indoors.

A few heaters had been dragged into the warehouse, so the crowd were split into even groups huddled around each one, munching and chatting.

'Great,' I said, nodding.

'Really?'

'No, bloody embarrassing, but it's done, hey? Any burgers left?'

'Yeah sure, but Jason wants to do the car scene before it starts raining.'

'Okay,' I replied, starting to feel less like a rock star and more like a clothes model. I didn't want to complain but I was cold and needed a bit of headspace.

I felt eyes on me and Lisa as we grabbed some greasy burgers from the van in the corner. It was weird. Most of the crowd were mates of the band, so they should be used to this, but I felt separate somehow. Was this what being famous felt like? Always on the outside?

I caught Mike's eyes and he gave me a wink. I remembered his 21st birthday party round his parents' house and decided that was what this felt like. I was just the birthday boy, nothing more.

'Why is everyone still here?' I asked.

'We need them to make the streets look busy,' Lisa replied. 'It's Sunday…'

'Right, yeah,' I said, feeling the need to get away from the stares. 'Come on, let's go outside.'

'I've got a better idea!' Lisa said, her eyes glinting as she jangled some keys in my face.

'Stephen will kill us!' I said as we slipped into his Karmann Ghia.

'He'll be fine,' Lisa said. 'Just don't get any ketchup on the seats!'

We munched in silence for a minute before Lisa said, 'So how's it going then?'

I raised my eyebrows.

'It's not that bad is it?'

'No,' I replied with a smile. 'It's a bit relentless… it's good to have a minute to let my head settle.'

'You haven't changed have you?' Lisa said and kissed me on the cheek. 'We haven't really caught up properly yet have we?'

'No,' I replied. I was going to joke that we'd done plenty of 'catching up' last night, but this wasn't the time. 'I guess we should be used to it by now. What's it been? Six months this time?'

'Yeah, I left when you started recording. India was amazing. So much to tell you! Some great places I want to go back to… you'd love Goa, but if we go back, we should head to Kerala… you'd get some great photos down there.'

'I thought Cambodia was going to be the next trip? Angkor Wat.'

'Maybe,' Lisa shrugged in a way that made me feel excited and worried at the same time.

I guess I needed a bit of certainty. I wondered if it would be like this for ever, heading off on our separate ways to pursue our own adventures, then catching up for short periods. On and off. Would we ever settle into a more simple routine? Is that what I longed for? No, not yet. Neither of us wanted the simple life. Not now anyway. I'd had that in the bookshop and got into a funk, smoking weed and chasing girls.

'The gigs are going well,' I said.

As much as I'd enjoyed travelling with Lisa I always needed the adrenaline hit of the gigs. Sure, it would burn out one day and I'd go on another journey somewhere alien to get my creative juices flowing, but I needed that buzz right now.

'Cool. So, what else have I missed?'

'Well…' I started.

'You know the drill, keep it simple.'

I laughed, remembering the first time we met up after one of Lisa's travelling breaks and I'd started listing all the new albums, TV programmes, films and events she'd missed.

'Okay, okay,' I said. 'TFI Friday obviously… you were back after the Euros so you caught up on all of that… I tried to talk the guys into a *Three Lions* cover but they weren't having it.'

'Good shout,' Lisa said. 'That moment's passed.'

'The trip in Cornwall was cool – getting better at surfing… and The Fast Show's as good as ever.'

'Cool,' Lisa said. 'Next time you should say *this month I 'ave mostly been playing guitar*.'

'Ha! Yeah, sounds about right.'

Lisa finished off her burger and said, 'It looks like Jeff's organising some tours for next year.'

'Really?'

'Yeah, it doesn't just happen you know!'

'I know,' I replied. 'I just thought Jeff was going cool on us.'

'No it's not that-'

A loud bang made us both jump as a dark shape appeared next to me.

'Oi!' Stephen shouted through the glass. 'You get any muck on my seats and I'll have you hung, drawn and quartered!'

'Shit! You nearly gave me a heart attack you muppet!' I shouted back.

I was annoyed because there was so much I wanted to talk to Lisa about – the pressure and frustration, how everything with Beachhead was taking so long, yet going so fast… the lack of meaning in any of it, my songs. Music meant so much to me, I felt it in every fibre, but what about the people who bought it… was it just a distraction from their lives? A mood to fill the gap?

Stephen opened the door. 'Come on, out you get… we need to get started.'

'Alright, alright.' I clambered out.

'Don't mess with the car,' Stephen said. 'I've already had some weirdo try and flip the hood.'

A long line of people were filing out of the warehouse, towards the nearest street.

'You're needed on the back of the truck,' Stephen said, pointing at an old American-style van with a flatbed at the back. From here I could see Rob's drum kit and the heads of our guitars. James and Andy were climbing up.

'Right then.' I gave Lisa a kiss. 'Last shoot, then we can head off, yeah?'

'Yeah,' Stephen replied. 'Then I'll give you a lift home.'

'Cool.'

I joined the lads on the truck. 'This looks great!'

'Yeah, just don't fall off, eh?' James said.

'No amps, so I guess we're miming again,' Andy said, pointing at a couple of speakers in the corners of the wooden platform.

'That's right,' Jason appeared, wearing a long brown sheepskin coat over his seventies shirt. 'We'll see how it goes but I've fixed one camera here on the back.' He tapped a black box I'd completely missed. 'And we'll have two cameras on the street to capture the mood… carnival but moody.'

'Sounds good,' I said, nodding, not really knowing where he was going with a carnival atmosphere on a December day in East London, but he made bloody good music videos, so who was I to judge?

'Right then, let's roll!' Jason shouted and hopped into a rusty orange beetle.

I grabbed my guitar, swung the strap over my head and played a few chords. The rest of the band looked how I felt: loving it but trying not to be embarrassed by it. Grinning sheepishly at the bizarre nature of it all.

The van moved off slowly, rolling as it crossed potholes, then onto a good road. Behind us, the eclectic mix of cars, bikes and vans followed us in convoy with people hanging out of every vehicle.

Music suddenly blared out of the speakers.

'And we're rolling!' Jason called out through his megaphone.

'Alright then lads,' James said. 'Let's play it like we mean it!'

The van turned the corner into the most run-down street imaginable, lined with boarded-up shops and tipped over bins, broken windows and bent lampposts. And a hundred screaming fans who were now mouthing every word of *Shift* like they'd heard it a hundred times before.

'*We can't tell her cos that's her fella, living in the shadow of a broken storm…*'

The crowd swarmed, cameras dashed in and out, and the stream of cars followed. More singing, miming and playing. Over and over. We turned and had another run, then another and, three plays later, we rolled back into the parking lot where the crowd milled around the cars, probably for heat as much as anything.

Jason hopped onto our flatbed with his megaphone, speaking to the horde. 'Listen, I just want to say thanks again to all of you for today, it's been great.'

He knew how to work the crowd.

'You've been brilliant and you're going to look even better when we've cut the video – believe me!' He looked at me and gave me a wink. 'You want to say anything?'

'Yeah sure.' I took the megaphone, copying how he'd pressed the trigger to speak. 'You've been amazing today. Bloody freezing, so thank you so much… I…' They whooped again. 'We really appreciate it and can't wait to see the final cut. I know you're probably sick of the song now…' That got a laugh. '…but you know the words better than anybody else in the country!'

James was beside me, so I passed him the mic.

'Yeah, spread the word! *Shift* is out in the new year!'

Jason took the megaphone back. 'We're going to call it a day now, so thanks very much!'

The mass wandered around for a bit, like at the end of a gig, then started to move away in pairs and groups, away from the cars, some of which crawled away too.

I leapt down and Lisa popped over, gave me a kiss. 'Leave all the gear, the boys will sort it out.'

'Yeah, sure,' I replied. 'See you back home.'

The lads were already cooing over Mike's campervan and didn't hear me, so I jogged off to get my bag from the make-up trailer and found Stephen leaning on his Karmann Ghia.

'It looked pretty cool little brother,' he said and gave me a bear hug. 'Come on, let's get you home.'

'Wow, was that a compliment?' I asked as I slunk into the passenger seat.

'Maybe,' Stephen replied. 'But don't get used to it.'

We'd had plenty of discussions after we'd signed with Jeff, about Beachhead, weed, the music business… and he'd always been cool, so I'd never told him *I told you so!* after years of asking him to send a scout down to see us.

'Right then,' Stephen said as we pulled out of the yard and onto the road. 'Another gig Tuesday night… ramping up to Christmas.'

'Yeah cool,' I replied, genuinely looking forward to doing a smaller gig where I could actually see the crowd's faces. 'Are you still going to Mum and Dad's for Christmas?'

'Yeah, where else would I go?' Stephen replied as we sped up to join a new road.

'True, I just thought with your new fella and all that…'

'No, it's not like that I… that's odd… shit!'

The next few seconds lasted an age. Like when I wiped out in the sea. Long seconds as I felt weightless and the buildings around us moved strangely.

I stared at Stephen who was struggling with the steering wheel, his legs pumping the pedals. The engine screamed a C sharp as we spun and crashed into the side of a parked bus.

Then darkness.

Monday 16th December 1996

Smile – The Supernaturals

Flashing lights. Darkness. Pain. Fear. White. Everything so white…

'You've been here all night?' A voice asked.

'Yeah, I managed to get some sleep on the chairs.' A different voice replied.

Both female.

Did they know I was here?

I tried to open my eyes but they felt glued tight. I couldn't remember much but last night must have been good because this was one of the worst hangovers I'd ever had. My mouth was cactus-dry, my head ached, there was a dull throb in my lower back… and my left arm really hurt.

'He's waking up. Luke, can you hear me?'

A crack of light as I forced my iron eyelids to open. A face… a smile. Lisa! Yes, that's whose voice it was. She'd dyed her hair darker… and looked good as a brunette.

'Hi, Luke, I'm Doctor Daniels. You've been in an accident and you're in the hospital.'

I took a massive lungful of air, like I'd been underwater, and my eyes opened fully.

'Accident?'

Images came back to me. Red car. Laughing. Red bus. *Strike*. I turned and saw Lisa. Still blonde.

'Lisa?'

'It's okay Luke, everything's okay.' She sat on my bed and held my hand, her eyes tired: pained.

'What happened?' I whispered.

'What can you remember?' The doctor asked me.

More images came to me, but nothing concrete, then… 'Stephen! Is he okay?'

'You were in a car crash,' Lisa said. 'Stephen was driving.'

'Your brother's in the hospital too – we're looking after him,' the doctor said. 'But I want to see how you're doing.'

I stared at her, she was probably only a few years older than us, and I wondered if I should have done something more useful with my life like becoming a doctor, a teacher or ambulance driver, or…

'Tree surgeon,' I said.

'What?' Lisa asked and gave the doctor a worried look.

'It's probably the anaesthetic,' Doctor Daniels explained. 'Still wearing off.'

'I'm fine,' I said and tried to sit up but my left arm didn't move.

'Keep lying down,' Lisa said.

'But my arm…'

'You had a number of injuries from the accident,' the doctor said. 'Mostly bruises. Do you remember what happened?'

'Yeah, Stephen was driving… we hit a bus,' I replied, remembering it all clearly now, but I was more concerned about my arm. I looked down and could see Lisa's hand on my right hand, but nothing where my left arm should be.

'My arm!' I gasped and felt Lisa's grip tighten.

'It'll be okay,' she said, her large eyes glistening.

'But…'

'It's okay Mister Redfern,' Doctor Daniels said.

Using my surname made me feel worse, like really bad news was coming.

'Your left arm took most of the impact of the crash and was damaged.'

I tried to swallow, but my throat was still dry.

'You had a clean break in the wrist and I'm glad to say it has set well,' the doctor said and glanced to my left, above my head.

I turned my head slowly, wary of what I would see, and frowned, making sense of the contraption next to my bed. My arm was in a plaster cast, suspended in a sling.

'We've kept it elevated, but we can lower it now.'

'Oh,' I said, feeling relieved and confused at the same time.

'I'll go and get your parents,' Lisa said and gave my hand a squeeze before leaving the room.

I took in the room for the first time while the doctor loosened the sling, allowing my arm to drop. It was white, clean and larger than any bedroom I'd ever had. I was on my own too, which was strange. I thought the hospital wards were supposed to be crowded.

'There we go,' Doctor Daniels said, resting my arm on my chest.

It was tingling now and a sudden sharp pain burst through it, making me wince.

'It'll take six to eight weeks to heal fully,' she explained. 'And you'll need to keep it still to ensure the bones heal straight.'

Suddenly it hit me hard: I couldn't play guitar. Seeing the fresh cast and feeling the pain in my wrist. We weren't going to play the gig tomorrow night or any gig for months. I couldn't even pick up my acoustic and have a strum. I hadn't gone a day without playing for… as long as I could remember. Was this it? The end of all our dreams? The end of Beachhead, just as we were getting started?

'We can arrange some physiotherapy,' the doctor continued. 'And when the…'

I stopped listening as another reality came crashing down on me. I felt guilty that it was my second thought. Was I really that selfish?

'Stephen,' I said, cutting the doctor off. 'What happened to Stephen?'

'Well,' she started, her eyes hardening, weighing up how much I could take. 'He hasn't regained consciousness yet, but he has been operated on and the surgeon is happy with his progress.'

I could feel my heart speed up as she talked, then two shapes appeared at my door. My eyes met Mum's through the glass panel and a tear ran down my left cheek. My brother…

'Is everything okay?' Dad asked as he entered, holding the door open for Mum.

'Yes, Luke is fine,' the doctor replied. 'Just the arm. I'll leave you to it.' She said and left.

'We'll get you home for a bit,' Mum said straight away. 'We can look after you there.'

'You may as well stay for Christmas,' Dad said, raising a hand to stop any of my objections.

'Yes, bring Lisa too,' Mum added.

I just nodded, trying to take it all in. Forget Christmas and being stuck at my parents' house, I wanted to know how Stephen was and how the hell my band were going to play tomorrow's gig.

'Nice place this.' Dad drew up two white chairs by my side. 'Private.'

'Is it?' I asked, realising that was why I wasn't in a crowded ward.

'The record label paid for it,' Mum said and bit her lip.

'Jeff was here earlier, Stephen's boss,' Dad said. 'It's all covered in your contract apparently and Stephen's of course.'

'How is he?' I asked.

Mum looked away, a tear forming in each eye.

Dad petted her and said, 'He took a knock to the head and a couple of ribs broken, but the doctors say he'll pull through. Just a matter of time.'

I was feeling sleepy again but didn't want to worry my parents, so kept on talking for a bit.

'How about the car?' I asked, knowing it wasn't the most important thing, but it had been Grandad's so it had some sentimental value.

'The traffic boys sent it away,' Dad said with a sigh, while Mum came over to hold my hand. 'Would have been a write-off but because it's a classic model… plus they're going to give it a once over, you know.'

I didn't know, but didn't ask. My eyelids were getting heavy.

'Lisa said the boys want to come and see you later,' Mum said.

'Cool,' I replied and nestled into my pillow.

The next thing I knew, a nurse was waking me up, wheeling a tray of food over the end of my bed. A clock on the wall told me it was early afternoon. I yawned and looked around, expecting Mum and Dad to still be there.

'You've got some visitors outside,' the nurse said. 'I can ask them to wait until you've eaten if you want?'

I leant up to get a look through the window in the door and spotted a pair of Converse.

'No, that's cool, send them in.'

'Lukey boy!' James was first through, followed by Rob and Andy. 'Y'all right mate?'

'Good to see you awake, lazy bones.'

'How are you feeling?'

'I'm alright,' I replied with a smile. 'Good to see you guys.'

'Oooh… hospital food!' James took a look. 'Not bad actually.'

'Nice room,' Rob said, reclining in one of the curved designer chairs.

It was all a bit much for me and I focussed on Andy, who stood quietly to one side.

'So, did any of you see it?' I asked, trying to keep the mood light as I scooped into the mound of shepherd's pie on my plate.

'What, the crash?' Rob asked. 'No, we went out the other way.'

'Oh yeah,' I replied, remembering them going in Mike's campervan.

'Didn't find out 'til Lisa rang me,' Andy said, still looking concerned.

They all had a touch of hangdog about them: Rob couldn't make eye contact with me and James was still pacing the room. Was it the gig they were worried about? I mean, I was fine and I doubt they were that bothered about Stephen, so that had to be it.

'Listen,' I said. 'I can't play guitar for a bit…'

'No shit,' James said, eyeing my cast.

'…so what're we going to do about tomorrow night?'

'The gig?' Rob asked, like it wasn't the elephant in the room.

'We'll have to cancel,' Andy said, still glum.

'Or you could just sing?' James said. 'It's only a little gig, right?'

'No way,' Rob said and Andy backed him up.

'I reckon I could just stand there and sing,' I said with a shrug, sending a shot of pain through my wrist, making me wince.

'No, it's too much,' Andy said. 'You're still in pain.'

'I'll see what the doctor says,' I replied. 'But even if I'm drugged up and perched on a bar stool, we still need someone to play rhythm guitar… I mean, how can we do *Avalanche* without it?'

'Well, I can play those bits,' Andy said. 'Just have to mix it up a bit.'

'The gig's tomorrow mate,' James said. 'It's too late to re-work the songs.'

'Mike could step in?' Rob suggested with puppy-dog eyes.

'Nah,' I said, shaking my head, even though I knew it could work.

I finished off the rest of the food, thinking about Stephen and what he would say. The show must go on and all that, I guessed.

A knock at the door made us all turn as the door opened and a smiling face appeared.

'Oh, hi Jeff,' Rob said.

'That's what I like to see!' Jeff said, closing the door behind him. 'The whole band sticking together through times of crisis.' He focussed on me. 'How are you feeling Luke?'

'Tired, but okay,' I replied, pushing the tray away.

'Well you've got your appetite back which is a good sign.' He looked at the guys. 'Er, can you give us five minutes? Cheers.'

'Yeah sure,' James said. 'We'll pop back in a bit, yeah?'

'They've taken good care of you then?' Jeff asked when they'd gone.

'Yeah, thanks,' I replied. 'I appreciate it… I mean, we do… my family.'

'Don't mention it,' Jeff said, seeming genuinely humble. 'That's what the insurance is for, right?' he let out a little laugh. 'I saw your parents… they're concerned about Stephen, but I'm sure he'll be fine. This is one of the best hospitals so… but the shoot went well yesterday I hear. Every silver lining has a cloud and all that.'

I didn't know if it was Jeff's sudden concern, my tiredness or him getting sayings wrong, but I was confused.

'Listen, this gig tomorrow night, do you think you can still make it?' He asked. 'Just sing a few of your numbers? I've got someone coming and, well, wheels are turning. There're a few plans afoot…'

'Yeah, we were just talking about it,' I replied, seeing this was what it was really all about.

He could be genuinely concerned about Stephen but Dave from Skimrider was right – the industry was fake. Hype for hype's sake… well, for money's sake.

'We can work around a few of the songs and I'll just not play on the others,' I said.

'Great.' Jeff looked relieved. 'I've got some big plans… I'm hoping they'll be in place in time for New Year, but they're under wraps for now.' He was looking out the window while he talked, like dictating a message or talking to himself, then he snapped back to me. 'Any issues could de-rail the whole thing, so we need to keep on track, okay?'

'Sure.' I nodded, feeling the old pressure building up again.

'I'm just glad Stephen brought Lisa on-board – she's ace. I'm pretty sure everything'll run fine as long as she's around.'

I saw a shape at the door and Lisa's eyes caught mine.

'I couldn't agree more,' I said and smiled.

Tuesday 17th December 1996

Cut Some Rug – The Bluetones

Back in 1995 after I returned from Australia to sign Beachhead's contract, we had a few months before the studio became available so I re-joined Lisa, who had carried on travelling, in Thailand. We hit the north of the country, trekking out from Chiang Mai to stay at a village in the highlands. Lisa was keen to learn more about the various cultures in the hills, which had apparently migrated south from China over the ages, and I was after some inspiration. It was a great opportunity for me to build my photography portfolio and although I took some of my best portrait photos – children playing in the rain; misty villages; kitchen laughter – my interactions there brought home how important music really was to me.

We spent a night in one of the straw-rooved huts set on stilts, surrounded by giggling children and trees overflowing with bell-flowers. We'd eaten well and been entertained by the village dancers and then it was our turn… someone produced a guitar. I was drawn to it, but didn't want to show off, then Lisa gave me a wink and I played a cover of a Jamiroquai song.

They loved it: the villagers old, young, and in-between.

For the rest of the evening I was surrounded by young kids, sitting on my lap, chatting away or showing off their best moves. It taught me to never underestimate the power of music.

'Any fans of John Peel out there?' I asked, searching the thirty pairs of eyes fixed on me. Some smiled and I got a couple of 'Yeahs'.

We were playing in the kind of venue we used to play back in Brighton and, truth be told, I loved it. We were in a smoky back room of an old Victorian pub where the dark, scuffed floorboards creaked with every footstep and the paint hung off the ceiling in long, nicotine-stained strips. Punters leaned on iron pillars or against the poster-covered walls, pints in hand. No dancing and no mosh-pit here.

'You might have heard the next song on his show then,' I said and turned to look at Andy who had picked up my acoustic guitar but still had his electric guitar slung over his back.

I gave him a thumbs up.

'This new version might sound a bit different,' Andy said into his mic with a laugh.

I raised my plaster cast and got a few more laughs. I was feeling alright – the meds were strong – and, so far, this was working. The crowd were here to see us and the other up-coming bands, so they appreciated we hadn't cancelled on them. I'd been searching the faces for Jeff or anyone who looked important, but the pub was full of long-haired lads and lasses. Not a shirt in sight.

Andy strummed and I tried to ignore how he'd added an extra up-stroke to the rhythm I usually played. It felt weird singing without my guitar against my belly. Our first song had felt strange too but I got used to it, like when I recorded the vocals in the summer. Was the guitar a barrier? I wondered. Something to hide behind rather than an instrument that projected my emotions?

Out came the words and I focussed on them.

Unlike most of my songs, *Avalanche* had no real meaning: the words had just come to me when I'd come up with the chord progression. But today it felt different. The lyrics weren't just words to the audience. I sensed that at the last gig. They sang and yelled the lyrics like they really meant something to them. Now, concentrating on the words, all I could think of was Stephen. He was still in hospital, unconscious, and we were here entertaining people. It didn't feel right.

We finished the song and I took a sip of beer, which tasted weird due to the bitter pills I was on, and shifted my arm in its sling.

'That sounded good,' James said, nodding.

'Maybe we should do an acoustic set one day?' I replied away from the microphone.

I gave the crowd another scan, looking for Lisa this time. Memories of the gig the day after we met came back to me, when she hadn't turned up and I'd been annoyed with Mike for showboating… I'd bumped into Lisa at the club afterwards and we'd often joked how different our lives would have been if we hadn't met. Fate?

What was slowing her down tonight? I wondered. We'd had a few words in the hospital: nothing major, just how she wasn't keen on me doing the gig after leaving hospital, but that wouldn't stop her coming, surely?

A jolt of movement in the audience caught my attention and people moved away. Someone throwing up I guessed by the way someone was holding back a girl's hair. At least I thought it was a girl. The mod haircuts and surfer locks were interchangeable with women's haircuts in the smoky dim-lit pubs.

'Alright, thanks!' I said as we finished a heavier number.

'I'm not drowning out your lead anymore,' I said to Andy off-mic and gave him a wink.

'Yeah, good sound in here,' he replied.

Rob and James looked content too as we moved on through our set list, keeping it pretty much the same as when we supported Skimrider.

'This next one's off our new E.P.,' I said, remembering this what it was all about. 'Shift.'

I sang, trying not to remember the video shoot or the crash, focussing on the back of the room and any newcomers… no sign of Lisa or Jeff but then my parents sidled in and my shoulders slumped at the thought of Stephen in hospital. I just hoped they weren't bringing bad news.

A few songs later, we wrapped up the set, finishing on a high.

'Thanks – you've been great,' I said as the lads started stashing our gear at one side of the stage to make room for the next band. 'Look out for the E.P. and our album next year, cheers.'

No green rooms here. Everyone in the mini-crowd chatted as a Bluetones track played over the speakers but it felt eerily quiet compared to our usual gigs.

'See you out the front, yeah?' James said when his bass was packed away. 'I'll get some beers in.'

'Yeah, cool.'

I helped Rob with his drums then spoke to a couple of the punters who liked our stuff. This was cool: intimate. The next band, Krunch, set up, who I had no desire to watch. They'd never been social with us and barely spoke to us at the gig at the weekend. After what Jeff had said about them being hot on our tails, I was wary of them. As I mingled, Krunch's lead singer – some Canadian tosser called Kurt who thought he was Cobain's successor – strolled past and turned to his bandmate.

'Wasn't it worth it, eh? They're pretty crap as a three-piece.'

He glanced at me to make sure I'd heard. I tried to ignore it, but it stung. Here I was putting in more effort than he knew, physically and mentally, and he was poking me like I was some injured animal. I knew it was just for show: trying to take us down because we were one rung ahead of them up the ladder. Stephen had warned me about fake rivalries too. Easy to get carried away with stuff like that, so I turned the other cheek, deciding a pint and my girlfriend were a far better option than a pointless fight.

The pub's front room was even smokier than the gig room, full of large wooden tables filled with people rolling up and chatting tunes. I spotted the lads on a separate table to my parents, giving us some space, I guessed, and heard conversations as I wound my way through the tables. It was all music gossip: new albums; B-sides; singles; who was shagging who; who was fighting who. Even if you weren't into music you couldn't deny there was a real buzz about British Indie right now and it was bloody amazing being a part of it. I nodded at the lads, looking forward to our usual gig dissection later.

'It sounded good,' Mum said as I joined them.

'Thanks,' I replied. 'Not bad considering.' Dad pushed a pint across the table. 'Cheers. How's Stephen?' I asked.

'No change,' she replied, wrinkling her nose to hold back her tears.

'I'm sure he'll be fine,' I said, trying to sound reassuring. 'It's a good hospital after all.'

'Are you sure it's okay to drink with your meds?' Dad asked.

'Yeah, I'm fine,' I replied, enjoying the floaty-head the painkillers had given me.

'You really should take it easy you know,' Mum said.

'I know, I know… it's fine, honestly,' I said. 'Everything worked out fine tonight.' I looked over at the lads and Andy caught my eye – he had an odd look on his face I couldn't work out if he wanted to talk to me or not.

Dad looked tense too, which I put down to the stress of Stephen being in hospital.

'So, is the hotel okay?'

'Yeah, it's fine,' Dad said, nodding. 'Listen, I know the crash wasn't anyone's fault but it's come at a bad time.'

'Like there would be a good time?' I replied, feeling irked.

'I know,' Dad replied and looked properly stressed so I held back. 'I heard from my solicitor the other day.'

'That stuff with Knowles still dragging on?' I asked.

'He won't give up,' Dad said with a shake of his head.

I looked to Mum who was unusually quiet.

'And your Mum has a date for her court hearing,' Dad said.

Mum rolled her eyes, clearly not taking it too seriously, not that she wanted Dad to know that! Everything I knew about her case had come from Stephen: how she'd had been caught spraying Bob Dylan lyrics on the back of a terraced house further out from her usual territory: how the police were sure they'd finally caught the Pavilion Poet. Dad had only just re-joined the force so was devastated. Mum had said she was just a copycat – a bored house wife looking for thrills. She'd agreed to take art classes and pay for the clean-up, but the council legal team wanted blood and she was going to be hauled across the coals.

'Everything we do is being watched,' Dad said: his eyes serious. 'I'm not out of the woods yet with Knowles… he has his ways as you know.'

I nodded, remembering how Mellor had tried to set me up with a block of resin and raided my flat.

'And Mum's case is tight.'

He gave her hand a squeeze.

'What your Dad's trying to say,' Mum finally said. 'Is that we need to be on our best behaviour… all of us.'

'Nothing the solicitors can bring against us,' Dad said.

'Oh, it's alright,' I said, immediately feeling guilty. 'I haven't smoked in ages.'

'Well,' he replied with a squint. 'Let's keep every-'

A shape appeared at my side. My parents looked up and I expected to see Lisa.

'Luke, sorry.' It was Andy.

He held his mobile phone out.

'I just had a text from Lisa, thought you should know.'

'Ah, okay,' I replied, wondering whether I should get a phone seeing as everyone else had one. 'Is she alright?'

'Yeah, she's fine. She said sorry for missing the gig - she's out with some mates and's going to stay round theirs tonight.'

'Right, cool, thanks,' I said, feeling slightly deflated as Andy left us to it.

I was looking forward to spending more time with Lisa, but it made sense. She'd been out of the country for a while and had loads of friends to catch up with.

'Anyway, I also heard from some contacts,' Dad said.

I sighed, wondering what else he was going to lay on me.

'In traffic,' he explained. 'They're still checking the car.'

'Are they looking for anything in particular?' I asked, switching from Dad to Mum, who were both frowning.

'Who knows,' Mum said with a shrug. 'It was an old car, so there's plenty that could have gone wrong.'

'Yeah,' I replied. 'Wear and tear.'

Dad shrugged. 'But Stephen had it serviced last month, knowing he was bringing it up here.'

Nobody mentioned it but I was paranoid the car could have been tampered with. My stomach tensed as I had flashback. It had been a while: Shirley's dead body; a penguin book on my desk; Isaac's crazed look when he dashed out to kill me.

'I'm sure they'll just find a rusty bolt or something,' Mum said, resting her hand on mine.

'Yeah sure,' I said, taking a long swig of beer, ignoring my gut feeling and hoping she was right.

Wednesday 18th December 1996

Hey Dude – Kula Shaker

The next day, I took the bus home after visiting Stephen in the hospital and listened to tunes on the portable CD player I'd bought when Lisa and I went travelling. I needed that comfort. Something to remind me of cosier times. Abroad, I would watch the world go by while the English tones of Thom, Crispian and Louise reminded me of home. Now, staring at cold, grey monoliths instead of red deserts and rolling jungle, they still comforted me.

I framed a few good black and white photos in my head, but mostly it was winter drudge lit up by Christmas lights. Urban repetition. Still, it was good thinking time.

Stephen had been trussed up to a variety of bleeping, pumping machines when I'd seen him and it felt awkward sitting at his bedside, talking to him. It took me a while to get used to speaking in his presence without a quick remark or witty put down coming back at me. I told him about the gig… how weird it was not playing guitar and about what I wanted to write about next. Songs with more meaning. Then I mentioned the car and how I was freaking out. How I was paranoid someone had done something to make it crash.

Only when I said it out loud was I honest with myself - I couldn't shake the feeling that something had happened. I could feel it in my chest like back in Brighton with the *Penguin Killer* - stupid bloody name – like I did with Isaac. Not that I knew it was him back then but still.

This time I was alert and ready.

The bus weaved and wound its way past traffic lights and shops as I thought about all the strange things that had been happening lately. The fire-alarm at the Skimrider gig; Lisa coming back home; the car crash. Only two bad things which, as my Dad would say, didn't make a summer. Or something like that. I was tired and, as home came into view I rang the bell and felt the need for a decent smoke.

It was already getting dark and the cold air brought my thoughts into focus when I jumped off. Maybe I was just reading too much into a couple of odd things happening? When we were away, Lisa and I had talked through what had happened around the bookshop: the murders; the pressure; the survivor guilt. She'd said it was natural to be affected and, in some ways, running away to a completely different place might delay the healing process. When I'd argued it was all in the past and I had a new focus now with the record contract and Beachhead, she had just smiled and kissed me. We have all the time in the world, she'd said.

'Alright lads,' I said, walking into the smoky, dark lounge.

'Hey Luke,' they chorused back.

Blockbusters video cases were scattered on the floor and Ewan McGregor's face was on the telly. I went straight to the answer machine but the green light told me there hadn't been any new messages.

'How's Stephen?' James asked.

'Same,' I replied and collapsed on the sofa with a sigh. 'Is this *Trainspotting*?'

'Yeah,' Rob replied.

I watched Ewan climbing out of a toilet and felt my urge for a smoke quickly disappear.

'You heard anything from Lisa?' I asked Andy, sure she was more likely to text him than leave a message on the home phone.

'No,' he replied and checked his phone just in case. 'Nothing.'

'No worries,' I said, feeling a mix of jealousy and anger that she wasn't here.

Missing the gig was one thing, but surely she wanted to spend time with me? Especially after the accident. Wasn't she worried about Stephen too? I cast a glance at the answer machine again but nothing had changed. I looked at the boys – nothing had changed here either. They were stoned, transfixed on the telly. Andy passed me a smoke and I hesitated for a moment, wondering whether I should keep a clear head or not, but a twinge in my left wrist reminded me how tired I was. I needed to switch off for half an hour.

'We're heading down the King's Head for the pub quiz later,' Rob said.

'Shall we grab a pie in there?' James said.

'I could murder a curry,' Andy replied.

'They don't do curries in the King's Head,' Rob replied, and the conversation slipped away.

An hour later, we were occupying our usual table at the King's Head, half-stoned and full of pub pie.

'What are the five largest land-locked countries in the world?' the deep, cockney voice boomed through a crackling sound system. 'One point for each.'

'Bolivia,' Andy whispered to Rob who was writing down our answers.

'Switzerland, obviously,' James said.

'Uruguay?' Rob suggested.

'No, that's on the coast,' I said. 'Paraguay maybe?'

'Alright mister traveller!' Rob replied, scrawling onto the sheet of paper hidden by his arm. 'We haven't all had the luxury of spending months studying maps…'

I peered over at our rival team who were hunched over their answers like witches concocting an evil brew. They'd named themselves *Yesterday's News* so we called them the Chip-eaters, which still confused them.

'And that's the end of the Geography round,' the rotund quizmaster announced from his stool at the bar, the microphone bristling against his beard. 'Swap sheets for marking.'

It felt like being at school but after a few pints everyone's spirits rose and we were usually fighting over half points to try and win the weekly crown. It was good bonding time with the lads and broke up the week, which sounds weird considering we didn't really have a day job, but the week dragged without gigs. Anyway, it gave me something to write to Lisa about when she was away and we always stormed the music round!

'Question Eight… the Gulf of Bothnia is the northern most arm of the Baltic Sea, not to be confused with Bosnia in the Balkans.'

'Twat,' James mouthed, keeping an eye on the quizmaster like he was our teacher.

'Hey Luke, give us your arm,' Rob said, producing a felt-tip pen from a pocket.

'What? Oh, yeah,' I replied and pulled up my sleeve to reveal the fresh, snow-white plaster cast.

'A blank canvas!' Andy said and rummaged in his bag for a pen.

'I might have a go at the band logo,' James said and joined in, leaving me to write the answers.

'Just no Krunch logos okay?' I said. 'Can't stand those bastards.'

'The drummer's alright,' Rob said.

'Just because you think he's fit doesn't mean he's alright,' James replied.

'Whatever!' Rob replied, no longer bothered by our teasing.

I smiled and thought it was a good time to raise an idea.

'Listen, don't laugh,' I said, spotting the emerging smirks, 'but I was thinking about using a tambourine at Friday's gig, what do you think?'

They laughed.

'Like Liam Gallagher,' I explained. 'Otherwise it's just weird standing up there.'

'Percussion's Rob's department,' James said.

'Just don't fuck up my timing, okay?' Rob said.

'Maybe we should get you a keyboard too?' Andy said, smirking, pretending to play one-handed.

'Alright, alright,' I said. 'We're not doing eighties covers yet.'

'Let's just hope it's a better venue than last night,' Andy said.

'It was old school!' James said. 'Like the old times.'

'Yeah but Friday will be a proper gig again,' Rob said.

'Last night was rough,' Andy said. 'That girl throwing up… not good.'

'Two of them,' Rob said. 'I heard one of the lads with them say it was food poisoning, but they just couldn't handle their drink.'

'On a Tuesday night? Ha!' James said and finished his pint.

'My round!' I said. 'I'd go to the bar but I can't carry four pints.'

'I'll help mate,' James said.

A few rounds later I was half-drunk and a bit queasy. Probably the meds. I couldn't tell the lads but all I wanted to do was go to bed.

'You're a proper part of Beachhead,' Rob was saying to Andy.

'No doubt,' James added.

'Hey, if Lightback get their act together we can get them to support us, right?' Rob looked at me.

I shrugged and said, 'Yeah, sure, that'd be cool.' I thought about Stephen and felt the guilt rise inside. I hadn't thought about him for hours. 'I guess it's down to Jeff really…'

'So the scores on the doors,' the speakers burst back into life. 'Music round, no surprise topped by *Hendrix's Plectrum* with ten out of ten. In second place we have…'

'Right, I'm going to head off,' I said, squeezing out between the table and bench.

'Early night princess?' James said, grinning away.

'Ha ha, no, I just want to see if Lisa's called or if there's any news about Stephen.'

Andy pulled his phone out. 'Nothing here.'

'Cool, cheers. Let me know the final score.'

I pulled my coat collar high around my neck and stepped into the winter chill, breathing out a cloud of pub air. I stomped off at a pace, walking to keep warm and on a half-drunk mission. The thought of Lisa ringing or turning up when I wasn't home clawed at me and at one point I almost broke into a jog, but managed to avoid any unnecessary exercise.

The lights were flashing on the answer machine.

I rushed over, pressed the button and held my breath.

'Hi Luke, it's Janet,' said a voice I didn't recognise. 'Lisa's Mum… I was just wondering if Lisa is at yours? Just wanted to check she's still coming on Thursday night? Thanks!'

Odd, I thought. Lisa hadn't mentioned it but we'd not really caught up properly.

The light was still flashing, so I pressed the button again.

'Hi guys, it's Rachel from the label,' a squeaky cockney voice announced. 'Message from Jeff… the sound engineers have finished mixing and need some vocal work from Luke. Come to the studio tomorrow. Luke only. Ta.'

The machine beeped. I stared at it, waiting for the light to flicker again but that was it. Nothing from Lisa. Maybe she was at Jeff's place and would meet me there? A twinge of anxiety hit when I thought about what had happened. Maybe he wanted to clear the air? More thinly veiled threats more likely, piling more pressure on me. Like I needed that with Stephen in hospital… or maybe he had a new manager lined up?

My head was going into overdrive.

If I was going to sing tomorrow I needed to put an alarm on to catch an early train into the sticks, so I downed a pill and was out like a light. Didn't even hear the boys coming back celebrating our win.

Thursday 19th December 1996

A Design For Life – Manic Street Preachers

The rocking carriage shook my bones as the train rattled through the North London suburbs, so I tightened my sling to keep my wrist from bumping against my chest. It felt okay – just the odd twinge of sharp pain when I woke up – and I was getting used to sleeping with a rock for an arm.

It was strange not seeing Lisa there when I woke up. I thought I would have slipped back into 'apart' mode seeing as she'd only just come back, but I missed her heat. Even though she was staying at her mates I held a hope that she could still slip into bed in the middle of night without a word.

Maybe she knew about what Jeff wanted and was already at his place?

He was a bizarre man. Jeff. Hot and cold. One minute he was a sixties legend full of stories and inspiration, the next he was the demon headmaster. Maybe power had changed him? Or the pressure of the label? He'd built it up from scratch so probably felt the same about it as I did about Beachhead, but magnified. These were the good times for everyone in the music industry though – another chance at reliving the glory days of the sixties, surely.

I stared out the window, my view expanding as skyscrapers gave way to houses. Green spaces appeared between the urban areas and grew to eventually dominate the landscape: trees; golf courses; fields. Open spaces. My mind seemed to relax and expand with the change. London wasn't all bad. Concentrated. Dense with inspiration as much as anything, which was hard to switch off from, but I missed the sea. Nothing could beat chilling on the beach in the summer with the lads, or waking up early to catch the sunrise.

Grandad.

My routine with the sunrise photos came back to me and those months just after he died. Pointless nostalgia or part of the healing process, as Lisa would have said, I still didn't know, but I hoped to use one of the images in our album, maybe an inner sleeve or on the acknowledgements page. One of my travelling pics too.

I used to dream of shooting the album cover itself but I was used to having my dreams squished by the monolithic music machine now, so held little hope. I'd spent years designing and dreaming up album covers, tour posters and band logos… but the final decisions would come down to some faceless person in marketing. Where was *my* artistic expression? I wasn't just a song-writing robot, pumping out lyrics and melodies. My songs were emotions. Life distilled. Beachhead's album was a condensed, filtered view of years of experiences and dreams. It was going to be a balanced musical journey – not a cheap product to sell to the masses.

I sighed, letting my emotions settle.

Maybe I could craft a song from this angst?

The train pulled into the rural station for Jeff's village and I jumped off. Memories came back from the recording sessions. Nobody here to greet me this time, but I could see the taxi rank and the house wasn't far.

'Ah, Luke!' Linda, Jeff's wife, opened the door of their mansion-like farmhouse.

I'd expected a butler on my first time here, but this really was a family house – a family house with a world-renowned recording studio in the back garden.

'Hi Linda, are you okay?' I asked politely.

'Yes, yes. How are you, poor thing?' She let me into the warmth of the hallway. 'Any news on your brother?'

A fire was crackling in an adjoining room and the scent of fresh coffee was drawn through from the kitchen by the open front door.

'Err, no change with Stephen,' I said. 'But the doctors are sure there's no permanent damage so it's just a matter of time really.'

How many times had I said or heard that this week?

'Good, good,' she replied and ushered me through the nearest doorway into a cosy lounge full of plump sofas and vases of dried flowers. 'I'll let Jeff know you're here.'

'Thanks.'

I took the room in. It felt like the room my parents would live in if they had loads of money: patterned fabric; minimalist paintings; thick curtains. Basic, but expensive. I doubted Jeff or Linda actually used the room, but it felt cosy.

I let myself imagine Lisa and I living in a place like this. Would this be what we wanted? Old beams, stylish furniture? A rural retreat? A cosy hideaway to bring up the kids. A safe place to return to after our trips abroad? Why not live in the city where the action was? I could hear Lisa say. I remembered Jeff's town house near the label's office and could see he really did have it all.

'Luke!' Jeff strolled in, shirt sleeves rolled up. 'Good to see you.'

He shook my hand, seeming the relaxed version I'd seen before in his home. A totally different person to *City Jeff.* The real him maybe?

'Arm okay?' he asked.

'Yeah, no trouble,' I replied. 'I can feel my fingertips going soft already though.'

'Some cheese wire should sort that out!' he said with a genuine laugh. 'The gig went well so I heard? Without the guitar?'

'Yeah,' I replied, trying to work out who he'd sent to spy on us or who he knew from the crowd. Surely nobody from Krunch, who would have made some crap up. 'It was a bit strange, but we worked around it.' I said, trying to hold his gaze, but as ever, I looked away. 'I'm going for a tambourine on Friday.'

'Ah, yes, the last gig before Christmas, good idea.' He looked around the room, then said, 'Look, let's get on with business shall we? Grab a coffee and head over to the studio office? A few things to go through while the engineers set up.'

Across the yard, past a line of horses being fed by Linda, we entered a huge, black wooden barn: Jeff's studio. Two world-class recording suites and an office lined with gold and platinum discs.

No pressure.

'Right then.' Jeff reclined in his brown, high-backed desk chair and shuffled through a few sheets of paper. 'Album name.'

He stared at me with sharp blue eyes. He wasn't in a bullying mood like he'd been on the Thames boat, but I could see that Jeff hiding, just out of view. One push and he'd be here.

'I...' I started and picked a disc on the wall to stare at. 'I, err, had a few names, like we'd discussed, but the one we liked as a band was-'

'*We Attack At Dawn*,' he said with a hint of a sneer.

'Yeah,' I replied. 'It links to our name... a beachhead in terms of a war... rather than someone who spends too much time on a beach. A landing, like Gallipoli or something... bad example, but you know what I mean.'

I was rambling. Strong coffee. Always set me off. No, that wasn't it. I felt uneasy. Was it Jeff? No. It was being back here and what happened in the summer. With his daughter. The event hung over us. A cloud.

'Yeah, I get it.' Jeff replied, pulling a file off a pile. 'But the surfer side of the name fits well for the gigs with Skimrider, promotions and all that.' Jeff paused to flick through the papers. 'We added your name into the pot with our other ideas and the boys in marketing came up with a few other suggestions... mocked up some covers and they're looking good.'

He handed me the folder and sat back, fingers arched like a James Bond baddie.

'I know which one I'd go for,' he said with an arched brow.

I didn't feel like I could do this. Not now. The last thing I needed was another kick in the teeth. I had to clear the air first.

'Listen,' I said, leaving the folder on my lap. 'About what happened in the summer.'

One eyebrow twitched and he said, 'With Charlotte.'

It wasn't a question. He knew.

'I want to… I feel awkward about what happened – it was a mistake and I'd like to apologise.'

He remained stone-still. I felt my cheeks redden and my anger rise. I hadn't done anything wrong and yet I was apologising.

'Or am I missing something?' I asked. 'You said we could use the pool, so I went for a swim and didn't see her at first… sunbathing.'

'Naked,' he said.

I hesitated and looked away. 'Yes,' I whispered.

'Apology accepted,' he said and leant forward. 'Charlotte has a tendency for doing stuff like that – especially when a band's recording. She enjoys the… attention.' His eyes softened a touch. 'But that wasn't what I've been annoyed about.'

'What?' I said and felt a drop of sweat run down my side.

'It was the assumption that you'd made it.' He gestured at the discs on the walls. 'The presumption that because you had signed a contract and you were in my studio, your work was done. Well it bloody well wasn't.'

He thumped the desk with his fist. 'It bloody well *isn't* done. You work's just starting, Luke.'

I breathed in and sat back. 'I get that,' I said, starting to feel hounded. 'This is everything I've worked towards, I-'

'Just like every other songwriter who comes here,' he cut me off. 'But I heard you, the engineers heard you… it's on bloody tape for fuck's sake.'

We stared at one another in silence as I racked my brain to recall what I might have said.

'That's why I've been hard on you, Luke,' he said. 'Gee you up a bit. Make you see that *THIS IS IT*. Your only chance. You've got skill but no more than any other guy out there with a guitar and half a dozen songs. I wasn't kidding when I said Krunch are on your heels… plenty of others too.'

'But…' I wanted to shout back. To argue my artistic rights.

'There's no bloody but, Luke,' Jeff almost growled.

'I understand, but…' I tried, feeling like a schoolboy getting told off by the head teacher.

'Well, it worked didn't it?' he said with the slightest smile. 'You showed me you had fire in your belly when we were on the boat. I knew you were ready. Then after the accident, you rose to the challenge and I appreciate that Luke, what with Stephen still in hospital.' He glanced at the folder. 'Open it.'

I didn't know what to say. Jeff was blowing hot and cold, switching between personalities right before my eyes. Disorientated, I turned the folder cover, stared at the first page and swallowed.

'Ready or not,' Jeff said. 'This is happening, Luke. I heard the passion, and your unique view of the world, in your demo and I stoked that fire. I gave you time to expand your ideas and you did it, Luke.'

I opened the folder and stared at the solitary sheet of paper.

We Attack At Dawn

Beachhead

Large font over a black and white image of Brighton beach at sunrise.

My photo.

'I believe in you, Luke… the whole band, and we've got a bloody good album here.'

'Bloody hell,' I said and laughed.

Tears were forming in my eyes and I couldn't take my eyes off the mock-up. Everything I'd ever wanted had just come together before my eyes.

'Yeah,' I eventually said, still in shock. 'It looks great.'

I couldn't wait to show the lads and Lisa. Mum and Dad, and Stephen.

'Right then,' Jeff said, looking his settled self again. 'Let's get these vocals fixed.'

'Cool, okay,' I said. 'Erm, I was wondering. You haven't heard from Lisa recently have you?'

'No,' Jeff replied as he shuffled through more papers. 'She stepped in for Stephen but I'm not expecting to see her 'til next week. Why?'

'I haven't seen her for a couple of days, so…'

'Did you have an argument?' Jeff asked with a raised eyebrow.

'No,' I replied, trying not to get defensive. 'She was supposed to be at the gig but never turned up.'

'Really? I'd heard she was there… maybe not. I can call her if you want?' He pulled his mobile phone from his jacket pocket.

'Yeah, that would be great, thanks,' I replied, knowing it was time I got a phone like that. 'Just for peace of mind.'

He dialled, waited, then said, 'Just gone to the answer message. I'll text her and let you know. Come on, let's get you warmed up for the vocals. Just backing vocals mostly.'

'Great.'

The engineers were next door in the smaller suite and had the booth set up for me. The rest of the room was bare apart from a set of guitars set in stands pushed to one side. I glanced at my cast and tried not to count how many weeks it would be until I played again. I ran through a few warm up exercises. Sounds. Scales. Tried a few lyrics. Put my headphones on and could hear them chatting in the control room.

'… completed if we want to keep the same cut for the album.'

'Don't see why not,' Jeff replied.

I could see how easy it was to eavesdrop on someone here and how I'd been heard, but still had no idea what I'd actually said to put Jeff's back up. Was it that day we got stoned and tried some backward guitar?

'Right, we're going to start off with *My World*,' the engineer spoke to me. 'I've taken your vocals out, so we just need you to sing the whole thing through from the top.'

'Cool, gotcha,' I said.

The opening riff kicked in a few seconds later and it felt good to be of some use even with a broken arm.

The rest of the day slipped away with take after take: main vocals; backing vocals for a chorus; some new 'oohs and aahs' for another track. Halfway through I realised what I was hearing through my headphones was the actual, final mix of our album. I was hearing it for the first time – and the songs sounded bloody amazing!

'How's it going?' Jeff asked when I went back into the house for a bite to eat.

'Yeah, all good,' I replied. 'Sounding great.'

'Good, good. We'll get the rest of the band together sometime in the London office to listen to the full album.'

'Cool,' I replied and tucked into a baguette Linda had left out for me.

'Right, I've got some calls to make,' Jeff said. 'So if I don't see you later, have a good gig tomorrow.'

'Thanks,' I mumbled through my sandwich.

'Oh and by the way,' Jeff pulled out his phone. 'Lisa sent a message back… says she's fine.' He looked at his phone. 'She says she's out with some mates and's going to stay round theirs tonight.'

I nodded and he left. I munched away, glad Lisa had been in contact and thought about the last couple of tracks I had to lay down. Something with more energy to lift up a chorus.

Maybe I could call Lisa when I got home? I pictured the phone in our lounge and remembered her Mum's message. Her voice. Her concern. It was Thursday today - wasn't Lisa supposed to be going round her Mum's tonight?

I felt awful. Like having a raging hangover on the same day your full-on period cramps kicked in. I knew I wasn't on, but my belly throbbed in time with the pain in my head. I felt so tired. So drained. Like a night last year when Luke and I drank too much whiskey. My throat was dry and I couldn't feel my arms. I needed sleep, but something told me I had to stay awake. Something was… different.

I could smell incense and a tang of damp. Something old. Both scents were alien to me, but there was a steady rolling movement I recognised along with the deep rumble of an engine – I was travelling. Another overnight coach journey shaking my bones, I thought and moved to get comfortable, feeling a rough blanket against my cheek. Odd, I thought, picturing the tartan rug my Grandma used to throw on the lawn in the summer. Usually I slept with a jumper against the window, or something softer.

Music was playing and… there was a voice singing. A man's voice.

'…the life we knew… live without each other…'

Was it Luke? Were we back in the campervan? No. Too cold for Australia. A dream then? My head pounded trying to make sense of my surroundings. I summoned the energy to open my eyes to look for a bottle of water but all I could see were red and white shapes moving above me. Shadows flickered and I fell asleep again.

Five minutes or five hours later, I couldn't tell, I woke to the same nauseating view of flashing silhouettes speeding overhead. The low engine hum muffled all sounds but I could hear tinkling guitar emanating from distant tinny speakers. The voice again. Singing.

'Luke?' I tried to say but I barely managed a croak.

The voice carried on singing and I focussed on it, following its lilt up and down. Something told me to concentrate. I knew the song but couldn't remember the name. One Luke liked, but I couldn't remember him playing in the van. I could picture Luke on the boat on the Thames and his surprise. I was back in England, so where was I now? Where was I going?

The voice sang higher. Too high. I shivered.

It wasn't Luke singing.

Friday 20th December 1996 A.M.

High and Dry - Radiohead

'Hey Luke, you seen my Stone Roses t-shirt?' James shouted from upstairs.

'Yeah, it's in my wardrobe,' I yelled back from the lounge.

We were chilling in the lounge, watching music videos, each of us going through our pre-gig rituals like footballers before a big match. I couldn't put my finger on why, but I felt more anxious than usual and just wanted it over with, even though I knew once I was up on stage I wouldn't want to get off.

'So,' Rob continued with his tutorial. 'Seeing as you don't want to bang it against your injured hand, you can tap it against your leg.'

'Yeah, I kinda guessed that,' I said. 'It's a tambourine, how hard can it be?'

Rob stared at me for a second, brow knitted, then said. 'That's what you used to say about the drums before you gave it a go.'

'Yeah, yeah, I know! Drums are tricky, I get it, but you literally just tap this to keep time.'

'No,' Rob snapped and shook his head. 'You use it to build up the energy… pat in a verse, shake to rise up to a chorus, then double time. Energy.'

'Okay, got it,' I said.

It made sense.

'Just test it out tonight,' Andy said, slouched in the sofa opposite us. 'Plenty more gigs with your wrist in plaster, right?'

'Maybe,' I said with a shrug. 'I can't remember what Stephen had lined up for January.'

'I thought we were building up to the *Strike* release and then the album?' Rob said.

'Yeah, but I can't remember all the dates,' I said. 'I've just been thinking up to Christmas to be honest.'

James bounded down the stairs and into the lounge. 'Sorted!' He crashed next to Andy. 'Quick smoke lads?'

'None for me, cheers,' Rob said and pulled a little bag from his pocket. 'I'm saving my energy for tonight.' He gave us a smile.

'Going out after?' James asked.

'Yeah.' Rob had a twinkle in his eye.

'How about you Andy?' James asked.

'I'm keeping a clear head.'

'Me too,' I said before James could respond. 'It messes with my pills.' I tapped the plaster cast.

'Just me then,' James said with a laugh.

‘So when did Jeff say we’ll get to listen to the album?’ Andy asked.

‘Sometime before New Year,’ I replied with a shrug. ‘But from what I heard in the studio, the mix is sounding great.’

‘They kept all my breaks in?’ Andy asked, then looked at his phone.

‘Yeah, nothing was missing, just cleaned up,’ I said and remembered Lisa’s message to Jeff. ‘Listen, that message from Lisa, what did she say again?’

‘She was staying with her mates,’ Andy replied. ‘Still not heard from her?’

‘No,’ I replied, wondering if I should give her Mum a call, or try Lisa’s mobile.

‘She’ll be along tonight mate,’ James said. ‘She’s been travelling for ages so hasn’t seen her mates for a while, that’s all.’

‘Yeah, I know,’ I said with a glance at the answer machine.

It was a tic I’d developed these past few days, which went against the point of having an answer machine and made me wonder what I’d be like if I had a mobile phone, checking it every few minutes. Nine out of ten times there was nothing there, but this time.

‘We’ve got a message!’ I said and jumped up to check it.

‘I thought I heard something earlier when you were in the shower,’ Rob said, eyes fixed on the telly.

'Could have fuckin' told me,' I muttered under my breath as I picked up the handset and pressed the buttons to listen.

'Hi Luke, it's Mum.' She sounded chirpy. 'Stephen's come round and seems fine. He's talking. The Doctors are just checking him over.'

I could hear Dad in the background. 'Tell him we can pick him up to visit?'

'Yes, we'll pick you up this afternoon if you want? One o'clock? We're not sure when Stephen can go home… talk later. Love you!'

'Who was it?' James asked as I put the receiver down.

'Mum and Dad,' I said. 'Stephen's awake.'

'Nice one!' the lads replied.

I looked at the clock – twelve-thirty. My head was swimming as I tried to put everything into perspective. I'd been so concerned about the gig, the album and thinking about where Lisa was that I hadn't given my brother a second thought.

'And he's okay?' James asked.

'Yeah, he's talking so it sounds good.'

'Good reason to celebrate tonight then, hey?' Rob said, beaming.

'Yeah,' I said, feeling some energy building up.

I was feeling positive and had a mini-daydream of seeing Lisa at the gig and having a great night out tonight, but now it was all about Stephen.

-

'I'm sorry, I've just got no idea who you are,' Stephen said, staring at me blankly.

Mum and Dad had let me go in on my own after they'd had some time with him and Doctor Daniels who seemed pleased with his progress.

'You what?' I said, reading his face, searching for laughter lines. 'I'm Luke… your brother.'

'Luke?' Stephen looked properly concerned and turned to stare out the window, in deep thought. 'Luke… ah… Master Luke!' He said in his best C3PO and snapped back to me. 'Master Luke, I knew you would return!'

I shook my head slowly. 'I thought the accident would have knocked some bloody sense into you. Dick.'

'Ah, you missed me then,' he said and settled back into his plump pillows with a laugh.

'Yeah, massively.'

He closed his eyes and took a deep breath.

'Enjoying the drugs?' I asked.

'Ha, yeah. I'm just tired… can't remember much to be honest.'

'Well, let me remind you. We were in the car and you were drivin-'

'Yeah, I remember that bit, driving you home, then the skid. Sorry.'

I was taken aback. My brother had never apologised to me before. Maybe he was more injured than I thought.

'Look, the car was old,' I said. 'Anything could have gone… you were driving normally.'

'The steering went funny, I remember that,' Stephen said. 'Or was it the brakes?'

'Don't worry about it now,' I said. 'Just concentrate on getting better… if that's even possible? Stupid phrase. Like you can *make* yourself better!'

Stephen smiled but still looked weak. 'How about your arm?'

'Bit of a pain,' I replied. 'But we still played the gig. We're giving it another go tonight.'

'That's good,' Stephen replied, looking serious for a second. 'Jeff would appreciate that. How about Lisa? Is she doing okay? Work-wise?'

'Err… well, yeah, but I haven't actually seen her for a couple of days,' I said. 'She's staying at her mates apparently.'

'And she's coming tonight?' Stephen asked as he tried to sit up.

I shrugged. 'Not sure. She wasn't at the other gig or at Jeff's when I re-did the vocals.'

'Pass me my phone will you?' Stephen asked and started tapping away, then held it to his ear. 'Straight to answer,' he said. 'I'll text her.'

There was a knock at the door and Doctor Daniels came in.

'Hi,' she said. 'How are you feeling Mister Redfern?'

Instinctively I thought she was talking to Dad, then I went to answer, but Stephen spoke first.

'Not bad thanks.'

'Good,' she replied and checked the readings on a square computer screen behind Stephen's head. 'Just a few more checks to carry out but the bloods have come back. All looking good, but we'd like to keep you under observation for a couple more nights.'

'Right, sure. Sorry, it looks like I'll miss your gig,' he said, shooting me a smile.

'No probs,' I replied and held my cast arm up. 'No guitar, but you'll miss my tambourine skills.'

'Are you not going to ask my brother about his famous band, Doctor?'

She raised her eyebrows and shook her head. 'Let's just say, you're not the first patients we've had in here from the record label.'

'Ooh, juicy gossip!' Stephen said, sitting up another notch. 'Do tell.'

'My lips are sealed,' she replied, focussed on the clipboard at the end of Stephen's bed but the slightest smile on her lips told me Stephen would work his magic and have his gossip by the end of the day.

-

Mum and Dad dropped me back at my house, then headed to Stephen's flat to get it ready for his return after he said they could kip there. The lads were still milling about at home and had achieved little apart from ordering some pre-gig pizzas. Top of the Pops was on the telly, which had been muted due to the severe absence of any decent songs.

'Ah, No Way Sis,' Andy said. 'Finally! Turn it back up.'

'Anything new going on then?' I asked after I'd given them an update of Stephen's progress while pretend Liam crooned in the background.

'Just getting ready,' James said with a sly look towards Andy which suggested he'd had his pre-concert meditation session.

I smiled back.

'I've pumped a few weights,' Rob said. 'Ready for action.'

'Good, good.' I cast a look at the answer machine, which flashed manically. 'Any phone calls?' I asked, trying to keep my temper.

'Oh yeah,' Andy piped up. 'I heard it go a couple of times but didn't recognise the voices so…'

'Thanks,' I replied and held my tongue.

I tried not to look anxious, but stumbled on my way over to the machine. It had to be Lisa, but wouldn't Andy have recognised her voice? I picked up the handset so only I could hear and pressed the buttons.

'Hi Luke, it's Janet again. Hopefully you got my first message, I didn't hear back from you.' She sounded slightly out of breath. 'Lisa didn't come round on Thursday so I'm hoping she's at yours. Please ring me back on…'

'Shit,' I muttered under my breath. 'Oi, Andy,' I called over. 'Any chance you could try ringing Lisa again? Still no sign of her and her Mum's going crazy.'

'Yeah, sure,' he replied in an infuriatingly calm manner.

I waited.

'Straight to ans-'

'Can you text her?' I cut in. 'Please?'

'Yeah sure,' Andy replied.

I couldn't get my thoughts straight. What was going on? I could deal with her not being around, but knowing she was here, in London, and not spending time with me felt rude. Like she didn't need me at all. Maybe the promises we'd made had been pointless? We were giving each other space to have a real crack at what each of us wanted to do, without getting in each other's way. But we were still *together*. We shared everything. We were singing the same song.

'Got a reply!' Andy said, waving his phone in the air. 'She says she's out with some mates-'

'-and she's going to stay round theirs tonight,' I finished the sentence. 'Heard it before. It's bullshit.'

Anger was building. She wasn't even trying anymore, using the same reply and it felt like a punch in the gut – she was clearly pushing me away.

'That's weird,' Andy said, standing up and walking over.

'What?' I asked and James and Rob came over, peering over his shoulder.

'Look.' He showed me the screen.

It was the message he'd read out. The exact same message he'd received earlier in the week – identical to the one Jeff had too. Nothing strange there.

'What? I don't get it,' I said, ready to grab the phone and throw it against the wall in frustration.

'Look at who it's from,' Andy said.

The small grey screen only had a few words on it – the message and the sender at the top.

CHRIS

It took a second, then my body seemed to register it before my brain did. My knees went weak and I grabbed the nearest chair.

'What the actual fuck?' James said and we all stood there staring at the phone for what felt like forever.

'She's gone off with Chris?' Rob said and the truth nearly crushed me.

I pictured her face and tried to remember what she'd said the last time I saw her… was it in the hospital? Maybe she was going to break up with me but didn't have the heart after the accident. I'd had a recurring nightmare about Lisa meeting some burly South African or Canadian on her travels and ditching me… but Chris? How did she know him? I never thought she'd dump me for some Indie band singer from a coastal town… I took an involuntary gulp of air, realising I'd just described myself… maybe Chris was just like me, but a better prospect?

I looked up at Andy and said, 'Give me your phone.'

'Why? What you gonna do?' He asked.

'Ring him. Ring her,' I said, standing again, ready for real answers. 'Find out what the fuck is going on here.'

'I'll ring him,' Andy said, fiddling with his phone. 'Listen…' He held the phone out as it rang.

The four of us stood around the grey brick, holding our breath as a click sounded, the tone stopped and it switched to a message.

'I'm not available right now, leave a message, ta.'

Chris's farmer boy tones.

'Listen you fu-' I started, but Andy had already cancelled the call.

'That's not going to help,' he said.

Chris was one of Andy's best mates and I could see the anguish in his eyes. I wanted to pin him down and make him tell me everything he knew about Chris and Lisa, but I could tell he was a shocked as me.

'We'll get to the bottom of it mate,' Rob said.

I was fuming and grabbed a beer off the table and took a long swig. Anger was pumping through every fibre in my body and sharp needles pressed into my left wrist under the cast.

'Take it easy, hey?' Andy said.

'Yeah, hold it in mate,' James said. 'Save it for the gig.'

What the hell was going on? I had to find out the truth. Were we finished? Was that why she'd come back? It was feasible but the same question kept coming back to me - why Chris?

'Ring him again,' I demanded.

'I don't think that's a goo-'

I was too angry to muck about. 'Ring. Him. Again!'

I felt Rob move closer, like he had to protect Andy as I loomed over him on the sofa, but I was in complete control.

'Answer machine again,' Andy said.

'Text him,' I said. 'Text them both… I need to know what the fuck is going on,' I said through clenched teeth.

'Okay, okay…' he replied and started pressing buttons with his thumbs.

James rolled a spliff while we waited and the sounds of chart hits on the telly washed around us. I waited, watching Andy for any tell-tale signs that he knew what was going on, but his face was as blank as ever. Then it twitched. Eyes to the phone. Lips tightening, brow creasing, eyes squinting.

'What is it?' I asked, fearing the worst.

He held the phone up for me to read. It was a message from Lisa and it was the worst.

Tell Luke I don't want to speak to him. It's over.

Friday 20th December 1996 P.M.

On and On - Longpigs

There was a police car parked on our street when I got back from the gig and I felt a wave of panic wash through me. Rob had gone off clubbing and I'd stuck to the first bar we'd visited like a limpet, trying to wash away the memory of Lisa's text with copious amounts of cigarettes and alcohol. I'd been oblivious to James and Andy heading home early, so I'd ended up grabbing a cab home alone.

I eyed up the police car, knowing the chance of them visiting our house was about fifty to one, but my paranoia, or the beers I'd had, told me they were here for me. I took a deep breath, pushed my key in the door and opened onto a bizarre scene: two police officers, one male, one female, sitting at the table, each with a cuppa, chatting to the lads, who looked respectable for once. The lounge was spotless. No signs of used bongs, weed tins or rolling papers.

'Alright Luke,' James said with a little wave.

'Hi guys,' I said, hooking my coat on the peg. 'Another wet one out there.'

'Yeah, cats and dogs,' the female officer said.

'The Officers are here about Lisa,' Andy said, looking wide-eyed and slightly wired.

'Okay,' I replied, trying to keep it cool.

The female officer stood and said, 'We just need to ask you a couple of questions.'

'No problem, err…' I looked at the lads.

The mix of thinking about Lisa, the beers, the post-gig buzz and having two uniformed officers in the room, made me feel light-headed, but I'd known police officers my whole life with Dad in the force. They were just normal people. So I took a deep breath and settled at the table.

'Yeah, we'll give you some space,' James said, pushing his tea to me. 'Nice to meet you Libby, Oliver.' He shook their hands and gave me a wink as he walked past, ushering Andy out with him to leave us three alone.

He'd obviously worked his charm on them, knowing their names and I focussed on them as the real people behind the badge and stripes.

'Can you confirm you are Luke Redfern?' Libby asked.

'Yeah, that's me,' I said, pushing away flashbacks of the aftermath of Isaac's killing spree last year.

The interviewers had been kind but relentless trying to find out why he'd killed.

'We understand Lisa Jones is your girlfriend?' Libby asked.

'Yeah,' I replied, trying to detach myself from any emotion. 'Was my girlfriend, I mean, I had a text earlier and I haven't seen her for, what, three or four days now I guess?'

'A text?' Oliver asked.

'Saying she didn't want to talk to me,' I said, saying the words I'd tried to wash away with beer all night. During the gig and in the pub I'd had the music and crowd to focus on, but now it was all too real. 'She said it was over,' I said, the words sticking to my dry mouth, so I drank some tea, feeling the comfort of its warmth wash down into my belly.

'Right,' Libby said. 'Did you have an argument the last time you saw each other?'

'No,' I replied with a shrug. 'It's all pretty sudden to be honest. She'd just come back from travelling and we were looking forward to Christmas.'

'And when was the last time you saw her?'

'Monday, when I was in hospital,' I replied, raising my plaster cast.

'From a car accident, is that correct?' Libby asked.

'Yeah, my brother's still in hospital,' I said and realised it had no relevance. I was still a bit drunk. 'Err, she was supposed to turn up to our gig on Tuesday, but never made it – same again tonight.'

'And you haven't been in contact any other way since?' Libby asked.

I shook my head and said, 'Everything was just normal until the text. She'd been away for a while, so we were supposed to catch up, then the accident. We texted her… Andy, Jeff, Stephen, but she just said she was out with mates and staying at theirs.'

'Which mates?'

'She didn't say,' I said, looking down, thinking I should have asked who she'd been staying with but didn't want to pry – that wasn't how our relationship had worked.

I didn't know how much info to give them. My run-ins with Detective Mellor in Brighton had taught me to keep aloof in situation like this, but he'd come good in the end. Maybe being open was best? I tried to keep focussed.

'The message we had tonight, from Lisa, was from another phone – belonging to Chris, one of Andy's mates.'

We sat in silence while the officers digested what I'd said, Oliver writing in his notebook.

'So you believe she's currently with Chris… do you have a surname?' Libby asked.

'No, I…'

'Lisa has been reported missing by her parents, Luke, and her Mother says she has been trying to contact you, so we need every piece of information you have okay?' Oliver said.

I felt an urge to resist, fight back. This was not my doing, I wanted to tell them. I was not in the wrong here – I was the one who'd been dumped!

I sighed and said, 'I'll find out,' then called Andy downstairs.

'What's up?' he asked.

'What's Chris's surname?' I asked and saw my chance. 'And his phone number – can you write it down for the officers please? May as well add Stephen's. Jeff's too. And yours.'

'That would be great thanks,' Libby said.

Andy scrawled them on a pad on the table and Oliver copied them into his notepad.

'And his address if you have it please?' Libby asked Andy.

'What are you going to do?' Andy asked. 'I can talk to Chris if you want?'

'We're going to visit him and if Lisa is there we can close the incident,' Libby replied.

'Great,' I replied, feeling a sinking feeling at the thought of Chris and Lisa together at his place.

'Is that everything?' Andy asked.

'Yeah, thanks,' Oliver said and Andy bounded back upstairs to his guitar pedals.

'Can we have your landline so we can contact you?' Libby asked.

'Yeah, sure,' I replied, adding our number to the list.

'Great, we'll be in touch,' Oliver replied. 'I'm sure she's safe and everything will be fine.'

'Yeah sure,' I said, thinking my world had just collapsed around my ears and I had no idea what I was going to do next.

'Thanks for your help,' they said as I saw them into the hall and out the front door.

As soon as the door clicked shut behind them, I rushed back to the table, grabbed the list of phone numbers and shoved them into my pocket. A second later, the lads thumped back downstairs.

'What's going on?' James was first down.

'Nothing much,' I replied. 'They're going to call in on Chris and get Lisa to ring her Mum,' I said, acting as nonchalant as I could.

'Alright,' James replied, looking around the room. 'Look, it's still Friday night, we had a decent gig, so I say we smoke some weed and play some PlayStation.'

I nodded, wanting nothing more than to escape from this tortured reality.

-

A few hours later, after Rob made it home all eagle-eyed and beaming from ear to ear, James and Rob raced each other on V-Rally, sitting cross-legged on the floor while I kept an eye on Andy, slumped in his seat. He joined in as much as normal and had barely looked at his phone. I didn't know if it was paranoia from the weed, or the way he always defended Chris, but I swore he knew more than he was letting on. There! He looked down suddenly, pulled his phone out. Text message set to vibrate. He looked concerned.

'Right, who's up next?' James asked. 'Winner stays on!'

'I'll get you next time mate,' Rob said and crawled back to a sofa.

'Andy's up,' I said as a sound behind me made me turn.

The house phone was ringing! I was so used to playing messages on it, I wasn't sure if it actually worked as a proper phone.

'Hello,' I said, eyeing up the London number on the screen, ignoring the looks the lads were giving me and feeling the full effects of the last spliff. It felt like I was talking in a movie.

It was Libby, the police officer.

'Hello Mister Redfern, just to let you know we visited the address you gave us for Chris Lightback and Lisa wasn't there.'

I exhaled slowly.

'And neither was Chris,' she continued. 'We spoke to his housemates, but they told us he left a few days ago.'

'What?'

I hadn't read the note Andy had written – just shoved it in my pocket – so all I could think about was how Chris had named his band after his surname, Lightback. What a prick!

'Chris is not at the current address and his housemates don't have another address for him,' she said. 'Do you have a former address?'

'Err, no,' I said. 'He's from Folkestone I think so…'

I looked up and caught Andy's panicked eyes. He was shaking his head.

'I'll pass you over to Andy,' I said and handed him the handset, then returned to the sofa, keeping focussed on Andy's conversation.

'…in Suffolk, yes. No, not Folkestone in Kent.' A pause. 'Okay, I'll find the latest address I have for his Mum and send it to you. No, his Dad passed away. Okay, thanks.'

Andy put the phone down, killing the call.

'They're not there,' he said almost apologetically.

'I know,' I replied, trying not to get angry.

I had to focus. Chris and Lisa had left London. Lisa wouldn't answer her phone. Chris wouldn't either. They just sent meaningless texts. But I needed answers. I had to talk to Lisa to get the truth. She owed me that. My emotions were bubbling over with a mix of rage and focus. Part of me wanted to crawl into a ball and sleep, but a stronger part willed me on to fight: to find out the truth.

Something clicked and I knew there was only one thing I could do.

'When you find that address,' I said to Andy.

'Yeah.'

'Give it to me.'

Saturday 21st December 1996 A.M.

Beetlebum – Blur

The train's brakes squealed as it slowed to a halt alongside a desolate, wind-swept platform. The station sign came into view: Felixstowe. End of the line. Literally.

A grey, drizzly day enveloped me as I stepped off the train and pushed away thoughts of how long it had taken to get here: a series of dull stations; over-heated waiting rooms; cramped carriages. Finally I was here and all I could think about was Lisa.

I'd barely slept last night after Andy had given me Chris's Mum's address. Shadows of my dreams haunted me still, of Lisa and Chris together: their faces circling my mind like a bad pop song; a head worm, burrowing through my brain, leaving behind nothing but tunnels of pain and betrayal.

Yet, a part of my brain didn't accept it. There was more going on here, I knew it.

I had the address and knew I wouldn't be welcome there, so I needed a place to stay. The idea was to get to his Mum's house, confront Lisa and get some resolution, kip in a hotel, then back on the train tomorrow and home in time to spend Christmas with my family. This was an old seaside resort, I thought, so I was sure it would be littered with hotels like Brighton.

I buttoned my coat tight and crossed a grey car park with a Fire Brigade training tower looming over me. I had what I used to call my festival rucksack over one shoulder, but its smell reminded me of travelling now and the camping trip Lisa and I did in the summer we first met. Since spending time abroad, I was at ease about turning up in a new town with nowhere to stay – ready to explore! Not that there seemed much to explore here in deepest winter.

No, this wasn't about exploration. I was only after one thing; answers. If Lisa had run off with Chris, she owed me more than a curt text message. That wasn't her style. That wasn't how our relationship had grown. I had half a tree's worth of letters and postcards in my bedroom from her travels, describing her every waking thought, her plans and dreams. We shared them. That's why I was sure she wouldn't end our relationship without a frank discussion. An explanation.

I strolled past shoppers with their bags bulging with Christmas presents and turkeys, crackers and tins of Quality Street. I passed through what I guessed used to be the Victorian railway station, now an octagon of tiny shops, leading through to a supermarket. Despite the buzz and holiday cheer, I couldn't shake the feeling this was a dead-end town with few past glories. The sooner I got out, the better.

Finding a sheltered alcove, I took out the A to Z I'd bought at Ipswich station where I'd changed trains. The carriage had been full of long-haired students returning to their parents' houses for Christmas, which had been me just a few years ago, yet so much had changed since then. Secretly, I hoped one of them might recognise me as the lead singer of Beachhead but, in truth, few of them had probably even heard of us.

On the train, my mind had been pulled towards deepening my lyrics and creating some longer, stadium-pumping, slow build-up songs. I'd made some notes and had some new sounds in mind. Maybe some piano. Introducing a keyboard player could work. Or maybe I could play it with a broken arm? Once I got a room in a hotel I could write a bit more. Something I could really get my teeth into when my arm was healed.

Stop. Save that for later. Prioritise.

I flicked through the A to Z to the slip of paper with the address and planned my route. It looked near enough: down the high street, towards the seafront, where I could find a hotel. Easy. My spirits rose a notch. Get the truth and get out.

I strode off and tried to be honest with myself. The only reason I was feeling any happiness – the real reason I travelled all the way out here –

was because I thought there was a chance I'd be returning to London with Lisa tomorrow.

That was my real goal.

The high street was bigger than I thought it'd be. Filled with Christmas shoppers lining either side of the long road which meandered down to the sea. Bustling families; hunched elderly ladies pushing wheeled baskets; a gaggle of teenagers; a man with a large head and a peculiar bobbing walk. Mostly the very young and very old, no-one in between. They'd all left for more exciting places, I guessed as I spotted a record shop. I'd had a long journey and needed a reward, I told myself, then all I needed was a Woolworths or an Argos and I'd be ready for the next stage of my plan.

-

Picking through a bag of Liquorice Allsorts and with an important new purchase tucked away in my rucksack, I turned off the high street, into a set of roads lined with red brick terraced houses. I imagined families inside, sharing stories, chocolates and Christmas cheer.

The wind pulled at my coat, carrying a salty tang to me from the sea and I felt a wave of nostalgia. Brighton called me. This place wasn't so different, I thought as I breathed in the briny air and spied the seagulls wheeling above. This could be one of the back streets of Kemp town, I thought, remembering the hoarder's house I'd visited during Isaac's weeks of terror. Would Chris's Mum live in a place like that I wondered and checked the nearest street sign: Felix Road. I was here.

More red brick terraces. Even numbers, odd. I crossed the road and counted the numbers down to the twenties until I found number twenty-five. The lights were on, leaking between the curtains in the bay window at the front, warming the dull winter light.

I took a deep lungful of air just like before going on stage, exhaled slowly and pushed the metal gate open with a squeak, then walked up to the front door. This was it. I felt a twist of anxiety dancing with excitement in my stomach as the doorbell chimed inside the house. I heard the dull thuds of movement, then a woman's voice, followed by a swish and light poured through the window above the door. Locks clunked and clicked, the door opened a notch and a head of curly brown hair popped out. Two eyes stared at me, followed by a waft of tarry cigarette smoke.

'Yes, what is it?' the lady asked.

She was in her fifties so had to be Chris's Mum.

'Err, Mrs Lightback?' I asked, trying to use the professional voice I'd heard Stephen and police officers use.

'No, what d'ya want?' she replied.

'Oh, sorry,' I said, feeling a weight release from me just as a wave of confusion grabbed hold of my tongue. 'I, err, I was looking for Chris? Chris Lightback and I was given this address by his friend…'

'Chris?' the lady said. 'You've got the wrong place love. Yeah, he used to live here with his Mum – remarried, not Lightback anymore.'

'Oh, right. Sorry,' I said.

'She moved out last year after he went off to London.'

'Any idea where she moved to?' I asked.

'Well, yeah, I did have it written down somewhere…' she disappeared. I heard rustling, then she re-appeared with what looked like a water bill. 'You can take this round to her if you want? I keep getting these after her re-direction stopped.'

'Okay,' I said, taking the letter and staring at the handwritten address on the edge of the envelope.

15 Manor Terrace.

'Thanks,' she said.

'Is it near?' I asked before she could close the door.

'Not that far,' she replied. 'Five minutes' drive maybe.'

'Okay thanks,' I said, wondering why she hadn't delivered it herself.

The door closed with a crisp click and I turned back to the street, feeling a new weight on me. I'd built myself up for this moment and I'd got nowhere. All I'd achieved was being laden with someone else's unwanted bloody task! Great. Two steps forward, one back, as Grandad used to say.

I stared at the grey sky and shook my head. What next? I started walking down the road the way I'd came and went to pull out the A to Z but stopped. I couldn't take the letter now. I was hungry and needed to find a place to sleep. I was heading towards the seafront so I kept walking until I reached a clifftop road, peering over hedges at the public gardens which dropped away in a series of winding pathways and evergreen shrubs. There was a road at the bottom, a long promenade fringed by coloured lights strung along the coast like pearls and, beyond, the cold North Sea lapped against pebbles and patches of sand. It reminded me of Brighton in a way, just not as built up and with a narrower beach. Quite quaint really.

Lights bobbed way out to sea and my eyes were drawn to the pier I'd seen in the A to Z map. Lights were blazing, so I guessed the amusements in the main building were open. Not much happening on the pier itself though, apart from a large yellow and red slippery-dip slide and a few shivering fishermen. I felt the urge to descend the steps to the prom and have a stroll but I needed to find a hotel first.

A few minutes later, my traveller's instincts had paid off. A hotel stood before me in all its Victorian glory – the Waverley – with its own restaurant and bar. Perfect. Now I could grab some food and a beer. Screw the cost, I thought, this was important. Plus, if I was honest, I was enjoying some time alone. It was good to get some space from the rest of the band after living cheek by jowl with them. After living on my own, moving in with people had been claustrophobic. This was good. I was already feeling the creative juices flowing and fancied a bit of lyric-writing over a plate of some hot food.

-

An hour or so later, I entered the bar, enveloped in Christmassy warmth. Holly wreaths and red ribbons. Christmas beers at the bar. It felt early for a drink but it was already dark outside and the tables were buzzing with fresh-faced homecoming students kicking off their Christmas break, sharing first term stories and singing along to tunes over the speakers.

Blur's new song, Beetlebum, was playing over the speakers and a group in the corner, squeezed around a square table, were singing their hearts out, arm in arm. I felt a twinge of jealousy and wished I could drink my worries away with some mates, like the good old days, so I hit the bar, humming a new melody for some lyrics I'd sketched out while I was eating. I also had my new purchase in my pocket, primed and loaded and I was feeling pleased with myself… until a girl walked past with the same long hair as Lisa's and my chest tightened.

I took a deep breath and let the feeling subside.

Funnily, the song I'd written wasn't about betrayal or abandonment, but about new starts, freedom and being released. Maybe I was becoming reconciled with the idea of Lisa leaving me? Maybe I had accepted it. But I couldn't move on until I knew why.

It had felt odd writing a tune without my guitar to duet with me: I didn't have its harmony and emotion – the minor chords to add mood or sevenths to lead on to more – but I couldn't play it anyway. My arm's ache had died down only to be replaced by a tortuous itch that had started to creep in. Everyone's comments about knitting needles were starting to make sense.

'A pint of Adnams please,' I asked the barman when I made it through the crowd to the bar.

I wasn't really in the mood for going out but it was Saturday night and if Lisa was out with Chris it was worth a shot. I could confront her now and catch the early train tomorrow morning.

I drank my pint at the bar, but had to move as it became crowded as more heavily-coated students filled the room, to the consternation of older locals and anyone staying at the hotel, hoping for a quiet drink. I moved to a cosy corner and listened to the young-un's eager conversations, feeling a wave of nostalgia for my Uni days, listening to their talk of new bands and new experiences as they revelled in their adult lives opening up to them.

This was cosy – a warm pub, gloves, pints and mince pies - but it wasn't the same when you're on your own. Plus, I felt like an old man in comparison to these kids… the things I've seen, I wanted to tell them, thinking of singing crowds at my feet, coral reefs and video shoots. Instead, my mind took me to Shirley's dead face, looming buses and Stephen's car crashing.

'Alright mate, what happened there,' a guy with long dark hair asked, nodding at my plaster cast.

I was unsure if he was slurring slightly due to the beer, or if it was his accent.

'Broke it in a car crash,' I replied, immediately wishing I'd come up with a better reason: skateboarding; fending off a burglar; wrestling tigers; freak skydiving accident.

'Woah,' he replied, suggesting the real reason was adequate. 'Who's signed it then?' he asked, tilting his head to read the lads' signatures and comments.

'Nice logos!' He said, admiring Rob's handiwork. 'Blur, Supergrass, Skimrider…'

One of his mates moved in to have a look too, so I lifted my arm up for her to see.

'I recognise that logo,' she said, pointing to Rob's sketch. 'Is that your favourite band or something?'

'Ha, yeah, you could say that,' I replied.

'Ben-Cheed?' the guy said. 'Never heard of him.'

'Beachhead,' I said with a laugh. 'They're a band. He was drunk when he wrote it.'

'Oh, I've heard of them,' she said. 'They support Skimrider don't they?'

'Skimrider? Awesome band,' he said. 'I'm John by the way.'

He held a hand out and I shook it with more gratitude than I meant to.

'I'm Sarah,' the girl said, offering her hand too.

'Good to meet you both,' I said. 'Nice to meet other people into decent music.'

'Yeah, Skimrider are my favourite band,' John said.

'This week,' Sarah said and nudged him in the ribs. 'Next week it'll be Krunch or, who was it? Beachhead?'

'Yeah,' I said, laughing, wondering if these two were together.

In that moment it felt like I'd taken a step out of reality and was watching my life unfold on a stage before me. That was the only way I could describe it. Detached, yet fully present, and my ego had disappeared. I made a conscious effort not to brag or tell them who I was. No need to tell them I knew Dave from Skimrider or tell stories of our video shoot or recording the album. Because it didn't matter.

'Yeah, they're pretty good, Skimrider,' I said, feeling a warm glow. 'Dave's a bloody good singer.'

'Yeah,' they both replied.

'Great album,' John said.

'I think Carl can play one of their songs on guitar,' Sarah said, pointing at one of the lads.

'Ah, cool,' I said, wondering if he was a fellow musician or one of the three-chord players who could only play one song the whole way through, usually Wonderwall. Stop being negative! I told myself.

'I'm Luke, by the way,' I said, clinking pint glasses with each of them.

'Good to meet you,' John said. 'So, you on your own then?'

'Yeah, I'm just visiting. From Brighton originally.'

'Brighton?' Sarah said. 'That's where Claire's at Uni! You'll have to meet her… Claire!'

She called her mate over and we slipped into a conversation about Brighton nightclubs, bands, who'd played gigs at their Universities. More people joined in. Random discussions flowed with the ale and time flew.

Eventually, John and Sarah were sucked back into their group and I felt the slightly drunken urge to get outside and explore. If I was honest, I wanted to see if Lisa was in a different pub or down the seafront – she was never one for sitting around watching telly or doing nothing at home. So I left the warmth of the pub and headed downhill to the seafront road, resisting the pull of an addictive bassline coming from a seedy-looking club.

Saturday 21st December 1996 P.M.

Disco 2000 – Pulp

As soon as I reached the prom I could see where I needed to go. Flashing lights in the distance highlighted the place to be: the arcades. Surely the hub of any seaside town. Pool tables, shoot 'em ups, grubby carpets and the chance to win sixty pence in two pence coins. Or a place to score some weed, I thought as I felt the urge to numb my feelings. No. This was a new place. A new place to discover, maybe meet people. It might not be the kind of place that Lisa would go to, but it was somewhere I could find info on Chris… and Andy for that matter, seeing as he'd grown up here too.

The pier had seen better days; its glaring lights blinding me as I cut in between shuttered candy floss and doughnut shops which lined the prom, and up a concrete ramp. I swung open the red, glass-panelled doors and entered the smoky arcade, feeling like a cowboy. Eyes turned to me from pool tables and gambling machines. Pier kids roamed, searching for dropped pennies from the coin-pusher machines. A group of lads caught my eye: laughing around Time Crisis – a shooting game with a plastic gun and foot pedal.

Then the eyes turned away and the noise enveloped me, bringing back warm nostalgia. Not for Brighton, but for sunny Sundays with my grandparents. Bags of pennies. The chance of winning more money. The clatter of coins and shriek of delight. Sweets and salty air. Endless fun.

'Alright.' I nodded at one of the lads at the shoot-em-up game as I passed and chose a gambling machine.

One pound in. Five gambles. Easy money… for the establishment. Nothing for me.

Same luck at the next machine. I eyed up the pool tables where a few lads were playing. If my arm wasn't in a cast I'd have a game and chat to them.

'You a skater?' A voice asked in what sounded like a put-on cockney accent.

I turned to see one of the spotty teenager from Time Crisis.

'Broke your arm on a skateboard?' He asked.

'No, I…' I wasn't sure what to say and couldn't think of a decent alternative to the truth. 'Car crash,' I said and watched the kid's eyes widen.

His mates came over. None of them over fifteen, all smoking. Not menacing, but looking at me like I had to explain way I was here, on their territory. Like a pack of puppies. Easy to please and possibly useful.

'Where you from then?' The lankiest one asked.

'London,' I replied, trying to play it cool in my half-drunk way. 'Just looking for an old mate.'

'Who's that then?' the first one asked.

'Lightback,' I said, keeping up the Clint Eastwood stranger in town aloofness.

'Don't know any Lightback,' Lanky said. 'Wasn't there a Lightback in your brother's year, Damo?'

Damo, the spotty one, shrugged.

'We know someone who might know,' the first one said.

'Yeah, Tip'll know him for sure,' said Lanky. 'We can take you to him.'

'Cool,' I replied, feeling a mix of elation and anxiety as I followed them, weaving back through the phalanx of games machines and into the fresh air.

'He's just over the road,' Lanky said.

I breathed in a waft of chlorinated air as we passed the swimming pool and eyed up a pub, searching for Lisa's golden locks. The lads led me into a smaller arcade, up some stairs to a room teeming with pool tables. The lads beamed with self-importance as they nodded and smiled at the punters, leading me through the smoke to the far corner where a couple of leather-clad men stood. Between them sat someone I recognised: the man I'd seen walking through town with the strange, bobbing gait.

‘Wait here,’ Spotty said as Lanky went over to talk to the men.

I couldn’t read their lips but they were quick. A nod. Hands in and out of pockets. A switch. Weed probably. I was beckoned over and the lads vanished, leaving me facing the two large men.

‘I’m looking for Lightback,’ I said. ‘Chris Lightback.’

Neither man moved.

‘Why do you search for Chris Lightback?’ the man on the chair asked in a deep, controlled voice.

He was sitting at a slant with one leg over the other. Rolling paper and a packet of Golden Virginia on one knee. His over-sized head bent down at an unnatural angle.

‘He’s a mate from London,’ I lied. ‘He said I could stay with him if I was passing.’

The rolling stopped and his large head rose slowly until his sharp eyes met mine.

‘I doubt that very much, Mister…?’

‘Redfern,’ I said automatically, regretting it instantly. Why couldn’t I just stay calm?

His eyes dropped and his fingers resumed rolling.

‘Well, Mister Redfern,’ he continued. ‘I may have information of interest to you, but what I’m wondering is what you’ll give me in return.’

'I'm sorry?' I said.

'What do you offer me for the location of Chris Lightback?'

'You want money?' I asked, looking over my shoulder to make sure nobody was nearby.

'Not money, Mister Redfern,' he replied slowly. 'No. What I deal with is information and favours. Knowledge is power. I run this place you see… the stowe, it's mine, get it?'

This guy, Tip, was starting to freak me out. Menacing without being threatening. He reminded me of a character from a film I saw recently. Usual Suspects.

'Right,' I said.

'I do you a favour, you do me one back. Understand?'

'Yeah, I guess so,' I said, wondering what on earth he was going to ask of me.

'I'll tell you what,' Tip said, looking up at me again. His voice lightened and sped up. 'You give me your phone number and if I hear anything I'll let you know, okay?'

'Sure,' I said, pulling my recent purchase from my pocket: my new mobile phone.

Play it cool, I thought, as I pressed the buttons, trying to find my own phone number amongst the list of deceptively simple headings.

'Right,' I said and read out my number, which one of Tip's men tapped into his phone.

I was starting to sweat. The only reason I'd bought the phone was to track Chris and Lisa down – I'd typed in all the phone numbers Andy had given the police and added any others I knew – and now I was being drawn into some drug dealer's information ring.

A second later, two buzzes suggested he'd forwarded my number to Tip and the other meathead, then my phone buzzed and a new number had arrived by SMS.

'Thank you, Martin,' Tip said and the hulk on my left nodded.

'Great,' I said, feeling disorientated by the speed of this new technology and that this seaside gangster had a hold on me now. 'Thanks.'

'I'll let you know what I find,' Tip said, dipping his head. 'Do you need accommodation while you're in town?'

'Er, no, I'm fine thanks.'

'Okay, if not, just let Aston know and he'll point you in the right direction.'

The man on my right gave me the slightest nod and Tip turned his focus back to his roll-up.

Assuming the meeting was over, I ambled away with another meek, 'Thanks', and headed back downstairs and into the cool sea air.

I meandered back to the beach, straight onto the pebbles and breathed deeply, clearing my head. I had the new address for Chris's Mum and Tip might give me info if I needed it – at a price – so I had everything covered… but what I really wanted was Lisa. I wanted to dance with her and have a laugh. I wanted to forget the troubles of the world, my broken arm and the pressure from Jeff. I wanted to escape. Get out of my head for a bit.

I was still half-drunk and needed more beer. It was Saturday night after all and I was sure there had to be more life in this town, so I stomped back along the promenade and had almost reached the hill road which led to my hotel when someone called out my name.

Lisa? I swivelled on my heels to see a group of people smoking outside one of the seafront flats. Was this it? Were Lisa and Chris at a party?

'Luke!' someone called again and I spotted Sarah with John and their mates.

'Oh, hi!' I shouted back and strolled over, gutted it wasn't Lisa but happy to see some friendly faces. 'How's it going?'

'Alright,' John replied. 'We're just having a quick refuel before hitting the club.'

'What? The dodgy-looking one half way up that road?'

‘Dodgy music, definitely,’ John said, offering me a spliff, which I took without a second-thought.

‘Oi!’ Sarah said, elbowing him in the ribs. ‘It isn’t that bad.’

‘Yeah, if you like Baby D and Whigfield!’ John replied.

‘Sounds great,’ I said, raising an eyebrow.

‘Exactly!’ Sarah replied, not getting my sarcasm.

‘I prefer something with a bit of guitar!’ I said, handing the smoke along, remembering my conversations with Lisa and how we tried to open each other’s musical tastes.

‘Well, we’ll be lining up the shots as soon as we get in,’ John said. ‘You need to be plastered to dance to that crap!’

‘Shut it,’ Sarah said and I still couldn’t work out if these two were a couple or not.

‘It sounds like a good laugh,’ I said, feeling happy to be back with people I felt comfortable with.

This was just like travelling, I thought. New faces, new places, new experiences. Plus, there was always the chance Lisa could be in there.

‘I could use a drink,’ I said, trying not to invite questions about why.

‘Come inside for a bit then,’ Sarah said, hooking her arm around my unbroken arm and pulling me through the front door to the party. ‘It’s too cold out there.’

'Cool, cheers,' I said as we entered the warmth and sounds of the flat.

'Carl rents it and he isn't allowed to smoke indoors,' Sarah explained as we passed the kitchen, already full of empty cans, pizza boxes and people chatting. 'He gave up on Uni after the first term, so he's the only one of us working.'

'I bet he loves it when you guys come home,' I said as we moved into the main room, where Carl sat with his acoustic guitar, strumming a Radiohead tune I recognised… but he was making a pig's ear of it.

Seven or eight students sat around the room, drinking and singing along, and I felt like I'd come home... or maybe not? I felt different now, like I'd felt in the pub. Older, sure, but detached slightly. I nodded at the guys I recognised as Sarah handed me a beer can and we squeezed into a space on the sofa. These could be new friends, or more importantly to me now, these were my crowd. These were the album-buying, gig-going, lyric-learning, chord-deciphering public who bought Beachhead's output and paid my wage. Without them I was nothing.

'Oh, I still can't get that middle bit right,' Carl said when he finished.

'No, it sounded good,' one of the girls said.

I couldn't help myself. I didn't want to let on who I was, or start bragging about my band, but I knew where he was going wrong and could help the guy. Surely that was okay?

'It's an F on the second set of chords in the verse,' I said, receiving some looks.

'You what?' Carl asked, not menacingly, but with a hint of *what are you doing in my party?*

I smiled and tried to keep it simple. 'Then E-minor and G.'

The lull of music allowed conversations to light up around us and I watched Carl try it out, softly, on his guitar but he refused to respond. I wasn't used to not being able to play guitar or, I realised, the centre of attention. Or maybe I had always hidden behind the guitar, unable to socialise properly?

'Oh, hi Luke!' Claire came into the room and sat next to me. 'I was telling Steve about that bookshop in Brighton you mentioned and…'

I was pulled into the conversation and loved it. I kept an eye on Carl who, instead of trying something new, returned to his safe ground, like an injured animal.

'Okay, everyone knows this one!'

He strummed an E-minor and I sighed. Good tune but… I had to resist the urge to wrestle the guitar from him.

'Today is gonna be the day…'

I let go. We drank, sang and, during the lulls in conversation, my mind flittered back and forth, to Lisa, to Stephen, to Isaac, but the drugs and drink soon washed them into one colourless mess, like watered-down paint, and I was just me again.

An hour later, the whole party evacuated the flat: a gaggle of upbeat drunkenness and laughs. I was swept away with the wave, through the dark doorway of the club and into a mass of smoke and revellers. And despite my apprehension this felt good. I felt good. Joking. Laughing. Singing.

Dancing the night away.

- I'm Only Sleeping -

A pillow. A nice, soft pillow. And sheets. They smelt fresh. Clean. Something didn't smell good though… me. I felt sticky. I ran my hands down my top and could feel I was still in my clothes, which felt sweaty. How long had I been in these clothes?

These were the first clear thoughts I'd had for what felt like an age, as my mind fought to break free of a twisted mass of feelings, views and sounds which still haunted me. Images of moving lights, being carried, floating, drinking, sleeping - the pictures in my head merged and I was unsure if they were memories or dreams?

I rolled over and a delayed wave of pressure followed, like my brain was made of lead. Was I injured? Had I been attacked? I squinted, trying to make sense of my surroundings. Maybe then I could work on how I got here?

I focussed on an orange light coming through a set of pink curtains. A street light? It was night, but the streetlight gave some definition to the room. A picture of a vase of flowers on the opposite wall hanging over a mantelpiece. Ornaments. An old telly. I didn't recognise anything, but memories were coming back to me now… going to the toilet in the dark. Somebody had been there, talking. Out of sight. Talking to their Mum.

Where was my phone? I wanted to call Luke, to see how he was doing. Why wasn't Luke here? He'd wonder where I was. And Stephen. Was he okay after the car crash?

I sat up, feeling some strength return as my memories slotted back into place. I was so tired. Drained. I couldn't remember the last thing I'd eaten and my mouth was incredibly dry. An image of someone holding a cup to my lips came to me. Like I was ill.

Car. Dark. Singing. Kicking.

The journey came back to me in a rush of emotion and my head fell back onto the pillow. I'd fought back when he came to get me, lashing out with my boots, but he was strong. He'd covered my mouth with something soft and I'd passed out again.

Now this.

No, there was more. I remembered a shape… someone sitting in an arm chair, in the corner of the room, watching me. Never moving. Was that his Mum? How could a mother let her son kidnap someone? None of this was right. I was missing something, I knew that, but I was so tired...

-

When I woke next it was daytime and I could see more of the room. My thoughts were still with me and I was feeling stronger. There was a table next to me, and a glass of water, so I shifted my body ready to pick up the glass and felt hard lines beneath me. I was lying in a sofa, not a bed, made up with a sheet and duvet.

I reached over and carefully brought the water to my lips. Relief. It tasted slightly bitter, but I needed it, so drank more. I rested the glass on the edge of the sofa, breathing, my eyes travelling around the room: the telly; a Christmas edition of Radio Times; a tree in the corner covered in tinsel; a Quality Street box. My stomach grumbled at the thought of food and I summoned the energy to push myself up onto one elbow, but my head felt woozy.

A bang made me jump and I spilt water on my arm. Someone was banging on a door – the front door maybe? The sound echoed around the house and all I could think was they were trying to break in to get me. Panic seeped through me, my heart thumping. I could hear someone shouting. A man.

I looked around the room, searching for somewhere to crawl to and hide? More sofas, the room's door and an arm chair in the corner. My head was hurting from the effort and everything was blurring. The banging stopped and I swore I heard my name being called out. I recognised the voice. I recognised the arm chair too… his Mum's chair. Someone was sitting in it. I tried to focus. A shape. A skirt, shoes, glasses staring right at me!

My elbow slipped off the edge of the sofa, the glass dropped to the floor with a dull clunk and splash, and I passed out.

Sunday 22nd December 1996 A.M.

Broken Stones – Paul Weller

The wind shook the windows of my hotel room and, for a second, I thought I was back home. When had I started to think of our band house in London as *home* I thought as I peeped from under the duvet to discover my true location. I stopped thinking of the flat above the bookshop as home long ago and I guess I stopped thinking of my parents' house as home before that… definitely after they turned my bedroom into a reading room, so *home* had been an alien concept to me for some time now.

Memories from last night came back to me along with the taste of aniseed from the shots John had forced on us in the club. When we'd entered the dingy club, stepping gingerly across the sticky floor to the neon bar set to one side of the square dancefloor of locals, I'd thought about asking John or his mates if they knew Chris or Andy, but out came the tray of shots and the evening slipped away.

I burped and tasted the spicy kebab we'd had afterwards. It had been freezing outside but we'd had our beer coats on, stumbling through the streets arm in arm, singing. All I could really remember was snapshots of dancing, laughing and drinking. Good times. I'd been drunk enough to have fun and too drunk enough to dwell on Lisa and Chris.

I turned over and felt like my brain was rolling inside my skull, floating on a lake of pain. Water. I managed a few gulps then fell asleep again, I think, and when I opened my eyes again, I searched for a clock. Nothing. In a moment of inspiration, followed by Herculean effort, I dragged my jeans off the floor, broke my phone free from its pocket prison and focussed on the digits on the screen.

Eleven-thirty.

Not bad. I was pretty sure the club – tacky in more ways than one – closed at two and we'd roamed the streets for a good hour after, eating our kebabs in a hut in the public gardens.

The visions ran through my mind as I lay on the edge of the bed, pushing away thoughts that I'd said something wrong or annoyed someone. That was just the hangover talking but I remembered Carl and wondered if I'd pissed him off. I stared at nothing for a while, then at my bag, finally fixing on the letter I'd picked up from the lady in Chris's old house. My stomach turned and I felt the weight of the situation with Lisa press down on me. I had to be strong to get through this but right now I really couldn't be arsed. Last night had shown me that life goes on. Life could go on without Lisa, just as it had done before we'd met and for however many months she'd been away travelling.

Eventually, after some pills and more water, I made it to the shower, which was always a pain with a plaster cast. New signatures and pictures adorned it now and, somewhere in the recesses of my mind, an embryonic song formed, centred round how our soul is like a plaster cast, signed by those who come into our lives.

I pulled on some clean clothes and made it downstairs to the restaurant.

'Full English please,' I said to the waitress with way more enthusiasm than it required.

Despite last night's kebab, I was starving.

'I'm sorry,' she replied, handing me a menu. 'We've just switched to our lunch menu.'

'Ah, okay.' I read the header – Sunday Roast – and my stomach growled in anticipation. 'Oh, brilliant!'

The roast turned out to be my saviour. Pink beef, horseradish sauce, a trio of angular roasties, Yorkshire puddings, sprouts, carrots, parsnips… all covered in thick, life-affirming gravy. Full, I just wanted to sleep again, but I had a task to complete. There was no point being here otherwise. I thought about Stephen and my parents. Travelling down to Brighton on a Sunday would be a pain, so I booked the hotel for one more night, wrapped up in my warmest jumper and sea-breeze defying coat and headed out with the letter in my pocket and my CD Walkman pumping tunes into my hungover brain.

It was cold, but the fresh air woke me up and, as I walked along the flat promenade, my speed picked up. The grey sea foamed to my left as I passed families braving the cold to get to the arcades on the pier, and I gave Tip's pool-hall a wary look as I passed. What would he ask me to do if he did find Chris, I wondered? I regretted the whole situation but knew if I found Lisa at this address I wouldn't need Tip after all, so screw him!

I pulled out my phone and saw the date. The twenty-second of December – nearly Christmas! A flash of panic ran through me as I thought of Mum and Dad again. I hadn't been in contact for a few days and they were expecting me at theirs for Christmas but had no idea when I would be arriving.

I looked at my phone, checking the signal which flashed on and off, and looked around. This part of the beach was cut off from the main part of town by the hill where my hotel sat. Ahead of me sat a line of silent giant cranes, leering over tiny rows of houses like metal sauropods. Maybe the mobile signal would be better closer to the docks, I thought? So waited a few minutes before trying again.

'Bingo!' A full bar of reception.

I found the list of contacts and rang Mum and Dad's home phone.

Straight to their answer machine. Did nobody answer their bloody phones these days?

'Hi Mum… Dad, it's Luke,' I said, hearing the wind rustle on my microphone. 'Sorry I haven't been in touch, I… I've taken a little trip, looking for Lisa.' I paused for a second, wondering what else to say. 'I'm hoping to be back in Brighton for Christmas, so I'll see you then. Probably catch the train tomorrow. I hope Stephen's doing alright? I've got a mobile phone now, so call me if you want. Cheers, bye.'

I hung up, feeling hollow. I needed to talk to them. Maybe to get reassurance for what I was doing? I knew Lisa was worth the effort but was I just making a fool of myself? I needed to see how Stephen was as well, or just to chat about random stuff like how it might snow this Christmas or what the number one was. I'd missed that when I was travelling.

'Damn it.' I should have read out my phone number as well.

A new song started on the Walkman and I focussed on the prom ahead where a couple walked arm in arm pulled along by a tiny, enthusiastic dog. My mind immediately went to Lisa and Chris and I felt a surge of anger rise inside me. I stared at the sea as the couple passed, focussing on the song. On Paul Weller's lyrics. I wouldn't be kicked around. I was in charge of my own destiny.

I didn't need the A to Z to find the house because, according to the map, I just had to follow the prom all the way to the last street on the coast, so I kept on, walking into the wind, passing a new set of arcades and a wind-swept market, which had attracted groups of chip-eaters and scavenger seagulls. Then it was quiet until the prom ended and I hopped onto the coastal road.

Manor Terrace. It sounded posh. But it turned out to be an isolated strip of weather-beaten bay-windowed terraced houses separated from the bleak wintry sea by a line of sunburnt beach huts and fifty metres of desolate scrub land and windswept rubbish.

I fumbled the letter as I checked the numbers on the doors, counting my way up to fifteen. Here it was. I turned the tunes off, pulled my headphones down and took a deep breath. This was it. I just had to find out the truth and be done with it. Without giving myself time to think, I stomped up the concrete path and knocked on the front door.

Nothing.

I stared out to sea. The sky was already starting to darken. Dusk would be here soon, but the street lights weren't on yet and there were no lights on inside the house.

I knocked again.

Nothing.

I pushed the letter through the letterbox and pulled out my phone. This was my plan B. First I rang Lisa and put my ear to the glass door. Was that a bleep? No, just something squeaking in the wind. It went to the answer message and I cancelled it. Next I tried Chris's number… I listened for any sound – a tune or just a buzz.

It went to answer.

'Damn it,' I hissed and banged the door again but, remembering what Dad had said about Mum's court case, I didn't want to attract attention.

Still, my anger had risen and I felt like I was being ignored on purpose. I didn't deserve that.

'Lisa!' I shouted, pounding on the door again.

Silence.

I felt stupid. With a sigh, I walked away.

Not for the first time, I wondered if Lisa and Chris had gone somewhere else? What if they were here but had just popped out? Maybe I should find a place to wait and catch them when they return? I eyed up an old wooden shelter but knew I'd only last ten minutes in the cold wind.

Too many what ifs.

Paranoia was seeping into my thoughts now my defences were down. Was this a wild goose chase? Was I wasting my time here? I needed closure but could I have gone about this another way? Maybe Tip would get me some better info on Chris and I could track them down?

I stomped back the way I'd came and veered off the prom as soon as I reached it, onto the crunching stones of the beach, desperate to feel something. Ice-cold spots of salt spray spattered my face as I neared the foamy, yellow surf, and I wished I had a hat. A memory flashed back from Brighton the summer before last when Lisa and I split up after she'd bought her flight tickets. Was the same thing happening again? She was always doing random things… for her own reasons or sometimes just to surprise me, so why should I expect anything different now? Maybe she didn't want the inevitable argument so had just gone off. She'd been back from travelling for just a day and that had been her goodbye? But why the job at the label? That didn't make sense.

Ahead along the beach, a metal detectorist swept the fresh sand and a couple of wind-blasted fishermen set up for a day's fishing in their waterproof overalls. I wondered what Andy made of this place? He grew up here with Chris. Did he long to come back or was he glad to escape? I thought about ringing Andy and the lads, letting them know what was going on but the trip had been a failure – two empty houses, nothing else. All I'd achieved was delivering some re-directed mail and getting a hangover.

I felt a vibration in my pocket. Out came the phone, but the screen just showed the time – and a new icon in the corner. I wished I'd read the instruction manual now. I pressed a few buttons… no texts… phone messages! I pressed play.

'You have one new message.'

I took a deep breath to calm down and played it. Was it Lisa returning my call?

'Luke, it's Dad. We got your message. Glad you're okay.'

I could hear Mum in the background, 'Tell him Stephen's going to be out for Christmas.'

'Stephen's coming home for Christmas… I mean here, home, to Brighton, so if you can get here that would be great.' A muffled sound suggested he'd put his hand over the mouthpiece, then he came back, whispering now. 'Listen, Luke… I've heard back from the recovery guys and they found something with Stephen's car. They're getting a second opinion but… look, keep this to yourself okay? It looks like the brake cables were deliberately cut.' He sighed heavily. 'Call me when you get this.'

The phone beeped.

'Fuck,' I gasped and looked for the nearest bench to sit on.

The crash had been deliberate. I wasn't paranoid after all. I sat and stared out at the endless horizon of grey sea. Someone *was* trying to hurt Stephen or me – or both of us. Or Lisa? Maybe they'd seen us in the car together and wanted to hurt both of us? Did Lisa know the truth? Was she hiding from whoever was after us? No, she would have told me, surely. This was all I needed, Lisa leaves me and someone's trying to hurt me. But why?

I pictured Isaac's manic face as he leapt at me in the bookshop and felt a sharp strike of pain in my wrist. If someone was after me again, I had to be on guard. I had to be ready for anything. I'd been stupid. No more drinking. I couldn't trust anyone.

I looked at my phone again, knowing I should give Dad a call back, but the icon was still on the screen, so I pressed the button again.

'You have one new message,' the female voice said as before.

Probably Dad's message again I thought.

'Mister Redfern,' a deep voice said and I sheltered my ear from the wind. 'This is Aston. Tip has the information and requests your presence.'

A beep signalled the end of the message and I stared around, feeling I was being spied on.

One step forward, one back, I thought. It wasn't like I had a choice and the arcade was on my way back to the hotel anyway, so five minutes later, I was back in the pool hall standing before the self-named owner of the town, trying not to stare at his deformities.

'My people have been busy and have the information you're looking for,' Tip said, rolling a cigarette just like the night before. 'The correct address,' he said before I could protest. 'Which is yours for a small favour.'

I looked at each of his men and gave a little cough before replying, 'Which is?'

'I need you to deliver a package, then get out of my town.'

'Okay…' I said, feeling this was a trap, but knew I was out of options. I had to find Chris and Lisa and get back to Brighton, especially if someone was after me.

My spidey-senses were kicking in though. Paranoia. What if Tip was connected to the car accident? That wasn't possible, but my hungover brain was feeling defensive, so every option carried weight. Maybe I should just say no and walk away right now… get on the train and head back to Brighton? But then the whole trip would have been a waste.

What if Tip really knew where Chris and Lisa were?

'Martin will send you the first address,' Tip said, pausing to lick the rizla, 'and a second when you've picked up the package. When you've delivered it, you will be sent the address you're after.'

I took a second to take it in and nodded.

'Then you leave my town.'

My phone buzzed and I checked it.

'Now go,' Tip said, gesturing for me to go.

'Thank you,' I said, catching his eye for the first time.

There was pain in his eyes, physical or emotional I couldn't tell, but there was a fatherly quality to them as well. He meant well. He cared.

'Good luck,' he whispered and I left.

Sunday 22nd December 1996 P.M.

Setting Sun – Chemical Brothers

It was pretty cold outside and I'd spent half my waking day walking along the coast in the winter wind, so after I used the A to Z to see where Tip was sending me, I headed inland and straight into the first café I could find. My hungover stomach demanded sugar to help digest the roast and my head *needed* coffee. Strong coffee! So I found a warm corner in the café and recharged my batteries with a black coffee and a doorstop wedge of chocolate cake.

I sat in a back room, over-looking the rooftops including the club we'd danced in last night, and all the way up the prom I'd just walked. I could even see the row of houses where I'd delivered the mail. I didn't know if it was the hangover, the cake or coffee, but I felt numb to it all. I just wanted it over and back to normal. I wanted to be able to play guitar, to get that stage buzz and to have a proper go at touring our album. With Lisa.

Half an hour later, I had the sea breeze at my back as my inland route took me to the graceful curve of a Victorian terrace overlooking the sea. I hadn't seen the front, but the red-brick rear-end of the building had seen better days and were now a set of dodgy-looking flats.

I found the house number Tip's man, Martin, had sent me, pressed the doorbell on the aged doorframe and waited. Around the door, an ornate white stone affair told of a grand history. Probably from when this place was a resort, competing with Bournemouth and Brighton for train-faring sun-seekers. Now it was rank and peeling. A bit like this town, I thought.

While I waited, images of the car crash came back to me, what Dad had said about the brakes and about not getting into trouble. A cold rush ran through me and panic gripped my body. What was I doing here? If someone was after me, why was I following errands for some dodgy guy? Was I walking into a trap? Adrenaline started to take over and I felt twitchy.

'What d'ya want?' A gruff voice suddenly demanded from the other side of the closed door.

'Tip sent me,' I said after sucking in a deep breath. 'To pick something up?'

'Code word?'

'Portman Road,' I replied, remembering the text.

A chain rattled and the door opened just enough for me to see a pair of eyes – one bruised – and a small box wrapped in brown paper, which angled out through the gap along with a puff of sweet cannabis smoke. I took the package, its brown paper crackling in my fingers.

'The address is on the box,' the guy said and slammed the door shut, leaving me in the cold.

I checked it and prayed it wasn't too far to walk. My feet were starting to hurt after the miles I'd walked, but I set off straight away, not wanting to hang around where people knew I might be. I headed down to the beach, into a wooden shelter and checked the address in the A to Z.

Sunningdale Drive.

According to the map, it was in an area called 'Old' Felixstowe, but when I veered back into the town, past the grounds of a brick wall lined Girls College, I crossed a main road and found myself in a modern estate. Apart from a squat church and a pub, there wasn't much old about this part of town.

Thoughts about Stephen and the brakes came back to me and I looked at my phone. Plenty of reception up here, so I gave my parents a call while I walked.

'Hi Dad,' I said when he answered.

'Luke, where the bloody hell have you been? Your Mum's been going crazy worrying about you, especially after the crash and your arm.'

'I'm okay, honestly,' I lied. 'Is Stephen still alright?'

'Yeah, he's just got to rest, so he's coming back here for Christmas,' he said with a calmer voice. 'We'll pick him up tomorrow.'

'I got your message… err, what you said about the car?' I asked, not knowing what else to say. 'Are you sure?'

'Well, yes and no,' he said with a sigh and I pictured him standing in the hall, shaking his head. 'But they're pretty sure the cable was sliced. Stephen had it checked before he drove it up to London, so it would have been noticed and my contacts said it couldn't have happened during the crash. Look, there's nothing you can do, so we'll just leave it to them okay?'

'Have you told Stephen?'

'No, not yet,' Dad replied. 'Listen, you don't have anyone after you… with a grudge, do you?'

'No,' I said, shaking my head, running a list of names through my head of potential enemies: Lisa's Ex, Jim, who I'd dobbed in back in Brighton; Mike after he left Beachhead; that roadie who always gave me evils; Kurt from Krunch. No, only Chris Lightback had any real reason to be angry at me after we nicked Andy from his band, but I had more to reason to be angry at him for going off with Lisa.

'Okay, I'll let them know,' Dad replied.

He'd been overly protective after what happened with Isaac, especially after I told him and Mum about where my amateur sleuth skills had taken me, and yet here I was again, not telling anyone what I was doing; risking myself to find out what was really going on. This was different this time, I told myself, this was personal.

'Where are you anyway?' Dad asked. 'Folkestone? Why on Earth are you over there? I can come and pick you up if you want.'

'No, it's Felixstowe,' I tried to explain. 'Suffolk, not Kent.'

'Oh,' he replied. 'That's miles away.'

'Yeah, I know. I've just got to track Lisa down, then I'll come home… back to Brighton, I promise.'

'*Track* her down?' Dad asked, his voice shifting to the police tone he'd use to patronise me. 'Have you two had an argument?'

'No,' I replied automatically, which was technically the truth. How could I tell him she'd buggered off with some random guy and sent me one measly text? 'She's just with some mates,' I said. 'So I just need to find their place.'

Silence.

I crossed a road, recognised the curve I'd seen on the map, so took a left.

'Your Mum wants to know if you'll be back in time for Christmas?' he asked, as though he didn't have time for my stupid relationship issues.

'Yeah, sure,' I replied, trying to remember what day it was. 'I'll get the train on Christmas Eve at the latest,' I said, hoping this whole situation was cleared up by then.

'Okay, I'll let her know. Take care and keep your phone on, okay?'

'Yeah, I will,' I said, checking the road sign of the street I'd just entered. I was nearly there. 'Take care and see you soon. Bye!'

I pushed away the guilt I was feeling. I would get back to Brighton in time, but I had to concentrate on the here and now. Everything had gone to plan so far, but if this was a trap, I had to be on my guard. Tip wanted me out of his town and, from the way he'd talked, he probably had a few ways to get me out. But only after I'd done his work for him.

I entered a cul-de-sac of identical, slant-rooved houses with black tiled upper-floor walls. Very German. I counted the numbers and tried to look casual as I walked past houses with lights on, now dusk was setting in. I could see inside some. Families around the telly, playing games or setting up for a roast. Kids playing. Adults chatting. Other than a solitary dog walker I'd seen when I was talking to Dad, everyone was inside their homes, which made me feel better. Nobody around to see me.

There. I double-checked the address on the package, had a look around, and walked straight up to the front door. Pressed the bell. Waited. One car in the drive and no lights on in the house. Through the frosted glass of the front door I saw a silhouette move closer. I held my breath, wondering how many more stranger's houses I had to visit before I finally found Lisa. My heart leapt at the thought she was here! Did Tip know all along? Was the package just a test?

The door opened and an old lady stared at me with huge owl eyes, magnified by her glasses.

Shit, I'd got the wrong house! How was I going to talk my way out of this one? This was the last thing I needed.

'Have you got it?' She asked.

'Errr… what?'

'Have you got the package dear? My Arthur needs it now,' she said.

'Yes. Here you go,' I said, handing her the parcel.

'Thank you ever so much,' she took it and placed it on a dark wood telephone table at her side. 'Now, the gentleman asked me to give you this.' She handed me a slip of paper from beside the phone. 'I hope you can read my writing?'

I repeated the address in my hand and she nodded.

'That's right, dear. Thank you now,' she said and closed the door.

I turned and walked away in a daze. I had to keep moving but I was concerned for her and took a look back. Her silhouette was clear through the glass door, picking up the phone. She's fine, I told myself, but couldn't help wondering who Arthur was and what had been in the package. Was it the lady's drug-addicted son or going by the name, her husband, needing something extra to help with an illness? I assumed it had been drugs in the package. Depending on how much she'd paid for them would show whether Tip was a cruel underground businessman or modern day Robin Hood. From what I'd seen in his eyes and how he talked about his town, I had a feeling it was the latter.

My steps took me away from the house and I relaxed more, walking away an inch taller, ready to finally find Lisa. The endless search was almost over! Tip had fulfilled his bargain as far as I could tell, so now I just had to see what Lisa would say to me. I checked the A to Z and found the address was just a few roads away – not far at all. Maybe this would all be over before sundown? I needed this resolution.

My pocket buzzed and I pulled my phone out and answered it, assuming it was Tip or one of his men.

'Hey Luke, I found you!'

'Andy?' I said and looked at the screen where his name was spelt out.

'Yeah, I got your number off your Dad. We wondered what happened to you and never heard anything so…'

'Ah, yeah, sorry,' I said. 'I ended up chasing Lisa and Chris down… all uneventful so far but I've nearly found them, so it'll all be over soon.'

'I guessed you'd done something like that when you took the address but… look I'm on my way home, okay? I'm driving back to Felixstowe for Christmas. So we can meet up if you want? Where are you now?'

'It's alright,' I said. 'I've got their address and I'm nearly there.'

'Right, well, Chris might not be at the address I gave you,' Andy said. 'I tried ringing him again and got nothing, but then I remembered his Nana died recently, so he might have gone there.'

Something felt odd. I couldn't tell if it was the paranoia after what Dad had said about Stephen's car or Andy's connection with Chris, but I smelt a rat.

'Do you remember the address?' I asked, still walking.

'No, but I know she lived near my parents' house… somewhere down Ferry Road I think. In a bungalow.'

I looked at the piece of paper the old lady had given me: Ferry Road.

'That's great, thanks,' I said, still not sure whether to trust him or not. 'When will you be in town?' I asked.

'I'm about an hour away – we can meet up yeah?' Andy said.

'Yeah sure, give me a text when you're here.'

'Cool, see you in a bit.'

I checked the nearest road sign and could see I was nearly there. Andy's phone call confused me, but I focussed on my mission. There was no way I was going to hold off now after everything I'd gone through to get here. This was going to be a simple question and answer session, then leave.

The sun had disappeared behind the distant houses by the time I'd got to the quaint row of bungalows and found the number I'd been given. A soft light peeped around the closed curtains in the front room, which boded well, so I strode up the cracked concrete path more determined than before. I pictured Lisa's defiant face as I rang the bell. Cool but strong. Ready to tell me some home truths. It would hurt but it needed to be done. I had to know where I'd gone wrong.

No answer, so I rang again.

What if I'd been given the wrong number? I wondered. Maybe the old lady had written it down wrong? Car headlights lit up the front hedge as someone drove past and I rang the bell again.

Still nothing, so I knocked.

'Lisa?' I called out. 'Chris? Are you there?'

Nothing.

Fuck this, I thought and got my phone out to ring them again but stopped when new car lights appeared and I heard the engine slow. Was it them? I felt an anger rise and turned to face them but something made me stop. They'd avoided me this long, seeing me might make them drive off, so I ran around the side of the house and hid in the shadows. I would wait for Chris and Lisa to get halfway up the path first so they would be trapped.

The car slowed to a halt right outside the bungalow and I heard a man's voice.

'…agreed. Suspect seen in neighbouring streets.'

A muffled voice replied over what sounded like a radio.

'No visual. Repeat. Slim blonde male, five foot eight, mid-twenties.

Muffled reply.

'Will do. Over.'

It was the bloody police!

I had to think quickly – I had nothing incriminating on me, but how could I explain being here. There was no way I could get caught after what Dad had said about Mum's case. Shit! What if the police knew about Tip's schemes and had been watching me? They could have taken photos… they could have plenty of evidence. I had no idea what I'd delivered to the old lady but that was no excuse was it?

Two car doors clicked opened and slipped further back into the shadows. Footsteps closed in on me and an odd thought came to me - what if Tip had set me up? He wanted me out of town after all. Did he send the police after me?

The officers took the path to the front door out of my sight. The bell rang as I crept back deeper into the shadows until I bumped against a tall wooden gate. Carefully, I turned the handle, which clicked open with what sounded to me like a deafening snap. I paused, holding the gate an inch open, and stared back.

'What was that?' One of the officers said.

'Shit!' I hissed, pushed through the gate and closed it behind me a quietly as I could, but it was too loud.

'Here!' The officer shouted to his companion. 'Stop!' He yelled at me.

I slid a rusted bolt across the gate, hoping it would buy me some time, then legged it into the garden, desperate to find a way out. It was getting darker by the second and all I could see was shrubs on the other side of a long lawn, so I rushed over, sending a panicked look back to see torch lights blazing under the gate and arms reaching over to unlock the bolt.

I pushed through a swathe of bushes, branches scratching my face, until my cast hit a dark fence.

'Damn it!'

A clunk signalled the bolt being opened, so I used what strength I had in my one good arm to scramble up and over using the fence's cross-bars to climb up and over. The wood was hard to grip and I slipped as I rolled over the top, cracking my head on a plank of wood as my body landed in something soft and wet.

'What the…?'

The smell of compost triggered a set of memories. I'd fallen onto a carpet covering a compost heap set on the edge of a rambling range of allotments just like Grandad's. I'd caught my temple on the side of a pallet which held the compost in, but had no time to worry and set off running along the narrow paths between the patch-work of plots. I could hear shouting behind me but had to get away. I couldn't afford to get into any trouble and jeopardise my future with Beachhead and Jeff, or Mum's case.

After a minute of jogging I slowed down to control my breathing and took in the plots: some bare; others plump with brassicas ready for their owners' Christmas meal; others deserted apart from some well-dressed scarecrows.

Running out the entrance, I tried to work out where to go next, picturing the maze of roads I'd seen on the map. No time to check it now, I just had to get back to my hotel as quick as possible. If Tip had set me up, he had no idea I was staying there, so the hotel was my only safe place. It was nearly completely dark and I had to go by instinct.

The only way I knew for certain to get me back to the hotel was along the beach, so I followed my nose and headed for the sea.

- While My Guitar Gently Weeps -

Someone was there, in the shadows. I was being watched. I didn't want to look but I knew the shape was there. Silent and still. Sitting in the armchair.

I'd been asleep again but someone had cleaned up the spilt water and brought me a new glass. I could smell food as well. A pain rolled around my stomach, forcing me to open my eyes. It was light. A warm orange light, like when Luke and I had been camping… somewhere hot, near the sea. A door was half open. That was where the orange, electric light was coming from. Not the sun.

I pushed myself onto my elbow and could see a plate of food next to the water. Toast. The smell made me salivate. I *needed* sustenance.

But what about the person in the arm chair?

I turned slowly, wary of what I would see.

There they were. Still and silent. Asleep? I couldn't hear breathing but a shimmer of light glimmered off their glasses.

'Hello?' I whispered, my throat hoarse.

Nothing.

With slow, weak movements, I moved to a sitting position and reached out to take a piece of toast. Hard and smeared in cold butter, but it was the best thing I'd ever eaten. My taste buds wrapped around the dairy salt and sweet white bread, tasting every morsel. I went to grab the water but an instinct stopped me. Many of my recent memories ended with me having a drink. As tired as I was, my mind was still active and I needed to get out of here.

Still no movement or sound from the person in the corner. I wanted to ask them why they kept me here? What did they want?

A sound made me stop chewing. I gasped and my body almost jolted in shock. Someone was playing guitar nearby. Upstairs maybe? I recognised the song but couldn't quite place it. Beatles. A man was singing, but it wasn't Luke. A rush of questions flooded my head just like before. Where was Luke? Where was I? Where was my phone? What the hell was going on?

I felt my energy coming back – and my memories. This sofa. The car. The pub. The guy.

I took the glass off the table and smelt it. I had to drink, but didn't want to be out of control again. I needed the toilet too and couldn't understand why I hadn't wet myself.

I drank the water. I needed it. More toast. More water. I wasn't sleepy this time.

The music continued, reminding me of the pub where Luke had been playing. Standing at the bar – I could hear one of his songs and wanted to get in and see them play, it had been such a long time, but some guy had stopped me. Said he was from the label, Jeff had sent him, wanted to talk gigs for Beachhead. Bought me a drink.

I'd finished the toast and water, and needed the toilet. I felt better now, like I could stand.

'What do you want?' I asked the person in the corner. 'Who are you?'

Nothing.

If they were asleep, I thought, maybe I could get out? I stood slowly, waited to let a head rush pass, then crept over to the door. The guitar was still playing upstairs as I pulled the door open, squinting in the light and wincing at every floorboard or door squeak.

A normal hallway.

I shuffled forwards, realising I had no shoes on, and tried the first door I came to. The kitchen. Another. A cupboard full of coats and a hoover. Another. A toilet. Finally! I rushed in, feeling the relief of doing something normal.

As I weed, my thoughts congealed into manageable chunks. I'd clearly been drugged, several times probably, and given some kind of loperamide to stop me crapping myself, which explained why I was so dehydrated. I was so lost in my thoughts, I flushed the loo and washed my hands. When I stepped out of the toilet, into the cold silence, I realised my mistake. A thump upstairs, then a tirade of heavy footsteps thundered above me as someone ran downstairs.

In a panic, I ran into the dark kitchen and clawed at the back door. It was locked and there was no key. A man rushed in, grabbed me from behind and I lashed out. Elbows striking hard bone.

'Stop!' He growled, holding me in a crushing hug, trying to pull me to the ground.

I flung my head backwards, smacking him in the face with a crunch and a howl. His grip loosened and I ran for the front door but it was locked too. No key. I was trapped!

'Help!' I yelled. 'Help me!'

I ran back into the lounge where I'd been sleeping and ripped the curtains back to open the windows, but they were painted shut and too small to climb through. It was dark outside and I could see strings of coloured lights in the distance. Car lights too. Where was I?

A noise made me turn and I ran to the shape in the corner.

'Help me,' I shouted. 'You have to help me!'

I grabbed their shoulders, shaking them. But they were so light. Loose.

Light blinded me and covered my eyes as the man grabbed me from behind again in a bear hug, holding my arms against my sides. I could smell the chemicals: he was trying to drug me again and saw a cloth coming towards my face. I fought but my strength was slipping away. I stared at the person in the chair, wondering why they weren't helping but all I could see was cushions: a pair of glasses wedged onto a human shape made from cushions, wrapped in a cardigan.

He was too strong. He'd pinned an arm back and I was using all my strength to push his other hand away from my face, but I couldn't do it. I wretched as vapours from the cloth invaded my nostrils and rushed down my throat. I couldn't hold my breath and the smell was so strong.

A new sound. A thump. The man's grip loosened slightly and I heard him swear.

'I'm home!' A woman called from the hallway. 'Chris, is that you?'

'Hi Mum!'

Words blurred as everything went black and I fell onto the cushion dolly in the armchair.

'What the hell's going on in here? Who's that?'

'It's alright… we're just leaving…'

'Drunk… out of here… right now…'

Monday 23rd December 1996 A.M.

Place Your Hands – Reef

I didn't know who to trust. Someone was out to get me, that was clear from what Dad said about Stephen's car, and now the police were after me too.

I'd had time to think about it and, as I mulled it over, other events came to mind that could have been attempts to get at me. The fire alarm being set off at the gig. Was that meant to spoil *our* set rather than Skimrider's? Were the cut brakes meant to scupper the video shoot? Was this all the work of a jealous band taking things too far? Krunch maybe? Somebody was trying to stop Beachhead just as we were getting started and that really riled me.

What about Lisa leaving unannounced? Was she involved somehow? Did she want Beachhead to fail so we could start our lives together? No, we'd discussed it at length, plus that wasn't her style. None of this was.

I sat on my bed in my hotel room, staring out to sea, wondering whether I should just check out of the hotel and head straight to the train station now, or get a full English breakfast in the restaurant downstairs and book another night so I could sort this mess out once and for all.

What bugged me was who had given the police my description? Was it Tip? He knew where I'd be and he wanted me out of *his* town. Or the old lady I'd given the package to? She was straight on the phone after I left. My paranoia was strong and I suspected everyone. Even Andy, who knew I was in town and where Chris's Nana lived. Had he called me to check where I was? Was he in cahoots with Chris, his old school friend? He said he felt guilty for leaving their band, Lightback, so maybe he felt like he owed him something?

Last night, after the scramble away from the police, I'd followed the prom as far as I could, then had to drop onto the beach for a bit where the cliffs protruded out and jogged along the beach for a stretch before the prom started up again and took me back to my warm hotel. It had been a quiet Sunday evening, so nobody saw me. Scared and confused, I had sent Andy a text from the hotel to say I was busy and just stayed in my room, worried about venturing outside. I had a shower and ate whatever snacks I'd accumulated at the bottom of my bag.

But what now? There was no way I was going outside if the police had a description of me. I couldn't change my height or grow a beard, and I wasn't going to dye my hair… I could use a hat though? Some gloves too. My ears were nearly frost-bitten yesterday in the cold sea wind. Maybe that would be enough to keep me incognito?

I switched my phone back on, having charged it overnight and felt my stomach lurch. What if I'd missed a call from Lisa? The date and clock flashed up along with a couple of icons; just text messages, all from one sender, Andy. He'd arrived in town about the time I'd made it back to the hotel and replied to my text, checking I was okay. Nothing about the police or anything that suggested he was involved in what was going on. I felt bad, not trusting him. Would I always keep him at arm's length? Was he always going to be the newbie? He'd added a lot to our songs already, so who knew what it was going to be like when we started writing new material together. I sighed, making a vow to put more effort in to be his mate: more effort to listen to him and to appreciate what he'd given up to believe in our dream.

I rang him straight away and an hour later, with my room booked for another night, and my belly full of warm food, I met him on what he called the 'triangle' in the centre of the high street. I hadn't told him where I was staying and was happy to keep it that way for now.

'Nice hat!' he said with a laugh as we walked to where he'd parked his grey Golf. 'I didn't know you were into American Football?'

'It was the only thing I could find,' I lied, not wanting to explain a black hat was the least likely hat for the police to notice. Every other man wore a woolly black hat these days, probably inspired more by Cypress Hill than Gridiron. I'd have to turn it round maybe, hide the logo. 'Black gloves too!' I said, taking the attention away from my hat.

'Nice,' Andy replied and drove us out of the town, back towards the older part of town where I'd been yesterday.

'It's a bit warmer today though,' I said as we passed a police car driving the other way and my paranoia ramped up a notch.

'Yeah, depends on the wind in winter,' Andy replied. 'Sometimes we get smothered with snow straight from Russia but the rest of the time it's the warmest place in the country.'

'Really?' I said, watching the police car in the mirror, relaxing as it turned off.

Were they still after me? I wondered. And was Tip still trying to get me out of town? The sooner I got out of here the better.

'Sorry about not meeting up last night,' I said after some silence. 'This whole thing with Lisa… it's hard, you know?'

'Yeah, sure,' Andy replied. 'You and Lisa were close so…' he left it there, not sure what to say.

'Yeah,' I said, feeling the reality of the situation hit me again.

'I can only think it's drugs,' Andy said, catching me completely off guard.

'What?' I said, studying him as he drove: his eyes flicking from the road to his mirrors.

'Well, Chris studied Chemistry and… well, since I left the band, I'd heard he was getting back into chemicals, if you know what I mean? That's why I had to see him after our gig the other day – make sure he was okay.'

'Right,' I said, trying to piece together what he was saying. 'But Lisa's not into drugs.'

'No, but she might help him sell them?'

'Why her?' I asked.

Andy shrugged. 'Cos Chris is crap at that stuff? I don't know. I was just thinking about it when I drove back yesterday… what if he'd made some drugs but couldn't shift them and met Lisa at the video shoot.'

I thought about it and could see his thought process, but it was all what ifs.

'No, you're clutching at straws I reckon,' I said. 'Lisa wouldn't do that.'

I thought about how she'd helped her ex, Jim, sell the block of cannabis resin Detective Mellor had planted on me. She knew her stuff, had connections and was bold enough to do anything.

'I don't know. Like I said, it was just an idea,' Andy said.

If Lisa was doing some drug deal to get some extra travelling cash, she'd want me to have nothing to do with it… so she'd push me away, but why come here? Why Felixstowe?

A lorry rolled past us and it clicked. The docks. Tip. No wonder he wanted me out of the way. Maybe I'd been sniffing round something way bigger than I realised.

'Have you heard from Chris then?' I asked, trying to act normal.

'No, nothing,' he replied as we turned into a road I recognised.

I wondered if I should tell him about the police?

'His Nana used to live along here somewhere,' Andy said, pointing at the bungalows. 'Not sure what number.'

I'd been keeping an eye out for the whole journey, trying to keep it cool, and felt my heart pounding as we drew up to the bungalow, then past. The drive was still empty. Where were they?

'We could park at the end of the road and knock on a few doors?' I suggested, not wanting to give away that I knew which one was the right house.

'Yeah, cool,' Andy said and found a free spot.

Hat pulled down and turned round to hide the American Football logo, I got out and asked, 'Was his Nana's surname Lightback as well?'

'Err no, she was his Mum's Mum, so I'm not sure what her surname was.'

'Great,' I mumbled out of earshot, then said. 'Okay, let's just see if anyone knows Chris then – I'll take this side.' I pointed to the side of the road where the bungalow sat just a few houses down.

'Okay,' Andy replied and headed to the first house.

I flicked my collar up and walked up the first path, not sure how I was going to play this. What if Andy found out which house it was before I reached it?

No lights were on in the house I was approaching, which wasn't surprising on a Monday morning, but it was the Christmas holidays now, so surely there would be Christmas lights on a tree if someone was in? Either way, it gave me an excuse to move on to the next house, whose lights *were* on. I cast a look over my shoulder and saw Andy was in deep discussion with an old man at the first house. I couldn't be bothered with this charade anymore! This needed to be settled now so I could get back to Brighton for Christmas.

'Fuck it,' I whispered and strolled past the next few houses, straight to the bungalow I knew.

No lights on, like last night.

It was odd being back here, I thought as I walked up the path. Dirtier in the light. I felt guilty, like I was returning to the scene of a crime, which

I guessed I was – it was illegal to run away from the police when asked to stop, wasn't it?

I knocked and rang the doorbell, hearing its familiar echoing chime from within the hall.

Nothing, so I banged harder. I could see through the net curtains in the main window that the curtains were drawn, but that would be normal if the place was empty.

'Oh, you found it,' Andy's voice gave me a start, making me jump.

'What?' I said, trying to construct an explanation. 'Nobody in.'

'Yeah, that guy told me this was her place – it's been empty since she died, so…'

'Right,' I replied, wanting to yell at the sky, but gritted my teeth and pushed past Andy.

'Let's go,' I said feeling the paranoia build, eyeing up the street for twitching curtains. I wanted to get back in the car and out of sight. 'We don't even know they're here do we?'

'Where are they then?' Andy asked, toying with his phone. 'Look, I'll text Chris, tell him we're here and you just want to talk to her, okay?'

'Alright,' I snapped as we walked back to the car.

Was it time to sack this off and get the train home? I didn't want to leave the wound open, but this wasn't feeling right. Drugs. Police. What with Mum's court case coming up, it felt like I was walking into something bad that would help no-one.

I slumped into the passenger seat of Andy's car and stared up the road of parked cars, worried I'd see a white police car turn the corner and cut us off, but it was empty. My wrist ached, probably from the cold and the excursions last night, and my spirits had hit rock bottom. Andy seemed perky though.

'Why don't we head down to the pier for a bit, then come back?' He tried, but I didn't respond. 'Or, I know! The viewing point. There's loads of places I can show you.'

He glanced at me, read my mood and shut up.

'Or we can put the heaters on and wait here for a bit.'

We sat in silence. I kept my eyes fixed on the road ahead, waiting for any sign of movement – car, person, cat – anything, while Andy fiddled about with the menagerie of cassettes which sat in the well of his driver's door.

'Shall I put some tunes on?' Andy asked.

'Shh!' I held up a hand.

Someone was coming. A man, walking into the road from a side road. A man I recognised.

'Oh shit,' I whispered.

'You know him?' Andy asked.

'Kind of,' I replied. 'Martin or Aston, I don't know which.'

'Aston or Martin?' Andy repeated. 'Aston Martin? Really?'

'Oh yeah!' I said with a sniff of a laugh and looked at Andy, but he wasn't smiling.

'Luke, how do you know Aston and Martin?'

'Well, I…' My voice trailed off as I watched the large man cross the road to the bungalow.

Was he here to make sure I'd left town? I couldn't tell Andy what had happened. Maybe Aston was here to meet Chris and Lisa for their drug deal?

'Aston was at school with my older brother,' Andy said. 'And I've heard enough about him to… let's just say… no, let's not go there. You've only been here for a couple of days, Luke! How do you know him?'

'He's slowing down,' I said as the henchman strolled past the bungalow, eyes fixed on it and its surroundings.

'And he's coming this way, get down,' Andy almost squealed.

I slunk in my seat, cracking a knee against the side and pulled my hat down over my eyes.

'Lock the car,' I whispered, waiting for the inevitable knock on the window.

I heard a clunk and Andy whispered, 'Done it.'

All I could hear now was our breathing and the wind outside. No footsteps. And the knock never came. Slowly, I peeled back the hat and rose up in my seat. My phone buzzed in my pocket as I watched Aston walking away, going back the way he'd arrived.

'That was close,' Andy whispered.

I kept my eye on Aston, only checking my phone when he'd gone out of sight.

I had a missed call from Martin. No message. No text.

'I think we should get out of here,' I said.

'Right,' Andy replied. 'I know the perfect place.'

Monday 23rd December 1996 Noon

Begging You – Stone Roses

Andy drove us along a road that took us through the middle of nowhere, or to the edge of some science fiction hell, I couldn't tell which. Desolate grassland to our left and, beyond a tall fence on our right, a tarmac desert where monstrous machinery roamed, hefting huge metal cubes, lining them up like over-sized Lego blocks.

'This is where Suffolk ends,' Andy said, proudly, as though we were arriving at a major landmark like the Grand Canyon or the Cape of Good Hope.

'Cool,' I replied: my stock answer when I wasn't sure if I should be positive or negative.

Andy had taken the quickest route to leave the bungalow and Aston way behind, then along the straightest, longest roads around town through areas I didn't recognise, until we passed the strip of houses on Manor Terrace, but didn't let Andy know I'd been there.

'So these are the docks then?' I asked, hoping for a short answer.

'Some of it,' Andy replied. 'Gets bigger every year… bigger ships, bigger cranes too.'

I nodded, eyeing up the metal sauropods which dominated the view.

'How about all this then?' I asked, pointing to the left.

'Oh, it's a nature reserve, but has loads of World War Two history,' Andy said and pointed at a couple of low hills. 'Buildings under them apparently and loads of gun emplacements on the beach, but the fort's the best bit.'

'Fort?' I said as we turned a corner and a huge red brick, grey-rooved building appeared out of nowhere. 'Awesome.'

'Landguard,' Andy said. 'We used to play down there when we were kids, Chris, me and our mates. We'd mess about on those towers.'

I nodded, taking it all in. It would have been a great place to play war games or hide and seek; the open concrete buildings and steps running up the twin watchtowers. There was a defiant quality about the towers, standing tall in the face of the wintry elements and time.

'I should have brought my camera,' I said. 'We could get some great band shots over there… for the album sleeve notes.'

'Yeah, good idea,' Andy replied, as we swung around a corner and the road ended abruptly with a small car park where he parked up with an amazing vista in front of us.

'Wow.'

A huge grey, mile-wide river swept past us, dividing us from the ferries and church spires of a town on the other side. To our right, the immense cranes leaned out and over some of the biggest ships I'd ever seen; fishing for containers from the improbable skyscraper city of metal boxes sitting on each vessel. I'd thought Brighton had maritime connections but it was nothing compared to this. Felixstowe was proving to be way more than I thought it was.

'That's Harwich,' Andy said, nodding at the distant spires over the water. 'The old Navy base, which the fort used to defend, but it's all just car and foot ferries now. These huge ships are coming to our docks… that ship's come from China,' Andy said, pointing out one of the hulks, 'probably via Rotterdam.'

'That's a lot of stuff coming in,' I said. 'And going out.'

'Loads,' Andy replied with a smile.

I thought about the drugs business Andy thought Chris might be building. He knew his chemistry apparently, which I assumed included what I thought of the dark side of drugs… pills, powder and all that. This place was the perfect spot for distribution to Europe. He just needed permission from Tip and he'd be sorted. But what about his band? Surely Andy leaving hadn't scuppered Chris's plans so badly that he had to resort to drug-dealing? It didn't add up. And why had Lisa agreed to help out? I didn't think she was that desperate for money.

Andy scrambled through the cassettes in his door and, like a magician with a rabbit, proudly held up a tape. 'How about some Roses?'

'As long as they're geological, no weapons,' I replied with a smirk and the tape went in with a click.

We sat in silence, listening to the first tune. Feedback built up, then Squire's haunting guitar. A touch of rewind, Brown's call to action and the bass and drums exploded around us like we were under aerial attack.

'Fucking brilliant!'

Andy cranked it up and we tapped along, watching the behemoth ships slipping by.

'I can't wait to see our album cover,' Andy eventually said, turning the music down and pulling us back to reality.

'From what Jeff showed me, it's gonna look great,' I said. 'They should have it all ready for when we have our first listen through.'

'Can't wait,' Andy said and looked down at his lap.

I felt a twang of guilt. I shouldn't have seen our album cover on my own… we should have shared that experience as a band.

'Yeah, it'll be cool,' I said. 'Sorry you guys didn't get to see it when I did, it was just the right timing with me going there to re-record some vocals.'

Andy said nothing and the air felt heavy.

'Look,' I started, not sure where I was going. 'I'm sorry if everything with Beachhead hasn't been how you imagined it, I-'

'Why do you think that?' Andy asked, his eyes fixing on mine.

'I don't know, I just… I guess, seeing what you gave up to join us and what you said the other day at the Skimrider gig made me think we weren't good enough and…'

'No,' Andy said, his face lightening. 'It's been great. All of it. Sure, I wish the guys from Lightback could experience what we've done, but that's in my past now, honest. It's been great. I prefer your tunes as well to be honest.'

'Cool,' I said, returning his smile, but thinking about Chris. 'The others from the band – they'll get through it, or find something else I guess.'

'Yeah, it was tough for them but what doesn't kill you…' Andy said, leaving the phrase hanging.

Cars came and went, pulling up beside us, joining us for the view, some people getting out for walks. A family of four: two older parents with two grown-up brothers walked past, wrapped up in their hats and scarves and I thought of Stephen and my parents. I felt the pull to be back in Brighton and was ready to ask Andy to drive us to the hotel to grab my gear and give me a lift to the station, when I recognised one of the brothers. John. I remembered how he'd been with Sarah on Saturday night, how they'd laughed together, danced together, shared a kebab… yet they remained stubbornly single. Sure, they were at different Universities, but they had a lot in common. All John had to do was make a move, show his feelings for Sarah. But I guess he didn't want to look stupid or spoil their friendship.

I felt a song brewing but pushed any potential lyrics away.

I thought of Lisa and was torn. Should I stay or go? I hated putting effort into something and giving up at the first sign of it not working, but when was the point where you said enough was enough? When was a project dead, a waste of time?

I sighed. What it boiled down to was, had I put enough effort into getting Lisa back?

'Do you really think Chris has set up a drugs lab?' I asked Andy.

He laughed, then said, 'Now that's a sentence I didn't expect to hear… no, I doubt he'd be able to do that.'

'But,' I started and stopped, feeling shocked, 'you said he was getting back into his chemistry and he could have asked Lisa for help selling his gear.'

'As a one off!' Andy said with another laugh. 'You know, looking for London connections, cos he wasn't from there. Probably bought too much or cut some to make more.'

I shook my head and watched John and his family strolling down the beach and out of sight. I felt anger rise again. I couldn't let this trip be a complete waste of time – I had to find out the truth!

'Right then.' I turned to Andy. 'Either Lisa's left me for Chris or she's helping him sell drugs or whatever it is… why hasn't she told me? I'm owed that, right?'

Andy raised a hand. 'Look, I don't know, okay? She sent you that text didn't she?'

'Chris sent the text not Lisa!' I almost shouted. 'And she's not the sort of person to shy away from stuff or be embarrassed.'

I couldn't shake the feeling I'd had when Isaac was on his killing spree. Whether it was a police gene I'd inherited from Dad or paranoia, it didn't add up and I needed answers.

'So?' Andy asked.

'So, I still need to find her.'

'Well, I was supposed to be going out for a run later but… let's go back to Ferry Road and take another look,' Andy said and started the car up. 'If they're there, you can get your answers.'

'Right,' I said. 'Yeah, cool.'

Ten minutes later, we pulled up in the same spot as earlier, and sat in the car, staring down the road. We'd passed the bungalow and the drive was still empty.

'We should give it a few minutes and then go and knock?' Andy said.

'Okay,' I replied but wanted to jump out, run up to the house and bang on the door, knock it down if I had to. Where the hell were they?

'I can ring Chris again, but he doesn't answer and-' Andy stopped and sat up like a meerkat.

'What is it?' I asked, squinting at the end of the road where a van had turned the corner.

'That's his van,' Andy whispered.

'What? Chris's van?'

Andy nodded.

For a second, I was frozen to the spot. Andy too. The tired-looking white van sped towards us, then swung into the bungalow's drive without signalling. He was in a rush.

I snapped into action, flung the car door open and ran up the street before Andy got out.

'Don't do anything stupid!' he shouted, but I was on a mission.

The van door slammed shut. It was obscured by a set of fir trees in the neighbours' garden but as soon as the van came into view I shouted, 'Lisa!'

I jumped the low wall and saw Chris with a Tesco carrier bag in each hand. The keys were in the front door, which was ajar, so I ran at it.

'Where's Lisa?' I shouted, barging Chris out of the way.

'No!' Chris shouted and dropped the bags.

I just pushed the door open and he rugby-tackled me into the hall, landing in a ball of elbows and knees.

'Luke!' Andy shouted from the drive. 'Chris, get off him!'

I'd landed on my good arm, so I couldn't fight back as Chris grappled and scrambled over me.

'My world, my world,' Chris grunted.

I waited for a punch to the head or a kick, but none came as he crawled over me and across the hall to the nearest door.

'What's going on Chris?' Andy said from the front door.

Chris ignored him, fumbling with his keys, repeating his mantra. 'My world, my world…'

Andy offered me a hand and pulled me up as Chris unlocked the door and pushed it open.

Everything went silent.

The stench of faeces and cheap body spray rushed out of the dark room as we peered in at the shape lying on a camp bed in the centre of the barren room.

A head lifted and eyes opened, staring right back at us.

- She's Leaving Home -

The Beatles. Always the bloody Beatles. What was up with this man? Their songs had haunted me in the van, in the first house and wherever I was now. The last thing I remembered was the fight and the woman shouting. Something about me being drunk?

I daren't open my eyes to see where he was now.

How many days had I been in this messed-up sleep-driven world? How many times had I asked myself that? Days must have passed and all I'd seen were snippets through my dazzled and blurred head. It was a never-ending nightmare which I wasn't getting used to. After the fight, I knew for sure I was in physical danger and had to get out at all costs. The drugs he'd used on me were taking its toll on my body and my mind, which felt loose… I couldn't hold a decent trail of thoughts together and… I needed the toilet. Despite the pain and the weakness which pooled in every bone, I refused to soil myself.

I forced some willpower to resurface. Eyes open. One day this will end. You will get through this.

The faint orange glow of street lights crept through the net curtains onto the bare walls of this new room I'd been deposited in. Empty. No, a water bottle, a bucket in the corner, a bowl of water, a towel and some clothes. This was new. What had changed? Was this his way of apologising?

I crawled off the unstable camp-bed, straight for the plastic bottle, happy to hear the top click open. I drank deeply. Fresh water. The light switch wasn't far but I didn't want to see my prison. Keep it in the shadows and maybe my memories would fade quicker, I thought and focussed on the bowl of water instead. Cold. A towel and some soap.

Other than freedom, all I wanted was to feel clean, so I undressed, had a strip wash, used the bucket loo, demeaning but it had to be done, and pulled on the new clothes. They were warmer than what I'd been wearing: thick tights; underwear; jeans; a long-sleeve top and a woollen jumper. Not my style but the labels suggested they were brand new and they smelt fresh. I felt clean now and could sense my normal mind returning.

There was a spare pack of tights at the bottom of the pile along with a pack of Custard cream biscuits, so I pocketed the packet and munched as I planned my escape, constantly listening for any sound or sign of the man coming back. A strength deep within me was taking hold. I would do anything to get out of this and back to my normal life. Back to Luke and London. I'd been in some scrapes before, sure, but nothing like this… this was unreal.

I moved back to the bed to lie down: the smell of my own waste wafting around me, making me feel like an animal in a cage; reducing me to my basic instincts. But my instincts were strong, I told myself. I thought of all the challenges I'd overcome: growing up with an overbearing mother and a distant father; the constant weight of proving an attractive girl could be intelligent; travelling to new countries alone. I could analyse each factor and visualise a timeline of pressures guiding my personality and choices one way, then the other – culminating with me right now. Stuck here.

No, this was not my fault. Not my decision. This was someone else's fault. That man – he chose to do this. Part of me wanted to say he would pay for it – that was right wasn't it? Justice. But I wasn't in control any more. I hated that. I had to admit I needed help. Luke. I always needed him in some way, even when we were apart. His adventures, voice and concern for me. He would help now. Together we were… I never liked to go over the top with our love for each other, but we fitted well. His weaknesses were my strengths and he gave me an energy I'd never felt before.

Snippets of my fight with my captor came back to me and, having seen him properly in the light now, the events in the pub were coming back to me. I didn't know his name but I could remember meeting him in what was probably the last memory of my normal life. He had sat down next to me in the pub and said he was from the label. I'd never heard of him but he bought me a drink… we chatted about Beachhead and music… he'd helped me walk out of the pub. So drunk. He must have drugged my drink.

Stupid girl! Maybe it was being back in England or the new job with the label, but I'd let my guard down. Bottles. Always drink bottles.

I must have fallen asleep again because when I woke again the colour of light had changed. My stomach woke me or maybe it was my dream… I'd heard a voice calling my name, I was sure. It had sounded like Luke. No, my mind was playing tricks, hoping for something out of reach. My belly was twisting and growling for more food, so I finished off the biscuits and water. Soft sunlight bled through the window and I felt the urge to look outside to see where I was. I had absolutely no idea what I would see. There was a beach last time. I felt stronger now. Wherever I was, this time I would get free and find help. Smash the windows if I had to.

With small, heroic steps, I stood up and walked to the wall and made my way to the solitary door, for a second, I thought it might be open. What if he had realised what a mistake he'd made and decided to let me go? Is that why he'd given me new clothes? Was I able to get out?

I turned the handle, but the door remained stubbornly closed.

Of course he wouldn't let me escape. I'd seen him. He was marked. He'd done wrong and knew it. I could recognise him, point him out in a line. I tried to think back to my Psychology lectures about captives… mind games and Stockholm syndrome. What did he want? That was the key. He hadn't asked anything of me, just held me prisoner. He'd only just started giving me food and water, so he clearly hadn't planned this… which suggested it wasn't his idea.

He had to be working for someone else.

Is that why he disappeared? Was that where he was now? Receiving instructions? The woman in the last house! His mother? She'd sounded shocked hadn't she? That's why he'd moved me. He was running out of options and getting desperate. What the bloody hell did he want?

I gasped, feeling my mind sharpen. I was in even more danger than I'd realised. His next step would be to silence me. Or was he saving me for someone else?

I banged my fists against the door, the hollow echo reverberating through my tired body. I banged again, happy to hear something; to feel something new; to cause something to happen!

A noise outside made me turn. A car pulling up outside! My instincts kicked in and I cursed the time I'd wasted sleeping and self-indulging. I should have been preparing. Frantically, I searched the room for a weapon – anything I could use. No furniture, just a worn-out carpet, bare walls and the old metal camp bed I'd been sleeping on. Even the curtain rail had been taken down.

I slumped to my knees, knowing I didn't have the energy to fight him one on one, and stared at the old skirting boards, peeling and cracked.

Voices outside made me turn. Someone was yelling. This was my chance! I clawed at the old wood, grabbing what I needed, then slipped back into bed, pretending to sleep.

Ready to attack.

Monday 23rd December 1996 P.M.

You And Me Song – The Wannadies

There she was. I had found her. Lisa!

But this was not what I had expected. I thought she'd be cosying up with Chris, drinking a cuppa on the sofa, watching telly. Not this. Not locked in a barren room with a camp bed and a bucket. She looked terrible. Like she was on death's door. Not beaten, but ill. Something inside had told me this whole thing was wrong but I hadn't thought Lisa had been abducted.

'Bastard,' I growled and grabbed at Chris, pulling him down and pinning him to the floor with all my strength.

A shape moved over us and I saw Andy step into the room, towards Lisa.

'Lisa, are you-' he started, but was cut off by a scream.

Everything around me moved too fast to comprehend. Sudden movements in Lisa's room while I struggled with Chris, who kept hissing 'My world,' through gritted teeth and, 'Nothing's gonna change, nothing's gonna change…'

Andy yelled and I heard a thump on the floor. Someone had fallen. What had he done to Lisa? Had that bastard been in on this all the time? He'd hidden it well and I'd fallen for it again. Was he trying to keep me away from Lisa, or had they been after me all this time? Was Lisa the trap? Was that why Andy had brought me back to the house?

A shadow leapt over me and Chris wrestling in the hallway, this time coming out of the room. Chris wriggled out of my grasp, crawling away from me. I turned to see Lisa running out the front door and gave Chris a shove but he lashed out, kicking me in the face and I reeled back in pain.

'Chris,' Andy called out from the other room. 'Help me mate.'

Chris stumbled to Andy, into the room where he'd been holding Lisa and I clambered to my feet, torn between giving Chris and Andy a good kicking and chasing after Lisa. I felt the cool air from outside and knew Lisa needed me, so I ran outside after her, glancing back to make sure I wasn't being chased.

'Lisa, wait!' I shouted, slamming the front door behind me.

In the fresh air, wide-eyed, I stared about, tripping over the bags of food Chris had been carrying. Their contents spilled out like the intestines of a gutted animal. I side-stepped them and ran to the road, checking both ways for any sign of Lisa. A dog walker was way down the street and someone was unpacking shopping from the car in their drive but I couldn't see anyone else. Where was she?

'Lisa!' I shouted, hoping she was hiding between the parked cars and would recognise my voice.

She didn't appear.

I stared back at the bungalow and at Chris's van. Should I steal it and get away? Or at least take the keys? Panic was taking control of me, shaking my muscles and teeth. What the fuck was going on? I took a sharp breath and movement caught my eye - a can of beans rolling across the drive. It was rolling *towards* the van!

I leapt into action, running around the side of the building to the bins where I'd hidden from the police. Lisa must have taken the same route I did last night. I carried on through the gate the police had broken to chase me, and into the bungalow's back garden. A packet of crisps lay on the concrete path. Breadcrumbs. I followed the trail through the garden and scanned the shrubs for any sign of Lisa. The colours were vivid in the daylight compared to when I'd last been here, but the panic felt the same.

'Lisa! It's Luke!' I called out and rushed into the undergrowth at the back where I'd scrambled over the fence last time.

I pushed through the branches with my arm raised, using my plaster cast as a shield. All the way to the back, to the fence.

And there she was.

Wide-eyed. Freaked out. Crumbs around her mouth and a bloodied shard of wood pointed at my chest.

'Lisa,' I whispered and held out my hands.

Her eyes focussed on me, lightening as she recognised me.

'Luke?' she whispered hoarsely.

'Are you okay?' I asked. 'Whose blood is that?' I blurted, pointing at the crimson shard of wood.

Seeing her, the real her, not the imagined version I'd kept in my head, switched something in my mind and every emotion connected to the thought of her leaving me disintegrated. This was the real her. She looked so delicate. Fragile. Crouched between the bush and fence, clutching biscuits like an abandoned child.

Lisa stared at the red wood, blinked and dropped it like it a hot coal.

'I… ah… Luke!' she mumbled and flung her arms around me, hugging me tight. 'Is this real?' She whispered.

'Of course it's real,' I whispered back.

Part of me still wanted to ask her why she'd left me and never called, but that was fading – she wasn't in a good state and it was clear none of this had been her choosing.

'Are you okay?' I asked, gently pushing her back so I could see her face. 'Did he hurt you?'

'I… I'm fine,' she said, meeting my gaze. 'It's really you, isn't it Luke?' She sounded hollow, distant, but was coming back and cupped my face with a soft hand.

'Yeah, it's me,' I replied, sniffing back a tear. 'I came to find you… to find out-'

'You came for me,' she cut me off, thankfully. 'How long?' She asked. 'How long have I been gone?'

'I'm not sure,' I replied honestly. 'Days…'

My heart was still pounding hard and my head was all over the place. We had to get out of here, but Lisa was not her usual self. She was tired, sure, but the way her eyes darted about, barely settling on one thing, suggested she was still freaking out.

'Here, take my coat,' I said, placing it around her shoulders.

She slipped her arms through the sleeves and stuffed the pockets with what she'd been carrying.

'I can't go back inside,' she said, staring through the bushes into the garden.

There was no sign of Chris or Andy yet, but I knew it wouldn't take them long to find us.

'You're not going back in there,' I said. 'Look, I know how to get out of here, to somewhere safe, okay?'

She nodded earnestly.

I tapped the fence next to us. 'We just need to shimmy over here first, okay?'

She nodded and stood up. We were taller than the fence and there were branches in the hedge to step on, so it would be easier than I'd made it in the dark!

Lisa peered over the fence, then back to the garden and to me. 'I got him though, didn't I, Luke? I got him.'

I hesitated for a second, not sure what to say. I didn't want to panic her, but she needed the truth, didn't she?

'Yes, well, you got someone,' I said, trying not to worry about Andy as I guided Lisa to step up to the nearest branch. 'But we still need to keep moving. Just be careful on the other side.'

I looked over as she climbed over, at the wooden pallets of the compost heap where I'd cracked my head, then I climbed over carefully. We made it. I took a full lungful of air and surveyed the patchwork landscape of the winter allotments. Empty as far as I could see.

'Come this way,' I said, taking Lisa's hand and pulling her towards the main track which ran through the centre of the plots.

'Who was it then, Luke?' she asked. 'Who did I stab?'

'Err… it was Andy,' I replied quickly, hoping saying it faster made it less real. I wondered how long he and Chris had been planning it all and felt weak at the thought. 'He was helping Chris I think,' I said, convincing myself as much as Lisa that his injury had been deserved.

Lisa stopped in her tracks. 'Chris?' She said, eyes fixed to the ground, brow furrowed. 'Was that the man in the pub?'

'What pub?'

'Where your gig was… he said he worked for the label, for Jeff, so I had to speak to him… part of the job, he said. Bought me a drink.'

'The gig in the Winchester?' I replied. 'You've been gone that long? Jeez.'

'How long?'

I shrugged and spotted a keen gardener digging a distant plot, so ushered Lisa along.

'Five or six days I think,' I said, trying to remember what day it was. Nearly Christmas, that was all I really knew.

We walked in silence for a while and the enormity of what Chris had done sunk in. Events were clicking into place now and I could see how Chris, with Andy's help, had pulled the wool over our eyes. Lisa had been gone for nearly a week and they'd been misdirecting us, putting us off the scent. Using Lisa's phone was clever but had given him away… but Andy had been the one to reveal it. Why? He gave me the first address too. Then nothing until he found out I was in Felixstowe and he rushed here to sort me out. Was it a trap? Had I been drawn here on purpose?

Chris must have cut Stephen's brakes. And the fire alarm in the gig? Chris had been there.

'Where are we going?' Lisa asked, pulling me out of my angry, paranoid inner-state.

'I've got a room in a hotel,' I said, staring at the sky which was already turning a shade of pink in the west. 'We just need to keep a low profile, head along the beach, I know the way.'

I did it before, I thought, and avoided the police, so we could do it again.

'Are you warm enough?' Lisa asked.

She looked snug in my coat and had found my gloves. I hadn't thought about it and shivered. My hat was keeping my head warm but my fingers were tingling.

'I know!' I said with a smile and nodded at a well-padded scarecrow.

A few minutes later, we left the allotments and were navigating through residential roads I recognised from last night's escape and took the same route, only now I was now sporting a scarecrow's dark blue ski jacket, which had seen better days, a musty woollen scarf and a pair of burgundy mittens. The sight had made Lisa giggle, which gave me hope she was feeling better.

'How did you know I was here?' Lisa asked after we had walked a bit further. She was clearly trying to make sense of what was going on, like me. 'I mean… how long have you been here?'

'Oh, only a couple of days,' I replied.

'Trying to find me?'

'Yeah,' I said, not wanting to explain how I'd thought she'd dumped me and the only reason I'd travelled all this way was to get some answers.

I felt heartless now. Cold. How had I really accepted Lisa would dump me like that? After everything we'd been through? People change and being apart can lead to people growing in different directions, but nothing had really changed with us had it?

I reached out to hold her hand.

'We'll get you somewhere warm, some hot food and then we can call the police, okay?' I said.

'Can't we call them now?' She said. 'I don't have my phone but we could find a phone box?'

I pictured Tip and the police who had chased me, my Mum, and Dad's warning about getting involved in anything that would tarnish our family's reputation – but being with Lisa made me feel different. Everything was different now. Life or death. Running away from the police seemed ridiculous now. Talking to them should have been my priority!

'We can call them now,' I said, watching Lisa's face as I pulled my new phone from my coat she was wearing.

'You've got a phone!' she said and almost laughed.

'Yeah, let's hope it's useful for once,' I replied and pressed buttons as we walked along a grassy strip between estates, fringed by pine trees bending in the salty wind. The sea was near.

I checked the phone screen but some of the usual icons were missing.

'No reception,' I said. 'It's been on and off around here, so I'll keep trying while we make our way back.'

We crossed a cliff-top road lined with sea-view mansions and jogged over the exposed grassland to a set of wooden steps which cascaded down beach-hut lined terraces to the prom and beach. The grey North Sea greeted us with a blast of wind and I thanked the naked scarecrow for his coat.

'Slow down!' Lisa cried as I jogged down the steps.

'Sorry, we need to keep moving.'

I eyed up the prom left and right, and back up the steps, making sure we hadn't been followed. A few people were shuffling along, wrapped up to endure a Christmassy walk, but no sign of anyone I recognised. I felt the same panic that had consumed me last night when I had jogged along here, hiding from the police.

'Come on,' I said, taking Lisa's hand.

It was just a few minutes' walk to where the prom ended, where we would have to drop onto the beach for a bit before the path started up again. I'd feel safer there, away from potential viewpoints.

'Do you know where we're going?' Lisa asked.

'Yeah, I did it last night,' I replied. 'And it was dark then, so we'll be fine,' I said as I surveyed the sea but couldn't see the sun, which was going down behind the grassy cliff which hid us from the road.

'Let's just keep going,' I said as I guided Lisa down the steps to the beach.

'The tide's pretty high,' Lisa replied and for a second it felt like we were back travelling in some far-flung destination, exploring, discovering.

'It'll be fine,' I said, checking the beach ahead which looked narrower than I remembered it.

Silhouettes of grand houses appeared on the cliff top set back from the eroding coast by acres of lawn or wind-swept garden. Not a bad spot. We climbed down onto the beach, then along the strip of shingle and sand.

'Can we go up these steps?' Lisa asked when we passed a solid staircase next to an array of bizarre concrete shapes set into the hill like large Lego blocks.

'No, it'll take us back to the streets,' I replied. 'Come on, we've just got to get around the corner and we'll be back on the prom.'

I held her hand and we picked our way across the wet sand, around a boulder, to a tall stone wall which skirted the grounds of the last house and garden along this stretch of beach.

We rounded a large lump of ancient concrete and I saw we had a problem.

'Oh shit.'

The tide was in.

'We've got to go back,' Lisa said, tugging my hand.

'No, it's not much further.' I pointed to where the wall curved away from us. 'The prom starts up just over there.'

I remembered this stretch of the beach had been stony, with a few boulders on the beach, but it had only taken a few minutes to walk. Now it was an impenetrable mass of rock and water, with the waves splashing against the three-metre high wall which protected the garden from the ravages of the sea. I looked up at the iron fence lining the top and had an idea.

'Look, we can climb here and shimmy along the wall – easy,' I said and pointed to where the concrete shapes were set at an angle into the wall, giving us a ramp to climb.

Lisa stared up, then at me and back to where we'd walked. Nobody was in sight.

'What about your arm?' she asked.

'I'll be fine,' I said, not thinking about it. 'We have to keep moving. If anyone follows us, they'll expect us to be near, so we have to get as far away as possible.'

'Yeah, I know,' she replied, looking frailer than ever. 'Can't we just wait it out somewhere safe?'

'It'll be night soon,' I replied, trying to keep calm. 'And it's getting cold, come on!'

I let go of her hand and climbed up the blocks to where I could see the top of the wall.

'It's fine,' I said, beckoning her up. 'You go first and we'll go at your pace.'

Reluctantly, Lisa joined me. She was nimble but slow.

'That's it,' I said. 'Up there and we can hold on to the iron railings, shimmy along… best get going while it's still a bit light.'

But the light was fading almost by the minute.

Lisa made it onto the wall, then tentatively worked her way around the corner and I followed. The ledge was narrow, so I had to slip my feet between each rusting railing with each step, but we soon got a rhythm going and in a few minutes we were on the most exposed part of the wall where the land curved away in both directions. Nobody could see us here.

Other than checking on Lisa as we side-stepped along the wall, I kept my eyes on the bizarre gardens the other side of the fence, where some Victorian had crafted mini-caverns and shell-lined walkways.

'I need a rest,' Lisa said after a while, panting.

'It's okay,' I said. 'Catch your breath, then keep it steady. We'll be there soon.'

Ten feet below us, the sea lapped against the base of the wall, splashing barnacle-encrusted rocks. One slip and we'd easily break a bone and get wedged between the rocks - there was no way anyone could get to us if we survived the fall and the tide was still coming in.

Lisa started up again with steady steps and I followed, wincing every time I had to use my left arm to take my weight. My right arm was aching too, but I was sure we were over halfway there.

'Look!' I shouted.

Lisa looked at me, rather than ahead.

'Over there, the lights!'

'Oh,' I heard her say.

Land was in sight – the strings of colourful bulbs which lined the prom were swaying and twinkling, beckoning us closer. Just a few more minutes of careful steps and we'd be on the prom, just a few minutes' walk from the hotel and safety.

'That's it, keep going,' I said as the scenery below steadily changed from rocks back to stony beach.

Ahead I could see a street light and a long concrete ramp for boats, then the beginning of the prom itself. Just a few more metres and we could climb down and be off.

Silently, Lisa lowered herself onto the concrete, panting heavily. I held my breath as she edged down. Her first foot slipped and she grabbed the railings again, making them shake.

'It's okay,' I said. 'Try it again.'

Slower this time, she stretched out and waited until her foot was flat before she put her full weight on it, then clambered down and onto the flat concrete.

I took my turn, following her example and was soon beside her, hugging her and feeling a small victory.

'We did it,' I whispered and kissed her ear. 'I'm sorry. I didn't know any other way and...'

'It's okay,' she replied, looking more resolute than ever. 'Let's just get somewhere warm.'

'Sure,' I said and held her hand as we walked up the ramp, to the road.

It felt strange being back in a built up area, with parked cars lining the road and I could see a pub in the distance. The wind was still cold and the darkness felt stronger in the orange street lights. The nearest light was only twenty metres away, leaving this corner of the road in the shadows.

'It's about ten minutes' walk along here-' I started saying but a noise from my right made me turn.

I raised my good arm instinctively but it was knocked away with a loud clunk, which swung me around. My elbow screamed in pain, so I cradled it with my broken arm and twisted away from the shape coming at me from the shadows, so didn't see the next blow coming.

Another hollow clunk and my legs collapsed beneath me.

- You're Not Alone - Olive -

Before all this happened, back when I was travelling in Asia and Luke was kicking off the Beachhead tour with his mates, I started picturing my memories and life-experiences like water flowing through a fine-mesh sieve. The influence of India I guess, but the image stuck and developed.

Most of the water drips through the tiny holes of the sieve, to be lost forever; the mundane, every-day memories: walking the same road; buying lunch; choosing shoes to wear; having breakfast; going to bed. All duplicated, routine happenings which make up the bulk of our waking life. Events which the brain doesn't waste energy distinguishing between when it retains memories during sleep.

There's grit in the water though. Small particles which clump together to fill an occasional hole, stopping the water from leaving. These are the things memories are triggered by: events; scars; music; odours; people. They block regions of the sieve, pooling the water to create a reservoir of experiences; everything which makes us human. These pools grow as we experience more, and accumulate to eventually define *us*. Good or bad, those pieces of grit create the boundaries we have learnt to govern our lives by.

What I've come to learn is my friends are grit – I'd never tell them that – they're more like shiny nodules of gold in the grit. They, along with family members, are the super drip-stopping, gap-clogging particles which allow my pool to grow, along with my personal development. They are the people who helped define me and, in the end, made me a less-shallow person. Even more so with lovers and Luke was no exception. He helped my reservoir grow, by both being with me and giving me the confidence to run free to experience more.

All of this filled my head in the few seconds of pure shock when Chris appeared from the shadows with a cricket bat and attacked Luke. He cracked him on his good arm and then the head, knocking him out cold.

I screamed as Luke collapsed on the floor and leapt forward, shoving Chris away, pushing him clear of Luke so I could check his breathing. He hadn't hit his head on the ground, but that was little relief after the knock Chris had given him.

'What have you done you bastard?' I yelled up at Chris, keeping him away with my words as I crouched protectively over Luke.

Chris was muttering to himself and took a step back, staring around like a wild animal.

'Can you hear me, Luke?' I whispered. 'Are you okay?'

His forehead was cold where I stroked it and a nasty lump had already risen on the side of his head, but no blood.

'Nothing's gonna change,' Chris was mumbling in a low monotonous tone.

He looked unhinged, so I knew I didn't have much time. Would he attack me now after I'd stabbed his friend? I shook Luke and talked to him, keeping an eye on Chris all the time. Physically, I couldn't defend myself against him with or without his bat, but I could cause some attention and maybe someone would come to our rescue?

'Help!' I shouted.

'Shut it!' Chris darted forward and pushed me off Luke.

I fell backwards, grazing my palms on the sandy concrete ground.

'Shout again and I'll hit him real hard, got it?' He hissed.

I nodded and rubbed my palms. Maybe I could rugby tackle him? Make enough noise to attract someone and keep Luke safe. There was a pub nearby so someone must be within earshot, but one look at the cricket bat and Chris's leer told me it wasn't worth the risk.

I could tell by the way he was acting that he was being driven by unseen pressures. Mentally, he was clearly all over the place, but so was I… no, I could still distinguish right from wrong. Basic, but that difference between us gave me an advantage, surely?

'Come on Luke,' I whispered and gave him a nudge with my foot. 'You need to get up.'

'Keep quiet,' Chris hissed again. 'I need you here – both of you. Or it won't work.'

I hadn't had a single conversation with Chris since he kidnapped me, so this was the first time I could try reasoning with him. If I knew why he was doing this I might be able to talk him out of it.

'What won't work, Chris?' I asked with a soft tone, making sure I used his name.

'Never you mind!' He growled, still pacing back and forth: his head flicking to us on the ground, then along the prom, checking no-one was nearby.

I thought of the person I'd stabbed to get out of the house. Andy. And wondered where he was.

'Where's Andy?' I asked.

Chris shook his head as though deflecting the question, so I asked it again.

'Chris, where is Andy?'

'Bloody traitor,' he replied.

Someone was walking a dog further down the prom, waiting while it peed against a lamppost.

Chris stared, ignoring me.

Luke had said Andy was behind my kidnap, with Chris, but I wasn't so sure. A wave of guilt swam through me at the thought I'd injured an innocent person. But I'd been defending myself, as was my right. Anyone else would have done the same thing.

'He's a bloody traitor, Andy. A turncoat! Stabbed me in the back,' Chris whispered. 'Left us in the lurch… we were friends since primary school. Started the band together. Founding members.'

The cricket bat swung slowly like a pendulum as Chris paced back and forth. Classic signs of a trapped mind, which made him dangerous.

'Best mate… thicker than water. Dropped us, for him!'

As he spoke and seemed to be getting more agitated. He pointed the bat at Luke and I leant over him, covering his body with mine, staring Chris in the eyes.

'I will hit him! Or you if you get in my way!' He said and raised the bat.

'No, you don't have to,' I said, edging back a touch.

He laughed, took a plastic bag from his pocket, picked out a pill and slipped it into his mouth, and then said, 'You don't even know where you are do you? If you ran off you'd have no idea where to go.'

I looked at the beach behind me, at the necklace of coloured lights leading away and the lights in the buildings beyond. Luke's hotel was out there somewhere, but Chris was right: I was completely lost. We were in a dark corner, at the end of the prom where the nearest road curved inland. Nobody came down here.

'Get off him now,' Chris ordered and took another step forward. 'I could just leave you here… leave you to fend for yourself, but I need more time.'

I slid back further, getting ready to run. If I couldn't save Luke, maybe I could get some help?

'What is it you want, Chris?' I asked.

He shook his head, rubbed it and answered. 'Same as everyone else,' he said, the closest I'd heard him sound normal. The anger had dissipated, leaving a *poor-me* tone. 'Same as him.' He pointed at Luke. 'Recognition. The ability to create and build something. To show I was here… to be applauded.'

That was it. It was all about his band? I was getting through, but I still had no idea how imprisoning me or Luke helped Chris with his band.

'How does this help?' I asked.

'He said it would.'

'Luke said that?'

'No,' Chris said, rubbing his head. 'He said it would… the man. The man that matters. He said I would get what I wanted if I helped him. So I tried, but it didn't work. None of it worked, so I kept at it. That's what they say isn't it? The people who make it *never* give up!'

He was talking in circles, winding himself up again and making no sense.

'Who told you to do it Chris?'

'It doesn't matter. It'll work though, I know it! Then we'll see what Andy does and the others.'

'Who Chris?' I raised my voice. 'Tell me who? They could be wrong. There must be another way. What you are doing is wrong!'

'No,' he said, shaking his head madly. 'It'll work. It has to work! My world!'

He was staring down the prom again and I looked at the empty view: a distant pub and a few abandoned beach huts which had been dragged off the beach for winter.

'I've said too much,' Chris said, laying the bat on the ground.

'I can help you, Chris,' I said, keeping my voice calm. 'You can stop this now and we can all help you. If this is about music, Luke will help you, I'm sure. Think about Andy – where is he now?'

Chris ignored me, fumbling with his coat pocket again.

'Andy needs you Chris,' I said. 'You have to go to him.'

'I needed him!' he replied, fixing his eyes on mine. 'And you've asked too many questions.'

I saw a scrap of cloth in his hand and knew what he was going to do. I scrambled to my feet and ran for the pub, my feet slipping on the sandy floor.

'Help!' I yelled, searching for anyone. 'Help me!'

But Chris was too quick.

He caught up and had the cloth over my nose and mouth the second he grabbed me. I fought, scratching and kicking. I flung out with all my animal might and grabbed at his face but, just as before, my energy slipped away as he smothered me.

The chemical stench invaded my lungs, burning, and my senses faded away.

Tuesday 24th December 1996 A.M.

Found You – Dodgy

Sounds and smells came to me: the swish of a thousand rolling pebbles; the salt in the air; distant water splashing; old wood and musty material. Then the aches came: the dull throbbing in my right elbow; a deep thumping in my head; the usual little lightning twist in my wrist.

What a hangover! I struggled to think of what I did last night, picturing John and Sarah's face and the sticky-floored club as I tried to get comfy, rolling over without hurting any vulnerable areas. The bed was rough and hard, but I was too tired to worry. This wasn't the hotel bed though was it? Did I end up kipping on their mate's floor?

I pictured Andy driving the car, the huge ships and cranes, then the bungalow, and Lisa's face.

'Shit!'

My eyes opened in panic and my body jolted into life as last night's events came crashing into my mind: Lisa in the bed; Andy screaming; our escape; climbing along the high beach wall; Chris coming out of the shadows.

'Lisa?' I said, my dry voice croaking. 'Lisa!'

I sat up, ignoring my pains, determined to make sense of my surroundings. I was in a wood panelled room with a bench next to me, covered in peeling paint. Piles of plastic beach toys sat in one corner next to some mouldy shoes.

Shafts of weak morning light filtered through gaps in the planks in one wall and my breath steamed in front of me. I shivered and pulled the old sand-covered blanket I'd been wrapped in tight around my shoulders. I had my hat and gloves on, and the scarecrow's padded coat which was probably why I hadn't frozen in the night. I tried to ease myself up, cursing having both arms injured. It didn't feel like my right arm was broken – I knew what that felt like – but it was properly bruised where I'd been hit. My head wasn't much better and I soon discovered an egg on one side and felt sick when I touched it.

Was I in a shed? I pictured the garden of the bungalow but couldn't remember a shed in there. Where else would Chris have taken me if he needed me out of the way? A seagull shrieked in the distance and the other sounds I'd been listening to started to make sense.

'Ah…'

I was locked in a beach hut.

Weak, winter sunlight crept through a crack at the bottom of a wooden door by my feet and the rest of the objects in the wood-lined room made sense now, from the piled-up deckchairs and quaint pictures of striped lighthouses on the walls, to the plastic buckets and old rugs.

The state of the paintwork was terrible. This place was shabbier than Grandad's old allotment shed and desperately needed some attention.

Happy I knew where I was, my mind started working overtime, running through recent events and working forwards.

Presumably, Chris had dragged me here after knocking me out and locked me away, but where was Lisa? Had he taken her back to the bungalow? And Andy? What about him? It depended on how badly Lisa had injured him, but if they were working together, Chris would have to take him to hospital, which wouldn't be fully staffed at Christmas. That bought me some time. If I could break out, I could get to the police and take them to the bungalow. We could save Lisa before it was too late.

I searched my coat's pockets but I'd given *my* coat to Lisa, so she had my phone! Still, I searched my pockets to see what I had on me hoping I could find something useful and get out of this A-team style. But apart for a few coins and a tissue, my pockets were empty.

'Damn it,' I hissed and crawled forward to push on the door.

It rattled the metal bar and padlocks holding the doors fast. I could see it cutting across the gap between the doors. Another way out then? I crawled to the old cupboards screwed to the back wall, hoping to find a hammer or tool to help me break out, but they were full of plastic plates and more aged beach paraphernalia. I pulled myself up to a stooped, standing position and faced a bottle of water on the makeshift sideboard. And a note.

Drink and be patient. Use a bucket if you have to.

'What the fuck?'

I needed the water but was paranoid it was drugged after what Lisa had been through. Chris was a nutcase. Who knew what he'd planned for me? He'd captured me… was that his plan all along? To get revenge for stealing Andy from his band? It hadn't even been my idea – Jeff had suggested we ask Andy to join after his scouts were sent out to find a replacement for Mike. That's what Stephen had said anyway.

Thinking of Stephen brought back my conversation with Dad. What day was it? Christmas Eve already? What would my parents do if I didn't turn up at their house?

I slumped back down on the blanket, despondent.

My parents would be expecting me to arrive today and here I was, trapped. Maybe I should have told Dad more about what was going on? But what about what he'd said about getting Mum into more trouble for her court case? I pulled the rough blanket tighter around me and rubbed my hands. So cold! I hoped the weak sun would warm the hut up a bit.

I pictured Lisa again and thought of our conversations last night. Where was she? I had to focus, get out of here and find her again. This was between me and Chris. Nothing to do with her. She was just caught in the cross-fire.

'Fuck it,' I said and grabbed the bottle of water.

I would get out of this, get my life back to normal: get my arm healed; play more gigs; write new songs; tour the album; share it all with Lisa.

Although we'd shared everything we'd done apart through phone calls, postcards and letters… all the gigs, recording studios – everything I'd ever dreamt of – it had all felt less fun without her there. Sure, there was always stuff I had to do alone, but with Lisa around, everything shone that little bit more. Every gig would have an extra ten percent energy because I was singing to *her*.

I needed her more in my life.

When all this was over, Lisa and I needed a proper talk. I wasn't going to propose or anything, but we could work out something new. Maybe Beachhead could tour abroad so she could keep travelling? Or maybe she'd like working for Jeff and settle down in London.

Settle down.

That phrase used to send shivers through me. It sounded like all the fun would be sucked out of my life. Grey, dull, no fun, same street, same faces, mortgage, bills, putting the bins out, responsibility, same, same, same…

But, right now, I was warming to the idea of a bit of stability.

A sound outside pulled me out of my thoughts. A bang. And another. And was that a voice? I'd been too paranoid to shout for help, but maybe I should? Someone could be outside and help break the door open to get me out.

I stood, listening like a hawk, ready to call out.

'Help me! Let me out!' A woman's voice shouted.

It was Lisa! She was nearby!

'Lisa!' I shouted. 'I'm here!'

A loud bang made me jump, shaking the hut, followed by another thump nearby. On the hut next door?

'No shouting, either of you,' a low voice growled

I'd heard that voice before, on the phone maybe?

'Keep calm and this will be over soon,' he said, replying to something Lisa had said.

The amusements opposite the pier came to mind, along with Tip, sitting with his two men either side of him. Aston and Martin. One of them had called me and told me the address. Was it him? How the hell had Tip got involved in this? Chris and Andy were linked, but how did the local drug-baron fit in? Unless Chris was boiling up chemicals after all?

I wanted to shout out, to fight, but if Aston was involved, we had just taken another step towards serious and I had to back away. My instincts told me to be quiet – and to escape. With Lisa. We could do this. I just needed to find a way to talk to her, to get my bearings.

I crept forwards and peered through the cracks around the doors and between the older planks. The sun was up, coating the sandy promenade with golden rays, the beach beyond looked bigger than I remembered it with the grey mass of sea bubbling away beyond. I couldn't be sure, but it felt like we weren't far from where Chris had clobbered me last night. A shadow caught my eye and the dark shape of Tip's man appeared, dressed in a dark long overcoat, walking slowly. Patrolling like a prison guard.

I shuffled over to the side of the hut closest to Lisa's and searched for a crack in the wall. Nothing high up, but I moved a pile of buckets and saw light by the edge of the cupboards towards the back. The owners really hadn't looked after their hut – there was rotten wood low down where the high tide must have nibbled at it.

Crouching down, I could see outside and the concrete ground in the space between our huts. I clawed at the worn away wood, pulling splinters inside and breaking them off until I'd created an inch-wide hole. I lay down on the floorboards to look through the gap. There was an open space of about two foot, then the white wood of her hut.

'Lisa,' I whispered, trying to project my voice as quietly as possible, which was virtually impossible. 'Lisa! Can you hear me?'

I had no idea how loud I was, but hoped Tip's man was out of earshot, or maybe the sound of the sea would cover my voice.

'Lisa, can you hear me?' I whispered a bit louder.

A shadow moved across the front of the hut, cutting out the sunlight under the door, and I held my breath. The line of dark continued and the sun came back. I waited. Heard the sound of thick soles brushing on the thin layer of sand and the shadow came back, then passed again. Tip's man was pacing back and forth like some bloody soldier. Maybe he had been in the army? I remembered Andy's reaction to me knowing Aston and felt the weight of my situation press on me a little harder.

I waited for a bit, gauged where he would be now: at his furthest point, past Lisa's hut, and whispered again.

'Lisa, it's Luke. Can you hear me? I'm in the hut next to you. Have you got my coat?' I blurted everything out, knowing my time was limited.

The line of shadow returned and I pressed my ear to the gap between the wall planks.

Nothing.

The shadow returned and I kept my ear still, calming my breathing and trying to filter out the swish of the sea, the seagulls and sound of slow steps.

'Luke, I can hear you,' came the words I was desperate to hear.

'I love you,' I said.

Silence.

I'd said it before to Lisa and we'd been open about our feelings, but usually she would say it back.

'Luke, can you hear me?' She whispered, clearly not having heard me.

'Yes.'

I focussed on the most important issue: escape.

'Have you got my coat?' I asked.

'Yes,' she replied.

'And the phone?' I asked, hoping Chris hadn't been careful enough to check the coat I'd given Lisa, assuming he already took her phone when he'd kidnapped her.

'No signal,' came the reply.

'Fuck it!'

What now? I looked at the door. Surely one sharp kick would break the wood, but could I get out quick enough to out-run Tip's muscle-head?

What if both of them were out there? They'd probably just knock me on the head, like Chris had done, and shove me back in my prison.

I stroked the lump on the head and winced at the twin pains from my elbow and head.

'…a way out,' Lisa said, but I only caught the end.

I kneeled up, grabbed the bottle of water and took a swig, feeling agitated.

I searched the hut again, trying to ignore the sound of steps outside and the moving shadow. The front door was a no go, the wall on Lisa's side had a few holes but would be in Tip's man's line of sight, and the other side would be the same, which left either breaking through the floor, roof or back wall. I felt like I was in Stalag Luft III trying to outwit the Nazis. The thought gave me hope. Maybe there was a way out? I stood and jabbed at the ceiling but it was solid and, from what I'd seen of Lisa's hut through the gap, the floor was only a couple of bricks off the prom, so it was the back wall or nothing.

From what I remembered, these huts backed onto the road, so if there was a way out, I would have a clear escape route across the road or maybe straight to a car I could hide behind. I pictured myself crawling out and under the nearest car, but knew I couldn't do that with my injuries… and Lisa! I'd have to get her out too.

It was too much to think about, so I concentrated on the cupboards on the back wall. Opening one, I could see they had their own backing, so I shook the unit to see how well it was attached… the whole thing moved – it was free standing! It had made a low scrape when it moved so I froze, checking the shadow was still moving across the sun line under the door… but the sun must have gone in because all I could see was a grey line.

I waited, holding my breath, straining to hear the footsteps, then carefully angled the unit away from the wall an inch at a time. The back wall looked as rotten as the side wall, so I made more space and wriggled behind to push and test the boards. One was spongy and I managed to work a long nail out, then used it to scrape away any small sections I could get my fingertips into.

I kept at it. Quietly, steadily. Images from Shawshank Redemption came to me and I considered straightening up the unit to cover my tracks, but time was short. Who knew what Chris, Tip and Andy had planned for me and Lisa? I had to get out and free her!

A foot-long section of a plank gave way, bending outwards with a crack, so I paused and held my breath again. I counted to twenty, then wiggled the plank again until it came away in my hands. I placed it to one side, then started on the next one but stopped. I could hear something. Not footsteps exactly, but something moving close to me.

Someone was at the back of my hut!

Warily, I crouched as low as I could and peered through the gap I'd created. I could see a car, the grey road and… a face appeared! Inches from mine, making me jump.

Higher State of Consciousness – Josh Wink

I had to get out of this bloody hut. Get free, find Luke and get the hell out of this place, fast.

I didn't know who the big guy outside was or how he was involved with that creep Chris, but things had only got worse since I escaped the bungalow. Luke had been attacked, I'd been knocked out again and I had the guilt of stabbing Andy weighing over me. I couldn't blame Luke, but his reckless climb along that sea wall had been typical of him not thinking things through properly. He was always rushing. I bet he still thought he'd rescued me rather than messing up my escape.

There. Now I'd purged my bad feelings, I felt centred again and could concentrate on more constructive thoughts. After everything I'd been through, my resolve had never been stronger. Maybe it was the change of scenery, the new clothes or the cold air? I couldn't tell.

The man outside had peered through the single gap of light between the front doors a few times, so my first step was to build a fake version me to give me time to make my escape. I bound up the blankets they'd left me, curled them up on the padded bench with cushions for a pillow, then I hid in the darkest corner behind a rack of deckchairs. The man had checked me twice so far without raising the alarm, so it had worked!

That's when I heard Luke's voice and whispered back to him through the wall planks.

I imagined him like a captive tiger in the next cage, desperate to get to his mate. If I knew Luke, he was bound to do something stupid soon, so I had to act fast. I had to get out. But this hut looked and smelt brand new: tight, pine boarded walls; immaculate painted benches with storage space underneath; baskets full of cleaned dining linen; lines of blue and white-striped bunting strung up. Even the indoor eaves had been painted.

I could tell from the shiny screws in the front doors that they were triple locked. Too dangerous that way, so I kept searching, finally eyeing up the electric hob on the worktop in the opposite corner. Electric. Not gas. Which meant batteries… or mains electricity? I crawled over, trying to position myself where I couldn't be spotted from the front door and found what I needed: a grey cable which lead to a neat wooden panel screwed onto the back wall.

'Sorry,' I whispered to whoever owned the hut and grabbed a Badminton racket from a box of sports gear.

I snapped the handle off at the neck and flattened the broken metal under my heel to create a flathead screwdriver, then set to work prising open the panel. The screws were easy work but it had been fixed from the outside too, so I chipped the wood away at the strongest points until, about ten minutes later, the panel finally came loose in my hands!

Checking I had everything I needed in Luke's coat pockets and grabbing the water bottle, I squeezed through the hole, replaced the panel behind me and breathed in the fresh sea air. I buttoned the coat up around me, its heavy material keeping me warm, and gripped my new metal weapon.

Crouching between the back of the hut and screened by a car parked beside me, I felt a wave of guilt wash over me for what I'd done to Andy. I stared at the sharp edge of the broken badminton racket. Would I be able to do that again? I wondered, knowing I might have to, but afraid of the after effects another violent incident would have on me.

A scratching sound caught my attention and I turned to Luke's beach hut. Going by the peeling paint and beach grime that had built up around his hut, it had not been well looked after. A pair of fingers appeared through a gap in the back, clawing at the rotten wood, and my instincts kicked up a notch.

Wherever I'd been - travelling, learning and studying – Luke had called or written, telling me of his wins and his lows, and I'd replied with mine and lifted him where I could with funny stories or encouragement. He needed it. He needed me just as I needed his humour and enthusiasm for life. Although sometimes I wondered if he really knew how much he had achieved on his own? No disrespect to the lads, but Beachhead was pretty much just an extension of Luke's musical skills… the rest of the group magnified what he created, sure, and he wouldn't have made it without their full sound, but it was Luke who gave them the energy and goals to aim for. I'd seen him in action, building them up, chivvying them along and creating a space for them to thrive. He needed that too.

I peered around the edge of my hut, keeping low, and saw the tail of the big man's coat as he passed my hut. I could hear Luke gnawing away on the wood at the back of the hut like a rodent, but was confident the man wouldn't hear from the front. The biggest risk was him seeing me cut between huts. Just a metre, but a sliver of shadow or a kicked stone could give me away.

It was too much to risk… so I walked away. Away from the huts, away from Luke, through the parked cars, and across the road, where I found another car to crouch behind.

Tears filled my eyes as I looked up and down the road, working out where the town centre was. I fumbled in the coat pocket and brought out Luke's phone: still no signal. I looked back across the road. A gap between the parked cars allowed me to see Luke's hands bending bits of plank out. He was making progress but the hole was still too small for him to crawl through. Could I really abandon him? Maybe this was the only choice? Surely I could get help before anyone noticed I was gone and before anything happened to him. A flash of white reminded me of the cast on his broken arm. He was in no position to defend himself, especially after the whack he'd taken from Chris.

I sat there, unsure of what to do, knowing if I went to help him I could easily draw attention to him. A car pulled up further down the road so I edged around the car to keep out of sight, hoping it was just a family on a Christmas walk, but when a large man, who looked remarkably similar to the one guarding us, stepped out, I knew our time was running out.

The man helped out someone out of the car. An old man? No, someone physically disabled. I sighed. They were just getting some sea air, but seeing the strong man helping him out settled my intentions. I waited until they'd walked onto the prom, out of sight, then jogged back to where Luke was clawing his way out of his hut.

His face appeared, red-cheeked and dishevelled.

'Hello,' I said, with a smile.

It was so good to see him in the daylight. His eyes smiled back but I could tell he was in pain.

'Hi,' he replied quietly, and turned away, checking on the guard I guessed. 'Nearly done,' he whispered and pushed at another rotten plank.

The hole was tall enough to crawl through but not wide enough, so I picked at one side, breaking away the rotten chunks as quietly as possible.

Deep voices came to us from the prom and we both froze.

'He's here!' Luke whispered. 'Tip's here!'

'Who?' I mouthed.

I had no idea who he was talking about, but his expression said enough. I bent the last plank up and Luke pushed his head through, twisting in silent agony as he forced his body through the gap. It was tiny, but I bent away any snags and tried to support his arm as he wriggled out, like a bug released from a chrysalis.

When he was on his feet I pointed around the car, to the other side of the road. He nodded and followed as I jogged, bowed-down, across the road.

'What now?' I whispered when we crouched behind the car.

This was as far as I'd made it before.

Luke kissed me, then said, 'Back to the hotel.' He paused to think. 'We can lose them… head up the hill here, then cut back towards the hotel.'

'What about the police station?' I asked.

He shook his head. 'I think it's near the railway station… what about the phone?'

I pulled it out. 'No signal.'

'We need to turn it off,' Luke said. 'Save the battery.'

'Okay,' I replied, not seeing his logic. We needed this phone until we got to the safety of the hotel, so I pretended to turn it off and stuffed it back in the coat pocket.

'Let's go,' I said, grabbed his hand and led him to the next car, uphill.

Tuesday 24^rh^ December 1996 Noon

Me and You Vs the World – Space

I felt alive! Scared shitless, but alive. Cold and wary of my injuries, but my legs were both fine and I was ready to run the hell away from the bastards who'd held us captive. I knew I shouldn't have trusted Tip and swore to trust my instincts next time. When would I ever learn?

Lisa and I were free and needed to get out of sight before they found we had escaped, then we could concentrate on the basics: keep safe, get some food and shelter, then contact the police. Assuming Tip hadn't got to them as well? What if Chris had connections with the local police? Maybe I should contact Dad first and see if he knew anyone in the Suffolk Constabulary.

No, focus on priorities: food; hotel; police.

'So, do you know where we need to go?' Lisa asked after we'd jogged up the road which curved away from the beach, out of view of the beach huts.

'Yeah, sure,' I replied as we passed a huge convalescent hospital, which had been hidden by trees.

Behind it I could see the terraced houses where I'd picked up Tip's package for the old lady. They looked pretty smart from the front.

Another example of Tip's eyes and ears around this place, I thought, but also a sign I was getting to know this town.

'To get back to the hotel we turn left up here, then head along the cliff-top road,' I said, pointing at an impressive Victorian building on the crest of the hill.

I remembered the road along from there with the gardens which cascaded down the hill, the ones I'd seen when I first arrived here. That seemed like weeks ago!

'I'm not happy staying on the roads,' Lisa said, slowing down. 'Is there another way to the hotel?'

I stared back at the huts and couldn't see anyone, then eyed up a low wall on the other side of the road. Maybe she was right? Maybe there was a safer way to get back.

'Okay, we can cut through the gardens,' I said, hoping one of the winding paths led where we needed to go.

Lisa pulled my hand, stopping me. 'It isn't going to involve scaling more walls is it?'

'No,' I said, trying to remember the gardens. 'It's just a few stony paths and shrubs, a few sets of steps, honest.'

'Come on then,' she replied, with a determined look in her eye.

We jogged over the road, skipped the wall and slid down a grassy slope to the beginnings of the beachfront gardens. A large shelter was on our left, while a series of lawns, ponds and winding paths meandered away from us, to safety, with the sea on one side and a cascading hill on the other.

We set off at a slow jog.

'What on earth?' Lisa whispered as a fake cave appeared, arching over the path.

'Wait,' I said, stepping into the half-shadow and peering back to check we weren't being followed. 'Just dog-walkers and day trippers,' I said, keeping track of who was wandering around. 'Let's keep moving.'

My mind wandered as we kept a slow and steady pace. If Tip had come out into the cold to visit the huts he must have wanted to talk to us, which meant his men would open the doors soon. Hell, they'd probably already discovered we'd already gone.

We skipped past a circular pond, more lawns, then took a raised, sheltered path past more ponds to the back of a large building.

'The pavilion,' I said when we slowed to a walk. 'A theatre I think.'

'Is there another way around?' Lisa asked.

'Not that I know of.'

We'd passed a path that curved up the cliff, but I guessed that would bring us out too short of the hotel.

'It's just a quick stretch in the open then we can get back into the garden,' I said, hoping I'd remembered it correctly.

'But it's right next to the prom,' Lisa said. 'They'll see us.'

The light was already fading as another speedy winter day slipped past. How long had we been knocked out for? I wondered as we stopped and I stood in Lisa's way to face her, trying to give her some hope.

'We've just got to go for it okay?' I said, feeling my confidence rise. 'They'll know we've got out by now, so must make the most of every second. The quicker we are the better, so we keep running, yeah? Or we find a hole to hide in right now and wait.' I gave her a second to think. 'After last night, I don't fancy freezing to death, do you?'

'No,' she said, gripping my hand tighter. 'I just want to stay away from those bastards. Let's get going.'

She set off, pulling me along behind her. Past the bins to a narrow strip of concrete between the theatre and the prom. We walked fast, but I felt vulnerable. I heard shouting and spun around. Someone was waving about a hundred metres back down the prom.

'Shit, let's go!' I shouted, pulling Lisa along.

We cut round the front of the pavilion, up the first path we could see and I tried to keep my breathing under control.

'Not up there,' I shouted, pulling Lisa back from a set of steps. 'Keep to the middle and it'll take us all the way up.'

We jogged round the back of an enormous water-fed clock and I cast a look back to see one of Tip's men, Aston or Martin, rounding the pavilion and now had us in his sights.

'Not much further,' I said, as we climbed up towards my hotel and towards a large white building on the right.

I could see the hotel through the gap between buildings, where the path came out on the hill of the sticky-floored nightclub.

'Nearly there,' I panted.

'No!' Lisa screamed and everything went into slow motion.

We skidded to a stop and I stared around in panic. A large shape stepped out at the top of the path, cutting us off. Tip's other man.

'I told you to stay where you were,' he said in his gruff voice and closed in on us.

There was no way we could take him on, even if Lisa and I were armed, plus he had the high ground. I turned to see the other guy closing in on us, narrowing the trap and leaving us few exit routes.

'Look, we're doing this for your own good, okay?' he said as he advanced.

No weapon, I noticed.

To our left was a twenty metre slope of shrubs and bare soil which led back down to the road, the prom and the beach. I looked back at the second man cutting off the way we'd come.

'We can't both go round him,' Lisa said, her eyes meeting mine for a second.

I recognised that look – she was determined to do something, which would mean something crazy!

'One of us could though,' she said with a wink. 'You go one way, I go the other.'

'No!' I grabbed her elbow and held her tight.

A new shape appeared at the top of the path behind the big man, blowing Lisa's plan out of the water. I guessed it was Tip, but this guy walked normally… there was no side-loping gait. In fact, I recognised something about the way this person moved.

'We just want to get back home,' Lisa shouted. 'Leave us alone!'

'We've done nothing wrong,' I added, shimmying to the edge of the path, keeping hold of Lisa.

'It's okay,' the man said. 'We've looked after your mate, he's in the hospital.' He turned suddenly, hearing the newcomer behind him, but was too late.

'Chris?' I said, frozen to the spot as he raised his cricket bat and attacked Tip's man with animal ferocity.

Weren't they in this together?

'Oi!' the second man shouted and ran up the hill to help his mate.

This was our chance.

'Down here,' I yelled and jumped down the slope, pulling Lisa with me, away from the shouting.

We scrambled down the dry earth, trying to slow our descent and not hit the handful of fully grown trees whose roots held the bank together. Lisa slipped and I held her up with my healthy arm; my elbow shrieking in pain. It wasn't enough and she stumbled sideways, pulling her with me. Skidding and tumbling, we fell and rolled the last five metres, crashed into an evergreen shrub at the bottom of the hill.

'Shit, are you okay?' I asked, picking myself out of the branches.

'Fine…. I'm fine,' Lisa said and was up before me, pulling me up onto my feet.

She looked stoked, like she'd caught an amazing wave. Untouchable, like anything thrown at her would just bounce off. There was movement up the hill where Chris and Tip's men were fighting but I couldn't tell who was winning.

'Where now?' Lisa asked, eyeing up the prom and street ahead.

'They cut us off so they must know I'm staying at that hotel,' I said, annoyed at so close we were to safety. 'And the police station is miles away so…'

The lines of coloured lights flickered into life along the prom; their multi-coloured glow drawing us to the pier, which stretched out into the grey sea like an outstretched arm. More people were down this end, heading out for dinner or to the pub, so we could be safer here. Maybe we could ask someone if we could use their mobile phone to call for help.

Lisa leaned on me, her head nestling against my shoulder. 'I really need something to eat.'

'Okay, okay,' I replied, edging us towards the prom and away from Chris and the men. 'I haven't got any money on me but maybe we can hide out for a bit, then double-back to the hotel?' I suggested.

We skipped to the prom and walked arm in arm as though everything was normal, mingling with other couples taking in the sea air, and for a few quiet seconds, everything settled. A cosy warmth took away the cold in my bones and I felt grounded; whole; full. Just me and Lisa. Like this was a normal Christmas Eve and we were on the way to the pub to meet some mates. In a flash, like an intense dream just before you fall asleep, a hundred ideal scenarios of our future life flashed through my mind. Cosy scarfed walks, road trips, castles, Christmas trees, gigs, presents, children, campervans, hot beaches, parties, campfires, baking, growing food, growing children, growing together. Growing old.

It was perfect.

A cold wind whipped up my scarecrow's coat and reality came crashing back down on me. I looked over my shoulder to see if we were being followed, but didn't recognise anyone. More people were coming out, heading to the pubs and clubs I'd been to on Saturday, and I remembered John and Sarah. We'd already walked past their mate Carl's place, but we could have given that a go, couldn't we? Too risky to double back now though.

'Shall we find a pub to get something to eat?' Lisa asked as we walked.

'It would be safe,' I said, thinking it through.

'And warm.'

'But no money remember,' I said. 'Tip's men must have taken my wallet.'

'Nothing in your coat,' Lisa said. 'Just the phone…'

Parts of my body ached while the rest of my body felt numb. The thought of food set my stomach growling. I'd been running on adrenaline since I woke up and hadn't eaten a thing all day, so God knows what Lisa had felt like after being drugged for days.

'Why don't we just go into the first pub or shop and ask them to call the police?' Lisa asked.

I shook my head and said, 'Tip knows everyone here, they'll tell him before the police get here.'

'So we just hide or hope a policeman comes walking down here?'

'No, I…'

She was right. What were our options?

'The man said they were doing it for our own good,' Lisa said. 'And they had helped Andy, so they must be on our side.'

I was focussed on where we could hide out, so didn't reply.

'And Chris attacked *them*,' she continued, 'so we should trust Tip shouldn't we?'

'Maybe,' I said, my tired head trying to work out what was going on. I thought about Andy. What if he really had no idea about all of this and had walked into the fire like I had? Had it just been Chris driving this all along?

'The men could have been lying,' I said. 'And if we believe them, we'll fall back into their trap.'

'But why?' Lisa sounded tired. 'Why are they, or Chris after me – and you?'

'I don't know,' I said with a shrug. 'Because we stole Andy from his band? Seems crazy but…'

'He mentioned a man,' Lisa said. 'Chris said something about the man would give him what he wanted… but it hadn't worked, so he'll keep trying and-'

'Stop!' I snapped and grabbed Lisa's hand to stop her walking.

A number of silhouettes were meandering further down the prom, past the swimming pool on our right. One figure stood out, turning on the spot, searching for something, carrying something long in one hand. It dangled and swung with his walk.

'Chris found a way past us,' I whispered.

'We can go back then,' Lisa said, pulling my hand. 'Back up to your hotel.'

'Yeah, but…'

I thought about Carl's place but still didn't trust anyone. Maybe it was the tiredness, but I just wanted to ring my parents or Stephen and see what they thought. Funny, I'd never been like that before. I'd always been independent, relying on my own judgement. But I needed them now.

We were right next to the entrance to the pier, closed up for the holiday, and the string of small shops which were set in the front of the building, usually selling ice creams; hot dogs; candy floss; doughnuts.

'Doughnuts,' I said.

'What?' Lisa shook me.

'I…' I paused as an idea took shape. 'We'll be safe if we hide out a bit longer, then we can head back to the hotel when it's properly dark,' I said, eyeing up the metal shutters on the shops.

One shutter caught my eye, flapping in the breeze. It hadn't been fastened down properly, so could easily be wedged open, giving us enough room to slip in.

'But everything's closed,' Lisa said.

'We haven't got long,' I said, walking straight for the shopfronts, waiting for the nearest walkers to pass. 'Come here,' I said and pushed Lisa against the wall to kiss her.

Classic film move.

'What are you doing?' she whispered as I tugged at the metal shutter behind her.

Behind was a wooden door made in two halves so the top could be left open in the summer for fresh air. The top half would be held tight by the bottom, but if that only had one lock, I could find a way in. I tried the handle and felt the Yale lock holding it tight.

Lisa bent her head round to have a look.

'If only we could…' I started, but she took over, pulling something from her sleeve.

She wedged it down the side of the door and, with a deft slap, forced the lock open.

'Come on then,' she whispered, then slipped behind the shutter and into the shop.

I leaned back to check on Chris, who still was heading our way but staring around wildly, then slipped in behind Lisa.

Tuesday 24^{rh} December 1996 P.M.

I Wanna Stay Alive With You – Ocean Colour Scene

It wasn't over yet and Chris was close, but it felt cosy and relatively safe in the little shop.

Just a few metres long, the narrow room had a waist-high counter along the left hand side, where the shutters wafted in the breeze. Cupboards lined the back wall, covered with posters of prices and different sweet snacks. The names and pictures set my stomach off growling.

'Don't make a sound,' I mouthed to Lisa after we'd softly clicked the door shut behind us.

She raised an eyebrow, signalling she was in charge and pointed to a dark spot under the counter between two fridges. I nodded and let her get comfortable before I joined her. The fridges were softly humming and pumping out a mild heat from the back, warming us up.

'Cosy,' I whispered and Lisa put her finger to her lips.

I couldn't hear anyone outside, no steps or chatter, but I pictured Chris strolling past with a crazed look on his face, eyeing up everyone he passed. I waited for the bat to crash against the metal shutters. He was hunting us like wild animals and we'd gone to ground. What if he'd spotted us kissing? Or seen a trailing foot disappearing into the shop? No, surely he had no reason to check the shops. He had no idea where we really were. We could have gone anywhere! We just had to give it time and wait it out.

As we sat, hunched under the counter, my mind flickered, high on adrenaline and flight or fight instincts. My thoughts twisted around Chris, wondering why he was doing this. What was in this for him? And who was this man Lisa mentioned? It had to be more than revenge, surely? Otherwise, he would have mentioned it. He had kidnapped Lisa and never given any demands and if he was behind the car crash he'd injured Stephen as well… was he just collateral damage or another target? Even when he captured me he'd given no clue as to what he wanted. Was he trying to capture someone else? Were we the real bait? Was he trying to catch the 'man' he mentioned? I wanted to ask Lisa more but had to stay quiet.

Lisa shuffled to loosen her coat and snuggled into my shoulder. I smelt her hair when I kissed her head and felt a sense of comfort wash over me. I was tired, probably from hunger more than lack of sleep seeing as how long we'd been out of it, unless the whack to my head had caused concussion?

My eyes adjusted to the low light in the shop and I passed the time by reading the contents of the boxes in the open cupboards opposite us: oil;

sugar; wafers. I thought about raiding the fridges but knew the light could give us away, so I held off. I wasn't going to fire up the doughnut machine and start frying up, but the box of wafers had my full attention. I wanted to point them out to Lisa, but she was cosy and we had to stay silent. I worked out at the rate Chris had been walking he was probably outside right now and I found myself holding my breath.

Everything sounded louder than it should as I strained to hear what was going on outside. Over the blood pulsing in my ear, I could hear a few people outside shouting 'Merry Christmas' and a few minutes later, someone called their dog, but that was it. I waited until Chris should have passed and wondered what time it was. Night time dropped so early here on the east coast it would be fully dark outside, which would give us cover. Maybe we could sneak out, get into the town and try the phone again?

'I need the loo,' Lisa whispered and I realised how quiet we'd been.

I searched the room for a pot or bucket and spotted a vertical line on the back wall behind a pile of boxes.

'There's a door,' I whispered, pointing to the boxes. 'It should take us into the main building and we can find the loos, maybe some food?'

Lisa shifted her weight, then crawled forward to the boxes I'd been studying. I rubbed my eyes and joined her.

'Let's take some food,' she said, opening the wafer box. 'They're wrapped so they'll be fresh.' She filled her coat pockets with the hand-sized white packets of wafers, resisting the urge to stuff her face.

She pulled a large envelope from her pocket and handed it to me.

'Don't laugh but you might need these,' she whispered.

I squinted at the thin package, making out a pair of legs on the front.

'Tights?'

'They'll keep you warm!' Lisa whispered. 'I've already got a pair on.'

'Ah, okay, thanks,' I said, slipping them into my scarecrow coat's pocket along with some wafers.

A yellow box caught my eye.

'Oh…' I gasped, dragging it forward. 'Flakes!'

'Oh my God, let's take the whole box,' Lisa said, wide-eyed.

'Okay.' I shifted the box to one side, then started moving the other boxes, making room in front of the inside door and blocking up the front door in the process.

A glare of light made me turn: Lisa had opened one of the fridges.

'Milk,' she whispered, grabbing a bottle as I rushed over to close the door.

'No light,' I whispered and held my breath, listening for any sounds.

Nothing.

'Come on,' I said, tucking the box of chocolate under one arm and standing to my full height.

I said a little prayer as I turned the handle of the new door and opened it with a squeak. Red lights, like demon's eyes, blinked from the dark space beyond and I tried to work out where we were, piecing together what I remembered from when I came in here on my first day in the town. This was the outer room where the older games were kept.

'This leads through to the main arcade,' I whispered and led Lisa through the phalanx of silhouettes: pinball machines and games for younger kids.

'Over here,' Lisa said and pulled me to one side where she'd spotted another side door.

I nodded in the dark and followed, guessing the main doors would be alarmed considering the amount of money that would be kept in the gambling machines.

'It's open,' she whispered and pushed the door open to reveal the main arcade hall.

We were in the far left-hand corner. The smell of stale cigarettes, dirty carpets and old electric cables invaded my nostrils. Lights blinked from random places across the cavernous spaces, filled with more sleeping robot silhouettes. Everything was lit by a grey liquid light drifting through a giant set of glass doors at the back which led out to the pier itself.

The light drew us over, where we stood for a while, arms full of snacks, staring out at the huge slippery-dip slide and dark, violent sea beyond.

'Wow,' Lisa said after a while. 'All that water… I really need the loo now.'

'They're over here,' I said, pointing Lisa in the right direction, then followed her, realising I needed to go too.

The Gents were cold, damp and stank of fetid urine and mould. Did anyone ever use these loos? The toilet paper felt like tracing paper and the loo seat was freezing but at least the graffiti was amusing.

The pack of tights from Lisa fell out of my pocket, making me jump and I stared at it, in two minds. It was cold outside and we'd found shelter, so did I still need them? Women's tights? I'd done some odd things in my time, but usually under the influence. No, this was different. No-one would know, I thought. Sod it. I needed to stay warm.

We came out at the same time, me walking like John Wayne and Lisa looking way more relaxed.

'That's better,' I said, putting my arm around her.

'If you say so,' she replied. 'I feel like I need another wash after being in there!'

'Yeah, it was a bit grim.'

'I'm starving.'

'Let's camp over there,' I said, pointing to the pool tables which sat in the light from the huge glass doors. We'd be hidden by the pool table but able to see if anyone came in.

'Chocolate and wafers,' Lisa said as we rummaged through the boxes like we were at a picnic. 'A Queen's banquet! Did you bring the wine?'

I laughed, spraying half a mouthful of flakes.

'We 'ave a bottle of Jersey ninety-six,' I said, offering the milk, then set to making crumbly chocolate sandwiches out of the triangular wafers and flakes, washed down with milk.

'I really need a proper hot shower,' Lisa said after a few crunchy mouthfuls of dry wafers. 'Or a bath, full of bubbles. Some chill-out tunes.'

'I bet,' I replied, feeling icky myself after just one night without a decent sleep or wash.

'Are you saying I stink?' she said with the slightest smile.

'Stink wouldn't be an accurate word,' I replied. 'No, that's too strong… *hum* might be better. Ow!'

A flake hit me in the eye.

We laughed properly for the first time in ages, then fell silent with a sigh.

'Why do you always get me into shit like this Luke Redfern?' Lisa said, staring right at me.

Into me, it felt.

'I…' I started but ended up shrugging and looking out to sea.

'I've been to some pretty dangerous places you know,' Lisa said. 'Especially for a white girl and yet I get into more scrapes here, at home, with you, than anywhere else. Always with you.'

I couldn't tell whether she was joking or not and felt the need to defend myself.

'I can hardly be blamed for what happened with Isaac, I mean, how did I know I was living next to a serial killer? And as for Chris.' I shook my head a looked away. 'Drugs, ego, dented dreams… who knows what's going on in his head?'

'He said the man told him to do it,' Lisa said softly. 'They must have promised him something big.'

I hadn't pushed her to talk about what had happened with Chris but she was finally opening up.

'When did he say that?' I asked.

'After he'd knocked you out… then he knocked both of us out. He said the man who matters told him to do it… and something about being rewarded.'

'The man who matters?' I repeated. 'So someone put him up to this.'

My first thought was Jeff, seeing as he ran the label we were signed to and Andy had left Lightback to sign with, but that was crazy. Maybe it was Tip? That made more sense. Drugs, money or whatever Chris needed. But why did he attack Aston and Martin?

'We should let the police sort this out,' Lisa said, resting a hand on mine. 'It isn't your job to solve every crime you know?'

'Yeah sure,' I said. 'But you have to admit stuff like this puts your life into perspective, doesn't it?' The feelings I'd run through these past few days were welling up in me; their shadows darkening my thoughts. 'I thought I'd lost you and now we're bac-'

'What? Now we're back… what? Back together?' Lisa said. 'Like we'd split up?'

I stopped eating.

'I thought I'd lost you,' I said warily. 'When you disappeared.'

'You came after me but, you thought I'd gone and what? You thought I'd left you?'

A sweat ran over me. I'd been caught out.

'I…' How could I explain this without sounding like a complete tosser? Lying never worked with Lisa, so I only had the truth. Time to be honest. 'Chris sent a text saying you had left me,' I said, focussing on a new packet of wafers.

'And you believed him?' Lisa said with a huff: her mind clearly working through the gears. 'And yet you still tracked me down.'

'Yep.'

'But you didn't know I'd been kidnapped?'

'No, I…'

Suddenly this was the last place I wanted to be. I'd been in arguments like this before with Lisa and she always out-manoeuvred me like a chess grand master, cornering me in seconds.

'So, you came here because…?'

I felt her eyes bore into me.

'Closure,' I said, meeting her eyes. 'It didn't feel right and I needed to know why, simple as that.'

Lisa held my stare for a long second, as though reading my soul. Then nodded.

'Sounds fair enough,' she said. 'I'd have done the same if you ever left me, you bastard.'

She threw a pack of wafers at my head.

'Ha!' I threw a pack back, followed by a flake and another food fight ensued.

When we stopped, we smiled and kissed.

As shite as these days had been and, maybe it was the sugar, but I felt good now. I had Lisa back and could see my trip to Felixstowe was going to end up way better than I ever thought it would. It had been worth the effort after all. I'd discovered a little about myself as well, along the way. Maybe all those dreams I'd had about me and Lisa would become our future after all? I wanted to tell Lisa, to ask her what she wanted to do next, but I knew she'd been through enough and was tired. We just had to get through tonight and then we would make our new plans.

'I know it sounds stupid after sleeping half the day away,' I said. 'But after all that food, I could easily fall asleep.'

Lisa let out a little laugh, gave a cat-like stretch and said, 'Yeah, me too.'

I smiled and couldn't take my eyes off her, leaning against my legs, lit by a grey, almost moon-like light which filtered through the glass doors. Only the sea was beyond, and our backs were to the land, shutting everyone out. It was just us.

After finishing my photography course a few years back, I'd stopped carrying a camera with me. Maybe it was what had happened with

Grandad and Isaac. Who knows? But there were still times I wished I had a camera to capture a moment. This was one.

'Come on then,' she said, breaking the spell. 'Let's find a safe place to kip.'

'Sure,' I replied, feeling the moment slip away.

Silently, we searched the rest of the arcade for somewhere comfortable to settle down. We found a couple of blankets in the tiny office where they gave out change for the machines, and gravitated to the darkest corner, furthest from any doors. We found a gap between two monolith games machines, built a nest and curled up together.

'I've no idea what time it is,' I said as I felt sleep pull at me.

'Not too late,' Lisa replied.

As I drifted off, I thought about getting a couple of pool cues as weapons or setting up some booby traps, Home Alone style, then pictured my parents and remembered it was Christmas Eve!

I sat bolt upright.

'Have you got my phone?'

'Yeah, why?' Lisa replied sleepily.

'My parents…' I said, but realised how stupid it sounded.

We couldn't even call the police.

'No signal,' Lisa said and, as I lay back down, I wondered if we should have left the pier when Chris had gone past? We could have kept moving and found a phone box or knocked on a house to ask someone to call for us? Things always seemed easier in hindsight, I thought.

'Merry Christmas then,' I said with a little laugh at our absurd situation. 'I didn't have a chance to get you a present,' I whispered.

'Because you thought I'd dumped you,' Lisa whispered back.

That cut me, but it was true. The shame weighed down on me. How quickly I'd cut Lisa out of my life as soon as I thought she was cheating on me. The only reason I was here was because I wanted to confront her and get the truth – to tell her she was wrong and that she needed me. I felt hollow.

'I bought you a present,' Lisa said, taking me by surprise.

'You what? Really?'

'Yeah, it's at the bottom of your wardrobe. Tucked at the back. I even wrapped it.'

'You're taking the mick,' I said.

'No, it's there,' she said in her calm, ready for sleep voice.

'Cool,' I said, trying to picture what was at the bottom of my messy wardrobe. Old socks and books, hopefully nothing dodgy she might have found. 'Thanks,' I whispered and kissed her behind her ear.

'Night,' she whispered back and we snuggled up, feeling whole.

This was what I wanted. Forever.

Wednesday 25th December 1996

Ready Or Not – Fugees

A beach. The warm sun. A cool breeze. Palm trees swaying. Was this a memory or a new place? Or a song? Yes, a song played out in reality. It's been a long time… a long time since… since what? A long time… the words appeared and the view faded away. A long time. The words become sounds. Sharp, evil sounds, piercing my head. A. Long. Time.

'What the hell's that?' I growled, opening my eyes to the darkness.

I stared at the strange space around me, full of looming shadows. Cavernous. It made me feel tiny, like a mouse hidden in the corner.

A. Long. Time.

The noise erupted again, coming from Lisa. A synthetic sound.

'I've got it,' Lisa said, sitting up behind me, suddenly lit by an alien green glow.

Her voice brought it all back and I remembered where we were. The pier arcade hall.

'Hello?' she said as though answering a phone.

I turned. She *was* answering a phone – my phone! I could hear a man's voice at the other end, muffled, but definitely a man's voice.

'Yes it's me,' Lisa said. 'Yeah he's here too.'

'What the… who is it?' I asked, my voice echoing in the huge room.

Lisa held up a hand to shush me and carried on speaking. 'No, we're not okay – I was kidnapped by Chris Lightback and now we're stuck on a pier after he knocked Luke out and imprisoned both of us.'

I could only hear the murmur of the caller's voice.

'Chris, yes. We escaped but had no signal, so couldn't call the police… please, straight away. Yes, thank you. I'll pass you over.'

Lisa handed the phone to me with the slightest of smiles and said, 'It's Jeff.'

'Jeff?' I said, putting the phone to my ear.

'Luke? Are you okay?'

Just hearing his voice set me off and I felt tears welling in my eyes. 'Yes,' I said. 'Well, no, I'm injured and we need help-'

'Everyone's going crazy,' Jeff said, cutting me off. 'Stephen's been on the phone…' the reception cut in and out as he spoke, '…the police… it's gone midnight, it's Christmas Eve or Day by now and nobody can find you. What's going on?'

'Yeah, I know,' I said, feeling like I was being reprimanded. 'Listen,' I cut in, 'this is not our fault okay? Chris has gone crazy.' I tried to keep calm and state the facts. 'He kidnapped Lisa, he was the one who cut Stephen's brakes and he is hunting us down.'

'Yeah, yeah, Lisa said that,' Jeff cut in.

'We're trapped in Felixstowe pier and we need the police right now.'

'You're cutting out,' Jeff said, so I was unsure how much he'd heard. 'We had a late Christmas Eve Mass… received a call from Stephen. Apparently Andy rang him – he's in Ipswich hospital. He told him what had happened.'

'Right, that's great,' I said feeling some relief that Andy was okay. 'We're on the Felixstowe pier in Suffolk,' I said, wondering if I should just hang up and ring the police myself now we had a signal. 'Please send the police.'

'So sorry,' Jeff was saying but a crackle had started, making it hard to hear. He probably couldn't hear me either, '-my fault after I spoke to Chris.'

'What?' I shouted, finger in one ear.

'I tried to gee him up a bit, you know,' Jeff said. 'Pain can inspire the greatest music… -spiration to some… re-form his band and I…'

'I can't hear you,' I said.

'…guess he …give Lightback a shot but… idea he'd turn on you… make you write the bes-'

'I can't hear you Jeff,' I said, almost shouting. 'Can you hear me?'

Lisa hadn't taken her eyes off me; her face turning from relief to concern through my conversation with Jeff. 'Move around a bit,' she said, gesturing towards the huge glass doors which led onto the pier.

Jeff's voice was cutting out more frequently now and I could only hear random syllables. I remembered seeing Jeff and Chris talking in the alleyway outside the gig after the fire alarm had gone off and thought about what Lisa had said about Chris's ramblings. Chris must have cornered Jeff that night - probably set the alarm off to get to him - then mis-heard Jeff's advice. Or heard what he wanted to hear.

'Jeff, can you hear me?' I said, trying to stay calm as I strolled to the big glass doors and stared out at the dark mass of sea beyond.

I tried to piece together what Jeff said. He and Chris would have both been drunk – maybe Chris had been on speed or something chemical – I could picture it, Jeff in his dominant, preaching mood, which would have had an even greater influence on Chris.

The low level buzzing sound in my ear suddenly stopped. I looked at the phone: just an inert lump of plastic now. I pressed a few buttons to wake it up, but it was dead.

'What's wrong?' Lisa was by my side.

'It's gone off,' I said. 'The batteries ran out.'

Lisa took the phone and pressed a few buttons.

Everything rolled around my mind. The police would be here soon, I told myself. Jeff sounded genuine, so he would tell the police where to find us. But what had he started? He *was* the man Chris had mentioned. He'd given Chris hope that Lightback would get signed if he was able to inspire me to write my greatest songs – and what was more inspiring than losing your lover? Half the world's songs had been written about that, right?

'I'm sorry,' Lisa said, looking up at me. 'I left the phone on so we could call when we got a signal…'

I was annoyed she hadn't listened to me, but it was too late. Jeff wouldn't have got through if we'd turned it off and what he'd said made me understand the whole situation. I could think clearly now I knew how we'd arrived here. I shrugged and gave Lisa a hug.

'It's okay. We wouldn't have heard Jeff's call if it was turned off so-'

'Shh!' Lisa said, pulling away from me: her face tensing and her eyes turning. 'I heard something,' she mouthed and pulled me away from the glass doors.

I strained to listen but all I could hear was the blood pumping through my ears. A delayed shot of adrenaline sent my chest thudding as Lisa guided us back through the rows of gambling machines to the shadowy corner where we'd slept.

We crouched down together.

'Someone's in the building,' Lisa whispered, close enough to tickle my ear.

I was tense again. Drained but on edge, like some frightened, hunted animal. Ahead of us, the odd red light blinked between the silent hulks of the sleeping coin machines which stood in rows like de-activated Daleks. My eyes strained: searching the gaps for anything that would give someone away, but all I could see were hazy outlines or shadows within shadows. Then a silhouette moved on the far right of the hall and I froze. I swallowed and a second later, my heart started thumping out a tribal beat.

Someone was in the room and had come in through the side door just as we had. Lisa looked at me and I nodded, putting a finger on my lips. The shape became clearer as it separated from the furthest shadows and walked into the open area at the room's centre, near the pool tables.

'I am he, as you are he, as you are me and we are all together…' came a haunting, half-whispering, half-singing voice.

It was Chris, no doubt. I didn't know his voice but I recognised an edge to it. He sounded wired.

As he walked past the end of a row of machines, I saw a shape by his legs slowly swinging like a pendulum: the bat he'd whacked me with. I clenched my teeth and felt my anger rise. I wanted to rush him: jump out of the dark and take him out, release all the rage I felt for everything he'd done, everyone he'd hurt – Stephen, Andy, Lisa… me. He had to pay for this, the arrogant bastard.

But I was injured. I'd seen what he'd done to Tip's men. Even if we took him on together, Lisa and I stood no chance. One of us would end up seriously injured and I couldn't risk that.

Lisa shifted her weight and the creak of her shoe seemed to echo around the hall.

Chris hadn't noticed.

'…see how they run like pigs from a gun, see how they fly…'

Lisa and I remained stone-still, crouched, eyes wide open. Unable to talk, I reached out a hand, found hers and gave it a squeeze. It'll be okay, I was trying to say. We'll just wait until he gets bored and give the police time to get here. Time was all we needed.

She squeezed back.

Chris had reached the place where we'd eaten our snacks by the pool tables and I cursed the mess we'd left behind. The crisp and crackle of him checking our discarded wafer packets told us he was on our trail. I leant to one side and could just make out his foot, toeing our debris: the plastic packets glowing white in the light from the glass doors.

'Goo goo g'joob!' He shouted and moved out of sight.

He was touring the hall now, peeking behind machines and hitting them with his bat, trying to scare us out. Methodically, row by row, he was closing in on us.

'I know you're in here!' he shouted as he rounded a corner, with a little laugh to himself.

Lisa tensed but we stayed silent and still.

'Luke and Lisa,' he said with what I imagined was a sneer. 'The perfect couple.'

I tried to project what Jeff had told me onto what I knew of Chris and how he'd acted, but all I could see was a jealous, childish boy-man, smashing anything he didn't agree with. Sure, we'd tempted Andy away from his fledgling band when Mike's departure left us without a lead guitarist. Beachhead were the better for it. That was business, as Jeff would say. We had adapted and improved. Couldn't Chris see he had to do the same? He needed to stop dwelling in the past and move on.

'You've had it all handed to you on a bloody plate,' Chris continued rambling. 'An easy life… everything given to you… you privileged bastard.'

Those words struck a chord with me, reminding me of how I used to think of Mike, spoilt by his parents and given everything he wanted.

Jealousy made fools of us all. It was just about perspective, I'd learnt that. There was always someone with more than you, I thought, imagining Grandad had said that to me once, and there was always someone who wanted to be in *your* shoes.

Chris's silhouette passed between the next row of machines and all I could think was if he had a torch or some kind of light he'd be able to spot us for sure, but he carried on, creeping, wittering and banging.

'Some of us had to fight for our chance in life,' he said, making me want to hit him even more. 'See how they fly. I'm crying…'

Who did he think he was with his bloody sob story? Sure, I was lucky enough to have a good childhood and both parents, but I'd been through shit too. Lisa's upbringing hadn't been a bed of roses either.

'And you want to take our chance away from us – snatch it… kill our one and only chance before we've had a real go…'

His voice trailed off, muttering and I took a long, soft breath to calm my anger. Was he trying to get me angry? To make me give away our position or rush out and attack? It wasn't going to work. He could spout his self-deprecating bullshit all he wanted. No wonder he hadn't written any decent songs if all he could think about was his own life and how he'd been let down. I wanted to grab him, shake him and… I was falling into the same trap as him. Rivalry. Competition. All that Oasis and Blur bullshit the media hyped up had been good for Indie sales, but it wound up people like Chris and made them think it was real and healthy. Just like Kurt and Krunch. Weak-minded…

I had to stop thinking like this.

Chris was singing again but I could only make out a few words.

'…Gideon's bible. Rocky had come equipped with a gun…'

I recognised the melody. Another Beatles song. This guy was obsessed.

'…drew first and shot…'

My legs were aching from crouching for so long, but I didn't want to move.

'Jeff told me what to do,' Chris's voice was clear again, louder, closer. 'How I could help myself by helping you, ha!'

The laugh was hollow.

'If I could inspire you… like you needed more help. Then I saw you two. Perfect, in a perfect car. On a bloody video shoot. You lucky bastard. You've got it all!'

I wanted to defend myself, to shout back, but it was pointless arguing with him in this state. Andy had said Chris was into pills again and he was definitely on something now.

'You can talk to me!' He yelled as he rounded another row.

I felt Lisa jump and we both fell back, making a bang that sounded loud enough to give our position away. But Chris didn't notice. He was bloody close now. The last thing we wanted was to get trapped in the corner. He was checking each row, following a strict pattern so it wouldn't be long.

Two rows left.

'If you're lonely you can talk to me!' He sang, then sounded like he was growling at himself.

Ahead of us was a clear path through the gap to the left of the machines. I pictured us creeping through. If we could get far enough, keeping the games between us and Chris, we could make it round the back of him and out the way we came before he noticed.

'Ready or not… here I come…' his voice had changed.

Deeper. Calmer.

'…gonna fi-nd you and take it slowly...'

Fuck this, I thought. I squeezed Lisa's hand to get her attention and nodded down the narrow alley, hoping she'd understand. She nodded back and, when Chris was the furthest from us, I leant forward onto my toes and crept forward slowly, keeping crouched. Lisa moved ahead and we made slow, steady progress, out of the corner. Ahead, the glass doors to the actual pier were on our left, but we needed to turn right, cut across the hall and back out the way we came. To where I hoped the police would be coming any minute now.

'You can't run awae-ay,' Chris sang as he stalked the last rows.

Slowly, we edged along in the darkness, waiting for Chris to move before we crossed each open gap between the rows of machines. I don't know how we made it. Dark clothes, timing, stealth. Or because Chris was singing and muttering to himself, clearly off his head.

By the time we'd edged back round to the open middle of the room, near the pool tables, Chris was on the other side, walking the last row, near where we'd slept.

'Have you seen the little piggies,' he sang, 'crawling in the dirt… Ha!'

Hollow bangs rang out where Chris was smacking something with his cricket bat – the machines we slept beside or the blankets on the floor? We didn't hang around to find out. Lisa was off, running for the door we'd come through and I was right behind her.

'Quick,' I hissed as she turned the handle and pulled the door.

It didn't budge.

I leant forward to help, feeling a sharp pain in my elbow as I tried, but the door was shut tight.

'It's locked,' Lisa whispered with an edge of panic. 'Or wedged shut.'

'But it was open when we came in,' I hissed back.

I wanted to shoulder barge the door and break free but both arms were useless.

'Yes, it's locked!' Chris's voice boomed from nearby.

'Shit!' I grabbed Lisa's hand and pulled her away to make a run for the main doors, but Chris stepped out of the shadows cutting us off.

He stood in the grey light, head tilted: no movement other than his swinging bat.

'So this is Christmas…' he sang and stepped towards us.

Wednesday 25th December 1996

One to Another – The Charlatans

'What are you on?' I shouted at Chris, stopping him in his tracks.

'A bit of this a bit of that,' he replied with a self-satisfied laugh.

He was so out of it, he was taking me literally, or trying to be funny, I couldn't tell.

I stared at him, recognising myself in that look and in that laugh. He was confident but it was all fake. The drugs buoyed him, creating a manufactured, assured version of him. The chemicals numbed whatever pain he was feeling, allowing his true self to rise up. That's what he thought, but, as Lisa had told me, the drugs merely magnified his traits at random: this wasn't the real him, as much as he thought it was.

'I have my own mix,' Chris carried on, enjoying his captive audience. 'Concocted for energy rather than creative pursuits… I've got other stuff for that.'

I struggled to think of what to say – everything I thought of sounded hollow or trite, plus he was bound to have an answer for whatever I said. He was like a schoolyard bully: all he really wanted was power. Which was exactly what he had. I couldn't defend myself physically thanks to my injuries and Lisa and I couldn't fight him together while he had the cricket bat.

'I've been experimenting,' Chris said. 'Cos you've got to get the balance right. Uppers for energy and downers to keep it going… stamina.'

Balanced was the last word I would use for him, I thought as he twitched, broke eye contact and stepped towards us. Lisa squeezed my hand and I gave her what I hoped was an encouraging look and checked the space behind us. Only a few metres between us and the machines on the back wall. Lisa wasn't saying anything and all I wanted to do was tear strips off Chris for the pain he'd caused, but if I said anything bad about him, his drugs or his music he would fight back and do something stupid. Like all of this hadn't been stupid enough!

I had to calm him down; meet him in the middle. Common ground.

'Sounds good,' I said, trying a little laugh. 'Got any left?'

I gave Lisa's sweaty hand another squeeze to let her know I had this.

'All gone,' Chris replied softly.

'We can get some more, yeah?' I tried.

'All gone.' His voice turned hard again. 'You don't know what you've got til it's gone, that's right, isn't it Luke?'

I'd lost him. He switched so quickly, I didn't know how to play it. Lisa and I stepped backwards, slowly running out of space. I had to keep him talking. Lyrics? He loved quoting songs, didn't he? The Beatles. I racked my brain for something relevant, then found inspiration.

'Life passes you by when you're making plans,' I said.

Chris stopped, his bat hanging limp by his side.

'John Lennon?' he asked.

'Yeah,' I said, feeling a ray of light shining through.

This could work!

'You're quoting John Lennon?' He asked again.

'Yeah, legend.'

'You… don't know. You don't know SHIT!' He yelled, tearing his throat.

Lisa pulled me back, but my eyes were fixed on Chris.

'That's not what he fucking well sang, is it Luke?' Chris almost growled. 'You should know better! You're a bloody song writer too. All this was to make you a better writer… a better performer – to give you inspiration. I'm inspiring *you* Luke! But it won't bloody work if you don't know your stuff. Argh! For fuck's sake!'

He leapt into frenzied action, swinging his bat over his head and straight into the nearest gambling machine, shattering its glass front with a deafening crash.

Lisa and I jumped back, knocking into the machines behind us. We had nowhere left to run.

'He never sang that, Luke,' Chris said when he'd calmed down. 'He sang… Life is what *happens* to you while you're *busy* making other *plans*.'

I was frightened and angry. I wanted to protect Lisa and take this git out, but we were trapped.

'It's from *Beautiful Boy*,' Chris said. 'Underrated… like me.'

'Oh for fuck's sake, give it up!' Lisa shouted, catching me off guard. 'You poor excuse for a waste of a man. Stop this shit now!'

Silence.

I didn't know what to do to help. Lisa had the moment and had stopped Chris advancing on us.

'This isn't going to work and you know it.' She used her calm, teacher-like voice. 'We spoke to Jeff and the police are on their way.'

'What? Really?' Chris asked.

'Yeah,' I said. 'Jeff rang me.'

'What did he say?'

'He said you'd got it wrong. You misunderstood what he said to you… he was trying to inspire *you*, Chris. He was showing you there was a way out of the mess you'd got into after Andy left.'

I was ad-libbing, but that was how I saw it. Jeff did try to inspire his musicians, through his many methods.

'Andy left… he left me behind,' Chris said, his shoulders slumped. 'We were mates from primary school. He shouldn't have left us behind like that.'

'You would have done the same,' Lisa said. 'You know you would. You should be glad for your friend. Happy for his success.'

Chris shook his head, staring at the floor and rubbed it with his free hand. 'No,' he whispered.

'You know it's true,' Lisa said and I wondered if she was talking to me as much as Chris.

We'd had so many discussions about how I wanted to make it in the music business and how she wanted to make a difference in her own way… and what we'd both give for that goal. To achieve something. To be something.

'You've proved you're dedicated,' Lisa said. 'And you'd do anything for your dreams, but sometimes enough is enough.'

I stared at Chris, wondering if I could have descended as low as him to achieve my dreams. What would I have done to get signed? What would I do now to make sure we're successful? Isaac had been the same, hadn't he? Destroying everything around him to give meaning to his late wife's novel. In the end, we were the same. I had destroyed Chris's band to give Beachhead a chance. Who else had I trampled on to get where we were?

No. I had never crossed the line like this. This was wrong.

'This is NOT enough,' Chris said, staring at us now, still shaking his head. Something had switched in him again. His body straightened and arms tensed, lifting the bat. 'My plans haven't gone well… and maybe Jeff was trying to inspire me after all. I tried to inspire you, Luke, and test to you. Make sure you're worthy. Plans change,' he said with a strange laugh. 'And you've given me an idea.'

'What?' Lisa asked.

'Not you, him,' Chris shouted, pointing his bat at me and stepped forward, within swiping range. 'Lover boy, hero saviour, singer, fucking hit song writer.'

He raised the bat and I held up my plaster cast to protect me and Lisa, but he switched hands and jabbed me in the stomach instead, winding me. He grabbed the neck of my jumper and hissed, 'Fight back and I'll smash beautiful Lisa's face in, got it?'

I coughed, fighting to breathe and tried to nod. Lisa was staring at us, horrified, tears running down her cheeks.

'You're coming with me, Luke,' Chris whispered and pulled me away from Lisa, walking me back to the centre of the arcade. 'You're going to make *both* of us famous.'

'What?' I tried to say as I stumbled, half-dragged along by the psyched-up madman.

'You gave me the idea… John Lennon,' he said as we passed the pool tables and our feet crunched on discarded wafers. 'We'll both win. Your album is recorded isn't it? You die and your songs will sell… dead singers always sell more records. And my name will be known. We'll be known together, forever. Famous. Infamous. A legend. Legends.'

'Don't do it,' Lisa said, following us but keeping several steps back. 'This is wrong, Chris.'

Chris switched arms and got me in a neck-lock. He kicked opened the glass doors which led out onto the pier and a gust of ice-cold air blasted us, rushing up my jumper and around my ankles.

'Get off me, you fucker,' I tried to shout as I struggled, slipping on the wet wooden planks as he dragged me backwards out onto the pier.

'Shut up!' Chris shouted, and whacked me across the knuckles of my outstretched right hand.

All I could see was Lisa's horrified face, tears streaming down her cheeks as she followed us outside.

Behind Lisa, the white building of the pier arcade glowed, and the lights of Felixstowe beyond: coloured pearls; streetlights; house lights; flashes of blue. I reached out to Lisa. Not for help, but to calm her, she needed me as much as I needed her. I wanted to tell her everything I'd been thinking about but never had the time or the place to tell her… how much I loved her and how I looked forward to spending the rest of our lives together. How it was time to stop being apart. Time to start building our future together.

'Let him go, Chris!' Lisa shouted as we veered to one side of the pier and past the huge slide.

She rushed forward and grabbed Chris's arm to release me but he lashed out with the bat. She dodged and held back again.

'Too late!' Chris replied, relentlessly pulling me along. 'You can go now Lisa, tell everyone the story.'

'Go!' I tried to shout, hoping she could get to the police before Chris had his way and killed me.

'Stop wriggling or I'll knock you out,' Chris hissed as we moved out into the last stretch of open pier.

To my right, over the railing, I saw the metal-grey sea frolicking and splashing in the winter darkness. I groaned as my shoes slipped with each step, trying to get traction on the ancient wet planks. The salt air and white water reminded me of surfing in Cornwall and I thought of Dave from Skimrider.

'It's all fake,' I said, grabbing at the arm around my neck so I could breath. 'Jeff… the recording deal… it's all fake…'

Chris had heard but didn't slow down. He randomly jerked left or right to keep me off guard as we carried on past shelters built for chip-eaters and fishermen. How long was his bloody pier?

'It's not fake,' he eventually said. 'It's all we have… us artists. Otherwise we're just left with the art, aren't we? What else is there? Nobody to hear our music. Does a tree make a sound when it falls in an empty forest?'

I felt like I was listening to a younger version of myself and cringed. So much bullshit. His ideas were built on idealisms, on dreams and a nostalgia for the future. Every artist wanted to carry on creating and be recognised for their art… music was the same but… I was losing grip on my thoughts. No energy left to fight or even talk… music was aural emotion. We poured our emotions into something that made people happy. Our songs were a stimulant. Nothing more. Dance. Sing. Cry. The music simply stimulated the listeners' emotions.

I kept my gaze on Lisa. She looked terrified. I needed to help her stay calm.

'Nearly there,' Chris said, tightening his grip.

'The police are here!' Lisa shouted. 'Luke, it's going to be okay, the police are here!'

Was she trying to trick Chris? My vision was blurring and all I could see was Lisa surrounded by a haze. A blurred halo and wings.

'Too bloody late!' Chris shouted back, then dropped me onto the planks with a bone-knocking clunk.

I couldn't do anything as he lunged at Lisa, swinging with his bat.

'Lisa!' I tried to shout, but it came out as a croak.

She was trying to buy time, but it was too dangerous. Chris swung again and missed. Lisa waited for another swing, then leapt in to rugby tackle him, keeping away from the bat and sending him stumbling backwards. I tried to roll onto my elbow so I could get up and help but my body didn't obey me, leaving me rocking on the salty timbers.

Their silhouettes merged, I heard a shout and a scream as the dark mass moved. One shape grew, coming towards me. Was it Lisa? Had she done it? I tried to focus and speak, but could do neither.

'Right then.' The deep growl told me what I needed to know. Chris grabbed me. 'Let's get famous.'

'Where's Lisa?' I tried to ask.

'She'll live to tell the tale,' Chris said, pulling me up by my coat.

We were at the very end of the pier where he leaned me in the corner of the railings like a boxer on the ropes. I'd always thought I'd find extra energy in situations like this, Rocky-style, or maybe a super power would magically manifest itself in me allowing me to fight back. But, no. I was freezing, injured and completely at the mercy of a nutter who wanted to make a name for himself.

'They'll find my songs too,' Chris was speaking to himself, hunched by my side. 'Music and lyrics by Chris Lightback. It's all there. They can release them too.'

I turned my head and blinked to stare at him. What was he doing? He sat hunched with a pen and paper. Writing a letter? A note or… a suicide note. That fired me up. The fucker was about to kill me for my apparent martyrdom, but this was all about him. His grab at the little limelight I'd acquired through hard work and sacrifice. I'd worked for that, not him. The whole band had. He could fuck off! I pushed up against he rails with my back, got some traction with my heels on the boardwalk and sucked in the cold air, desperate to fight back.

'Final words,' my voice came out like a croak.

'Your music will be your final words,' Chris said without looking up.

He put the pad of paper into a plastic bag and wedged it between the planks.

'What do you think of this place?' He asked, standing to his full height and baring down on me.

'I…'

'Loads of history. The pier used to be much longer, but they blew it up during the war.'

He was wittering but I couldn't tell if it was the drugs or if he was delaying the inevitable. I could delay him further I thought, hoping the blue lights I'd seen earlier were police cars and Lisa had been telling the truth.

'And we'll add to that history, Luke,' Chris was still talking. 'You'll put Felixstowe on the map!'

He grabbed me under my arms and turned me, to push me over the rail, so I kicked out, hooking my legs around his.

'No!' he shouted in my ear and punched me in the lower back.

The pain paralysed me for a second, then I fought to turn back and slip loose of his grip, but he'd turned me with my back against the railings. He shoved the heel of his palm in my throat and pushed my head back. All I could see was black sky as I tipped back, choking and fighting for breath, clawing at him with my hands. Black sky and dark waters. I heard the thump of waves against the pier's legs beneath us and smelt the salty tang of the winter sea.

'We'll go together,' Chris grumbled as we struggled, then he let out a pained yell.

I was released and my head swung round, back towards the lights. I fell limp against the railing, slumping down again, trying to fill my lungs with fresh air and get my bearings. Two shapes were beside me, fighting, leaning over the railings. I recognised my coat – Lisa! She fought with Chris, who was making an odd gurgling sound. I reached out, but they were too far away. I tried to focus and saw a shaft of metal sticking out of Chris's neck.

'Lisa!' I tried to shout and used the railing to pull myself closer.

Lisa had the better of Chris, pushing him backwards over the railings, but he was thumping her with his one free arm, while the other tried to remove whatever she'd stabbed him with. She stepped on the railing to get a better purchase and I watched in horror.

'No!' I shouted.

Lisa had Chris pinned but as she climbed her weight tipped them backwards and, in slow motion, they both tipped over the railing.

Like a finely balanced see-saw, there was half a second where they seemed to stop. I reached out and caught Lisa's eyes. She didn't scream, or say anything, she just blinked and, life sped up again as the momentum took them both over and into the sea below.

I yelled animal screams, pulling myself up the railings, staring through the old metal bars at the dark waters beneath the pier. A circle of white water marked where they'd hit, but it was soon washed away by the irregular waves which swirled around the legs of the pier.

'Lisa!' I yelled, spotting two midnight shapes in the water. 'Lisa!'

The sea wasn't as far down as I'd thought and I pulled myself up to stand, sure I could see a hand, maybe a face poking out of the water. Someone was yelling but I couldn't hear them. I looked around for a life ring, but the pier was empty.

'Lisa!' I shouted at the water again, not sure what I could do.

The stony beach and concrete breakwaters of safety were too far away. I knew Lisa was a decent swimmer but in this cold and with her clothes on she could drown if I didn't help her. She needed me. She'd fought for me when she could have escaped. Now it was my turn to save her.

I took a breath and pulled myself up until the top rail dug into my ribs.

This was important. Lisa was the most important person in my life. More important than anything or anyone else. She was my future.

I didn't have the energy to pull my whole body over, so I lifted one foot onto the lower railing, like Lisa had done, then leaned over the top rail, reaching out.

And fell.

East Suffolk Daily News

Christmas Day tragedy as bodies are recovered from water at popular beach

Residents of Felixstowe woke to tragic events at the resort's pier this Christmas morning as Police confirmed two bodies had been pulled from the sea.

Eye witnesses said Police and Ambulance vehicles had been at the scene from the early hours of Christmas Day, with unconfirmed reports that the situation began with an altercation between late night revellers out for Christmas Eve drinks in the town. Residents have long complained about the escalation in Christmas Eve revelry and renewed their calls for pubs to close early. One witness heard screaming from the pier and another reported seeing Paramedics attempting to revive an individual on the beach at the waterline.

Felixstowe pier's owner, Jason Whitton, said the property had been broken into and showed signs of vandalism, but repairs would be made when access was granted and the arcade would be re-opening in the New Year as planned.

A cordon remains in place around the building and the immediate areas of beach and promenade. All Christmas Day swims have been cancelled while Police continue with their investigations.

Police sources say the two deceased were in their twenties and the authorities were currently contacting their relatives for identification. Another person injured at the scene has been taken to Ipswich Hospital and is helping the Police with their enquiries. They are expected to make a full recovery.

Tuesday 31st December 1996

Champagne Supernova – Oasis

A week had passed. It felt like three months and, at the same time, like just a few hours since that night on the pier. In many ways I was still there with Lisa in the dark arcade, or in those midnight waters, desperately searching for her.

My memories were in pieces. The Doctors told me my body had gone into survival mode when I hit the water, conserving what energy it had, which wasn't much considering I'd only eaten chocolate and wafers that day. In its desperate attempt to keep me alive, my body had fought the cold with life-saving hormones as I swam like mad. The last thing on my body's list of priorities was to lay down that experience as detailed memories, so I'd only retained a few emotions, glimpses and images of my time in the water: the weight of my wet clothes pulling my down; the panic; the surging water splashing my face, giving me ice-cold headaches; the blurred lights; the dark pillars of the pier; a flash of colour; a hand disappearing under the water, too far away to reach; the endless depths of darkness beneath me.

But why me? Why was I the only one who'd survived? Maybe the tights Lisa had given me had acted like a wetsuit, keeping my kicking legs warm, and the scarecrow's coat had been buoyant, holding my head up, but had that been enough to keep me alive while Lisa and Chris had been pulled under? Or had Chris attacked Lisa in the water? Had I been too slow to jump in and save her? If I had been quicker, would Lisa still be alive?

The same questions attacked me over and over, and showed no sign of going away over these past few days. Some faded, then returned, but all of them kept eating away at me as I tried to make sense of what had happened and how I had reacted.

The Doctors may have been right about my memories, but I wondered how much of that night my mind was keeping hidden, sparing me the pain and guilt, leaving me in a constant whirlpool of emotions every hour, every day… and it was draining.

My parents were there when I woke in Ipswich hospital, and Stephen: the three of them surrounding my bed in a shared ward with the green curtain pulled around them.

'You always have to try and out-do me, don't you Bruv?' Stephen had said with a laugh, but I'd seen the concern in his eyes and the look Mum had given him. Dad had remained unusually quiet.

They had brought gifts and promises that the label would move me to a private hospital soon, but it wasn't until the next day that they told me about Lisa, when the Doctors were sure I was out of the woods. That conversation had been seared into my brain. There was no way I'd be able to forget it.

'The police told us what happened,' Dad said and I knew something serious had happened because he was using his police voice.

'How you jumped in to save her… how you tried to save Lisa,' Mum said. 'They were on the pier by then you see. They saw you jump in.'

I'd squinted, trying to remember. I could almost feel the cold, wet railing.

'And you tried you hardest, Luke,' Stephen said as Mum placed her hand on mine. 'You did everything to save her, but Lisa didn't make it.'

I shook my head and stared at my brother as the words sunk in. No. A lie.

'They've got it wrong,' I said, a tiny part of me thinking it could be one of Lisa's tricks.

I expected her to walk in with a bunch of flowers like last time I was in hospital, after the car crash.

'No, Luke. Lisa drowned,' Dad said, fixing his eyes on mine. 'Along with… the man.'

'Chris,' I said, feeling anger, emptiness and numbness fill my chest in equal measure.

Even with the people who loved me the most around me, I disappeared in that moment. My mind slipped back into the dark waters and it felt like something within me at my very core… my soul, my ego, I didn't know what, had split in two or shrunk into a hard kernel. Everything that was me had been shorn away, leaving only the basic core of me, and my pain, behind.

I had stayed there, in my head, ever since.

Days, nights, sleep, hospitals, car journeys, my parents' house, presents, sleep, and now, back in London.

New Year's Eve.

Stephen, Mum and Dad hadn't left my side throughout. I couldn't remember us four being together for this amount of time for years and it felt good. Comforting, like being protected in a cocoon. Just like when we used go on holiday together when I was a kid. One unit. A team.

James and Rob had visited me in the second hospital and told me all about Andy, who had been recuperating at his parents' house in Felixstowe and was recovering well. It felt surreal, like I wasn't really part of what was going on around me. That's was why I didn't argue or push back when they said Jeff had planned a New Year party for the label at some swanky river-side location in London. Jeff had called me, of course, to offer his condolences and support, but in my eyes a shadow still hung over him. I couldn't explain why, but because Jeff had been involved in Chris's plan I felt he should take some of the blame. I needed to see him in the flesh before I was going to move on.

I didn't want to tell anyone yet but after a week of self-analysis, with my broken arm and with Lisa's death weighing heavy on me, I was resolved to give up music. No more gigging. I was going to pull the album from sale to avoid Chris getting his name linked to it. I didn't want the album or touring to feed my desire to succeed and distort me like it transformed him. I had to do everything to avoid turning into him, churning up the lives of those in his path. I'd seen a part of me in him: the arrogance and determination, and it scared me. Beachhead were about to go big and with that extra pressure I could easily turn into Chris. This was enough. The recognition, the recording, the gigs. It had all been great, but it was time to stop now before more people were hurt. New year, new me, new life.

If I was honest, I sensed a bit of Isaac in me too – the numbness he must have felt after his wife had died and the desperation to make amends. I couldn't afford to go down that path either.

'Right, here we are then,' Stephen said as our black cab pulled up outside an imposing white stone building near the Thames. 'It used to store fish, or tobacco, or something,' he said with a smile.

'I bet it smells lovely,' Dad replied, letting Mum get out before him.

It was one of those tiny normal events that set me back into pain. I would never be able to show that simple gesture of love to Lisa. I would never be able to do anything that showed her how much I loved her. Never touch her again, see her smile, smell her perfume, kiss her, hold her hand. I'd spent months without Lisa, while she was away travelling, so I was used to her absence in my day to day life, but slowly I was coming to terms with the fact that this time she wasn't coming back. Knowing that, everything reminded me of her and I couldn't escape her loss.

'Who's playing tonight?' Mum asked Stephen, keeping us talking.

'I've heard there might be a special performance from…' Stephen's words merged with the sound of the party as we entered the lobby and the security staff checked our invitations.

'What time is it?' I asked Dad, who checked his watch.

I had been getting used to reading the time from my phone, but hadn't bought a new one since the pier… even asking the time reminded me of her.

'Nine thirty,' Dad replied.

'Ah, Mister Redfern,' one of the doorman said, sending my heart racing – he sounded just like Tip.

Dad and Stephen turned, but backed off when they saw he was talking to me and handed me a sealed envelope.

'He's in the VIP lounge,' the doorman said. 'In the far left corner.'

'Thanks,' I said in what had become my half-whispered voice this past week.

'…last time you can have a dance before they put you in prison,' Stephen said, teasing Mum.

'The hearing isn't for another three weeks, thank you,' Mum replied, taking it in good humour.

Even that reminded me of Lisa. Of how her funeral would be before then.

'And the lawyer advised us the maximum penalty would only be…' Dad had returned to police-mode, protecting Mum.

I wasn't listening. I opened the envelope and pulled out a card. It was from Jeff, asking to meet up before his speech.

'I'll see you in a minute,' I told my family and headed off, skirting around the main dance hall, which was littered with groups of people chatting and dancing to a band on stage I vaguely recognised.

There were at least two hundred people here. Way more than on the boat event a few weeks back. I kept my head down, hoping not to bump into anyone I knew. My paranoia was strong as I felt people's stares and heard their whispers, but I soon found the door and slipped from view.

'Ah, Luke!' Jeff saw me as soon as I entered the plush, sofa-lined room. 'Excuse me,' he said to his important looking guests and ushered me into quiet corner, with one hand on my shoulder.

This was my chance to tell him I was quitting, but I wanted to hear what he had to say first. He sighed, as though gaining courage, which wasn't like him, then his eyes met mine. I held them for what was probably the first time, searching for his true feelings.

'Luke, I'm so sorry,' he said and I saw that he meant it.

The show of emotion made my eyes water, but I held them back, keeping my eyes on his.

'Lisa was an amazing girl… an amazing woman. She will be truly missed,' he said.

'Yeah,' I said, sniffing a tear back.

'Original,' Jeff continued. 'Great energy. And what happened,' he shook his head, 'I'm so sorry Luke. For your loss and for anything I did that may have led…'

He was getting choked up now, genuinely, and I felt the urge to stop him.

'No, I-'

A waitress arrived with a silver tray of champagne flutes. Jeff took one and I glanced at them lost in what I was about to say. I couldn't remember what meds I was on or whether I could drink or not – I just thought of Lisa. How she'd loved champagne, not that we'd had it often, but she would never turn down a glass, so I reached out and took one.

'It was all him,' I said eventually. 'Chris. Not you. He was always going to do something…' I wanted to say *stupid* but that was nowhere the level of what he had done.

Jeff nodded and stared off with a frown. 'You know, I've always tried to encourage the artists at my label to produce the most spectacular work of their lives.' Our eyes met again. 'You're album is great, Luke, and I truly believe, one day… once you're past all this, you will create something exceptional. Some people thinks it's a game, but it isn't, not to the true artists.'

I thought of Dave and his distaste for the music industry but let Jeff continue.

'The ability to touch a listener's soul with a melody or lyric is a rare gift that should never be undervalued… who can calculate the true value of music?'

'I don't know,' I replied, wondering if Jeff could tell I was ready to throw it all away.

'But you have the gift, Luke. Make the most of it.' Jeff raised his glass. 'To Lisa.'

'To Lisa,' I replied and drank, feeling the bubbles on my tongue and a subtle taste that made me think of meadows.

Something else Lisa would never experience again. I felt bitter. This toast was just another futile gesture for a life stolen from us. Pointless nostalgia or a step in the grieving process? I couldn't tell… but the alcohol did feel good. I took another swig and felt my body unwind.

'Listen,' Jeff said, sounding more business-like. 'I'm going to mention Lisa tonight, okay?'

I nodded, not sure what to say.

'I want tonight to be a celebration of her life as much as a celebration of this year,' he said. 'I know we'll have her funeral and a wake, but tonight should be for her too.'

'Okay, yeah,' I said, taking another sip.

'And I've got more news… I'm not sure if Stephen's mentioned it, but we've lined up-'

A shape appeared beside us.

'So sorry, it's time,' the suit said and Jeff stood up.

'Right, yes, err, sorry Luke.' He shook my hand. 'Time for the speech… I'm sure Stephen's told you – great stuff. We can talk it over later.'

And he disappeared, leaving me wondering what on earth he was talking about.

I spent a few minutes soaking up the VIP room, sipping my champagne, but after a few looks and behind-hand whispers, I left to re-join my family.

'Hey, Stephen,' I spoke into his ear so he could hear over the deafening music. 'What's this surprise Jeff's got in store?'

Stephen shrugged and said something back but I couldn't hear, and saw the lads coming over.

'There you are!' Rob was first to give me hug.

'Back on the booze – always a good sign,' James said and gave me a hug. 'Missed you mate.'

'And you,' I said, realising how much I needed these guys in my life.

They got it. They'd been with me all the way: they felt the pressure; rode the waves; hit the walls; broke through those walls. What I'd have given to have them with me on the pier.

Another shape moved through and offered a hand.

'Andy!' I said, seeing flashbacks of Lisa jumping at him.

This was the first time I'd seen him since before Christmas.

'Luke,' he said sheepishly.

I grabbed his hand and pulled him in for a hug, whispering, 'So good to see you mate.'

Tears ran from my eyes, I couldn't stop them. Fuck anyone watching, this was real life.

'Easy,' Andy said, pushing me back with a smile and patting his side.

'Sorry!' I said and let go. 'How are you?' I asked, trying to focus on him rather than the flashbacks from Felixstowe.

'I'm doing alright,' he said with a nod.

I recognised something in his eyes. He'd been to the same places as me, in reality and mentally. Something neither of us could put into words, but something we shared. Somehow, just knowing that made it feel easier to bear.

'How are you?' he asked.

'Pretty shit to be honest,' I said, knowing I could be candid with him.

'Listen, I had no-' Andy started but I cut him off.

'I know, it's okay. Nobody could have guessed what he would do, right?'

Andy shook his head. 'I blame the drugs but…'

'It's more than that,' I said, turning to the stage, to the band up there, playing, radiating – receiving the focus of the room and giving it back, both barrels, through their music.

Their energy pulled me in. I wanted to be back up there, to feel that surge again. Suddenly my vow to quit felt hollow.

'A lot of things are addictive,' I said, but I doubt Andy heard me.

I gave him a smile. James and Rob were behind us, having a laugh with Stephen. And my parents, arm in arm, giggling. I loved them all. And yet, I realised how little I really knew any of them, especially Andy. Maybe it was time to spend more time with them and getting to know them properly – not just sharing experiences with them. Because if I didn't do it now, I never would.

The band finished their song with an elongated drum roll and Rob nodded at me with raised eyebrows.

'Next album,' I mouthed back with a wink.

'Thanks, thanks,' the guy on stage said. 'That's it from us – cheers. Happy New Year!'

A flock of waitresses streamed through the crowd, handing out more champagne so I took a glass as Jeff made it up onto stage and took the mic.

'Thanks guys. Thanks everyone… bloody brilliant. Can't wait for you to hear their next album, from what I've already heard it's gonna be amazing.'

The crowd cheered and I felt my stomach tighten. As much as I wanted to be on stage, singing, playing, I was worried any attention I got from Lisa's death was going to send me into a spin, so I gulped more champagne and edged towards my parents.

'Now, tonight,' Jeff was in full entertainer mode. Cool hippy, open shirted experienced music man. 'Tonight, is about celebration, yeah,' he let the crowd cheer. 'We're celebrating a great year for the label.'

More cheers as he listed number one singles, albums and new releases. No mention of Beachhead, but Skimrider got a big cheer.

'But more importantly, we need to celebrate you,' he let it hang and I felt my eyes well up. 'Everyone in the music industry who has made this period of our lives bloody amazing. The nineties, eh? Seriously, I haven't felt anything like this since the sixties!'

Even Dad gave a cheer for that one.

'And tonight, we also want to remember those we lost this year, so please raise a glass to a special lady who recently passed away. Lisa Jones, who…'

It felt like I had stepped out of my body. A rush of emotion so strong took hold of me and squeezed everything else out, leaving an empty vessel behind. Just a pair of eyes. Seeing. Thinking. All the terrible things that had happened to me rushed back: the sea; the pier; being attacked; Chris; the bookshop; Shirley; Grandad; Isaac. I saw his pain again. Like mine. He'd lost his wife and had been consumed by grief and a twisted determination to build something to her memory – I couldn't go down that path, just like I couldn't let my dreams consume me like they had taken over Chris.

I felt trapped, stuck between the extremes – who the fuck was I anyway? Should I give up music? Jeff had faith in me didn't he? I needed to be on stage. Everyone around me wanted us to succeed. What would I actually do if I gave up Beachhead?

'…next year will be an even more important year for our bands.'

I tuned back into what Jeff was saying and switched my empty glass for a full one as another waitress walked past. I looked around, spotting a few journalists I recognised from the boat, then saw Dave from Skimrider, who caught my eye and gave me a nod.

'Lots of great albums and tours in the pipeline for next year, but none more exciting than the confirmation I've just received… I can now announce than ninety seven is going to be a great year for two of our favourite bands!'

A cheer.

'Skimrider are gonna tour America!'

The crowd cheered and I could see Dave and his band, hands in the air, soaking it up. It's all hype, I remembered him saying, and could see now that was how he stayed cool under the pressure. He played it down. Ride the wave. Go with the flow. Pretend it doesn't really matter. Surely, deep down, he was just like me and wanted nothing more than this.

'And with the launch of their debut album, *We Attack At Dawn*, I'm more than proud to announce that Beachhead will be supporting Skimrider on their American tour!'

Everything went crazy around me. The lads bundled into me from one side as my parents hugged me from the other and Stephen grabbed me, shouting something in my ear.

What the fuck just happened?

'Good luck lads – a great band. The album is sounding bloody brilliant too!' Jeff said. 'There they are.' He pointed at us. 'Great bunch of lads.'

'You look shocked,' Stephen said. 'Didn't Jeff tell you?'

'No, I… err… we were talking about Lisa,' I said, my head a buzz of thoughts.

'It's gonna be great – bloody amazing opportunity,' Stephen said, half drunk. 'After the UK release and mini-tour here in the summer… and I'll be coming too of course.'

'Of course,' I said with a smile, but my mask had slipped back on.

What the fuck? America? Supporting Skimrider? This was everything I'd ever wanted, but it was happening so fast… and without Lisa. We'd said, in a perfect world, we would combine our dreams and travel together and now it was happening too late. She would miss all of this.

I downed my champagne and focussed on one of the guitars, hanging in a stand on stage. Waiting to be played. Like me, with my broken arm. Full of potential. Waiting to come back. Could I do it? Was I ready to take this to the next level?

I watched the lads chatting excitedly: Rob ecstatic; Andy beaming; James talking with wild hands. Stephen was introducing Mum and Dad to someone from the label, smiling, laughing.

They were all the most enthused I'd ever seen them. The picture was way bigger than just me. This was for all of us. And if I couldn't manage any part of this, they would all be there for me. Just as I needed to be there for them when they needed me.

Jeff left the stage. Music started up. New Year was approaching. Resolutions.

A time for new starts?

No, what really counted was being here and now. *We* were here, now. And it was time to make the most of it. It was time I started to make the most of every bloody second.

I walked over to the lads, giving Mum a peck on the cheek as I passed.

'Right then lads,' I said. 'I've got an idea for this new song…'

Wednesday 1st January 1997

Original – Leftfield

The next morning, I woke up with a head full of thoughts. New and old. A hangover. Pains. Physical and emotional.

It was nineteen ninety-seven and I wanted to grab it with both hands and make the most of it, but my head was still stuck in nineteen ninety-six. Lisa came to me, as she did every time I woke, and I pictured her with me, cuddled up like when we were hiding in the pier. Our conversations came to me… the last things we'd said to one another; everything I'd wanted to say and didn't have the chance.

I gasped and sat up. What Lisa had said in the pier came back to me!

I flipped the duvet off me, leapt out of bed and rushed straight for the wardrobe, flinging the doors open. The bottom was full of old books, trainers and summer clothes, boxes of Lisa's letters and – there – a large square of red paper pressed against the back of the wardrobe. She had wrapped it after all! I reached out and stopped, my fingers an inch away, fighting back the tears, trying to control my breathing.

This was my last connection with Lisa. This was it. There was nothing else after this. Did I really want it to end here?

It had to.

I picked it up, feeling the weight of a LP inside, and read the label.

Dear Luke,

It might not be the best track on the album, but track five is my gift to you,

because every time I hear it I think of you.

I love you.

Lisa x

I laughed, remembering our old 'best album track' arguments and tore the wrapping paper off, recognising the album instantly: *Leftism* by Leftfield.

I had it on CD and we'd listened to it constantly on our coach trips across Australia when Lisa was slowly converting me to her taste in dance music. It wasn't all about guitars, she'd joked. And I'd said I never felt like I owned an album until I had it on vinyl, so this was her way of saying she was going to stay in London? The questions multiplied. Was she planning on working with the label indefinitely? Ready to stop travelling? Was she saying she was ready for us to settle down?

I'd never know.

I pulled the record from the sleeve and put it on the player, moving the needle straight to track five, *Original*, and listened to the lyrics, imagining Lisa singing them to me.

Will it ever be the same again?

You're original, with your own path.

She was original too. More original than I'd ever be, I could tell that from the first time I'd seen her in my book shop. She did things other people only dreamt of. Her energy lit up everyone around her. She'd burnt out too fast though. Our future had burnt out.

Because a dream starts and a dream must end.

That was the line I didn't want to hear, but needed to.

I made my mind up.

This year, Nineteen ninety-seven, would be for Lisa. I would live it for her. For everyone I'd lost. For all those wasted lives who would not have been lost in vain if I could make the most of every heartbeat and make a success of Beachhead. I was determined to live to my full potential. To experience everything. Fall and get back up again. Live to the limits and never let go.

Ready or not, I was determined to make this year my best yet.

THE END

Printed in Great Britain
by Amazon

86399120R00183